W9-AMX-297

FALLS OF GARD

FALLS OF GARD

by

LAURA BLACK

St. Martin's Press
New York

Library of Congress Cataloging in Publication Data

Black, Laura.
  The falls of Gard.

  I. Title.
PR6052.L32F35   1986   823'.914   86-1874
ISBN 0-312-28009-2

First published in Great Britain by Hamish Hamilton Ltd.

First U.S. Edition

10 9 8 7 6 5 4 3 2 1

FALLS OF GARD

Chapter 1

'We do not behave so in Scotland, Arabella,' said my Aunt, 'whatever you may have become used to in Australia.'

'I am truly sorry, Aunt Honoria,' I said. 'I was not thinking.'

This was not quite true. I had been thinking. I had been sick with longing for the clear sunlight of New South Wales, and the cool white columns of Government House; for my happy-natured father, and my gentle mother, and my two younger brothers and my little sister; and for the cheerful freedom of life in that exuberant colony. Thinking so, I had taken up the bone of a mutton chop, in order to pick off with my teeth the delicious well-browned remnants. This was not frowned upon in Sydney, even in Government House: unless to be sure there were visiting grandees, as there often were (for my father was hugely popular); then, of course, we all tried to mind our manners; except that often the grandees themselves liked picking up their chop-bones, or chicken-drumsticks, and were happy to find themselves in a place where this was allowed. It seemed to me (as it seems to me still) a more sensible method than struggling with knife and fork. But they did not behave so in Scotland.

I wiped my fingers, in shame, on my damask table-napkin. I reasoned: why equip people with copious squares of damask on which to wipe their fingers, and then, by enacting these rules, make the damask perfectly unnecessary? There was no purpose in saying this to my Aunt Honoria, or my Uncle Ranald, or my Cousins Henry and Grizelda. Least of all, perhaps, Grizelda. They would not have understood a point that seemed to me so very logical; or else they would have understood it all too well; and either way their opinion of me would have dropped still further.

1

It seemed to me sometimes that their opinion of me could drop *no* further – that it had already reached rock bottom.

I was in a most peculiar position. I was living in my home, the home of my family for centuries, an ancient place where I had spent much of my childhood, a place of great and sometimes breathtaking beauty; and I was homesick for a raw and alien country on the other side of the globe. I was living with my close kinfolk, whom I had known all my life; and I was homesick for a brash young city full of aggressive strangers. It seemed no less odd to me for knowing that it was quite usual. In that heyday of Empire, in that year of 1866, families were scattered to the ends of the earth by the needs of Army or Government. And little boys came all the way back to be schooled; and girls when not quite so little came back to be polished and presented. It happened all the time; I knew it; and I supposed that thousands of hearts were broken every year, and thousands of pillows were wet every night.

The dining room at Callo House was full of the golden sunshine of April in the Highlands; it was not my Australian sunshine, which seemed to purify what it touched, and to cure the wounds on men and on the countryside. The room was comfortable, like all the Callo rooms – too comfortable, like all of them, thickly carpeted, as though the sound of a footfall would be an offence, curtained with swags of heavy-weight brocade, as though the sun were admitted on sufferance, and must not presume, the walls lined with pictures in important frames, which seemed to lean inwards oppressively and threateningly, and all the space thronged with massive furniture of which the cushions were too soft and too numerous. It was not the kind of comfort I had grown used to, of big airy spaces, and a few bright rugs from India scattered on a scrubbed expanse of stone or wooden floors. A person could move in those Australian rooms. A person could run. The children had races in the rooms of Government House, I sometimes starting them and judging them, and sometimes joining in. To run in any room of Callo House would have been unthinkable. You would bark a shin or break a knee against great obstructions of mahogany and ormolu; and you would be in disgrace again.

I was still some weeks short of my eighteenth birthday. I

was still in the way of wanting to run. I was – I had been – in the way of wearing clothes in which running was possible. But – 'We do not behave so in Scotland'.

I escaped from the dining room when I could, since it was one of the days when escape was possible. There were fewer and fewer of such days. My Aunt Honoria and my Uncle Ranald had not all at once realised how appallingly my education had been neglected in Australia, how savage and uncouth I was, how utterly unfitted to take my place in an adult world of tea-cups, and balls, and the unremitting search (which must begin almost at once) for a husband. I had disembarked at Southampton in March; I had been conveyed to London, and thence to Edinburgh, and by a complicated route to Crianlarich, which was as far as the railway helped us, and so by carriage to Glengard, where Callo House frowned at the river: and, from the moment of my entry into the gloomy hall, I had unwittingly unpeeled myself, like an onion, revealing to my horrified aunt and uncle layer upon layer of barbarism, each more shocking than the last.

My embroidery was a botch. My box of watercolour paints had been unopened for years, except to turn my little brothers into Aborigine warriors in warpaint. On the pianoforte I could strum only strenuous dances, to set those brothers leaping. I danced, but in the manner of Sydney. I became confused among spoons on the dining table. (Government House had plenty of silver spoons, but my father never minded what spoon anybody used.) I had not read the poems of Southey. I was totally unskilled in the art – at which Aunt Honoria was expert – of talking to a stranger for hours while saying nothing: in Australia I had been used to conversations in which good stories were told, and fascinating things were said about new places and discoveries, and people who had not good things to say were content to listen to those who had.

Such a savage colonial hoyden could not be launched in Perthshire and in Edinburgh, without hideous embarrassment. Fortunately, there were five months between my arrival at Callo in a shower of steamer-trunks and carpet-bags, and the ball that would be given for my eighteenth birthday. Those months were there to be used, for a desperate labour of polishing, refining, rendering presentable the almost hopeless material I represented. Privately, I did not believe it could be done. It was clear to me that Aunt Honoria sometimes doubted if it could be done. But her sense of social position was so acute, that she spared no effort, in any direction, to make me into an object of which she might not be entirely ashamed.

My Cousin Grizelda saw from the start, and said often, that the whole labour was in vain. It was not obvious whether she was pleased about this, or sorry.

I was not friendless. I had the five greatest friends of my childhood, who became my friends again, which might not have happened at all. Some came back as I had come back (though not from as far) and some had never gone away. I was reunited with them not all at once, but according as they found themselves in Glengard.

It was almost certain that the first I would meet again would be Mariota Seaton; because she was the one who never went away, and never had been away. I heard this from Aunt Honoria. I thought it strange and sad. Aunt Honoria did not find it so. Grizelda had scarcely been away either, since Uncle Ranald inherited Callo from his father, my grandfather.

I did not believe that Mariota would have changed, as the men I had known as young boys had probably changed beyond any recognition. She was the closest to me in age; of our little childhood regiment, I was the youngest, and she, a bare year older, the second youngest. She floated about in a dream, as a child, beautiful and indolent and listening to fairy music none of the rest of us could hear. At least, that was what she said she was doing, but Geoffrey Nicholls said it was an excuse for doing absolutely nothing. It was something she had inherited from her mother, who, since Mariota's birth, had lived almost entirely on a chaise-longue. Mariota's mother was the Countess of Crask (so that Mariota was styled the Lady Mariota Seaton), which in the eyes of people like my Aunt Honoria gave her the divine right to do as much or as little as she pleased. She did not claim to be listening to fairy music, but to suffer from every debilitating disease known to the Faculty of Medicine. Geoffrey Nicholls was as cynical about her indolence as about Mariota's, but not in

Mariota's hearing. None of us risked too often or too greatly infuriating Mariota, because we liked being asked to Crask Castle, half way up Glengard from Callo House.

This was not because Crask was comfortable, clean, smooth-running, or apt to produce delicious meals at short notice. It was none of these things. But it was a joy to go there, for the warm welcome, gentle humour, and indulgent kindness of the Countess, and the unpredictable and sometimes outrageous enthusiasms of the Earl. None of us other children had ever met anybody in the least like either Earl or Countess. We all came from normal and conventional backgrounds, in which mothers and grandmothers were busy and efficient housekeepers and full of charitable works, and fathers and grandfathers were professional men (like my own soldier father) or conscientious landowners. The Crasks were made of different substance. You could not imagine the Countess engaging a housemaid or planning the menu of a dinner party; you could not imagine the Earl supervising the digging of a drain, or the despatch of bull-calves to market. It was hilarious for us to go there. There was some sadness in it, too. Even as young children, the rest of us realised that they were the least practical people in the world, and that from apathy, neglect, other-worldliness, and disastrous investments they were bound to find, one day, that their ugly little castle had crumbled into the river.

I was sure, years on, that Mariota would not have changed; I was sure her parents would not have either. I wondered if, when I went there – as I surely would – I would see visible signs of further decay. More dark patches on the walls, perhaps, where pictures had been sold; more steadings roofless, more farms let go, more chairs with broken legs, fewer servants and those more sluttish. I supposed it must all be just so; but Aunt Honoria would have none of this; she valued her friendship with the Countess of Crask almost as much as she would have valued friendship with the Duke of Lomond, in his great castle far away at the head of the glen; but unfortunately the Duke had been bedridden for years, and Aunt Honoria had never even met him.

I was lucky to escape, that afternoon of the mutton chop.

Perhaps it was because it was one of the moments when Aunt Honoria despaired of turning me into a lady, or back into one. The thought of another lesson in deportment oppressed her, I daresay, as much as it oppressed me.

I would have ridden. It was an afternoon for going far and fast, for letting the Highland air blow away my homesickness – for letting it blow away the imprisoning, disapproving atmosphere of Callo. I had been used to riding here as a child, on a variety of shaggy Highland ponies, set about by my grandfather's anxious grooms, and often contriving to escape from them to join Mariota and Geoffrey Nicholls and our other friends. I had been still more used to riding in Australia, sometimes several times a day: for on the way to places even quite close to Sydney the bumping and bucketing of a carriage on the unmade roads was worse by far than the bumping and bucketing of my father's lovely local-bred horses, the 'Walers' which were almost pure thoroughbred, which were the racehorses of that time and place, and which were sold in their thousands as remounts to the army in India. So almost my first act when I arrived at Callo – the very first moment when I found myself left to myself – was to run round to the well-remembered stables (already dressed as I was in clothes unsuitable for running) to see what horses my Uncle Ranald had.

There was nothing that could conceivably be a saddle-horse for me.

Within a day or two I found out the reason for this calamitous state of affairs. The family never rode for pleasure or exercise. Aunt Honoria had never, I think, sat a horse in her life. Probably Grizelda never had. Uncle Ranald, as befitting his notions of his importance, went always upon wheels. Other lairds, as I remembered from childhood, went often to the School Boards and Hospital Boards and Sheriffs' Courts and such on horseback; my grandfather did. But not the present Sir Ranald Gordon of Callo. His consequence required frock-coats, and brocaded grooms, and a wealth of gleaming harness. He believed himself a person of awesome importance in the county, and he believed this importance should be evident. All this I learned within two days: it was part of the atmosphere one breathed in Callo House. Within two days I was struck, as though by a gauntleted hand across

6

the face, by the contrast with my father; he was Uncle Ranald's younger brother; he was a Major General; he *was* a person of awesome importance in the Province of which he was Lieutenant Governor; and he never cared a button whether this was evident or not.

Solemn Cousin Henry, who was said to be assuming responsibility for managing the estate, was certainly obliged to ride a horse to visit some of the places he said that he must scrutinise. I was shown his horse. The grooms pointed it out to me with a kind of shame. They remembered as well as I did the energetic days of my grandfather (and they remembered me as well as I remembered them, which was a joyful surprise to me). Henry's horse was a kind of gigantic armchair of an animal, which looked as though it had never been kicked into a trot in its life. By looking at that horse, and knowing that its owner had chosen it for himself, you learned very suddenly a lot about that owner.

I asked Aunt Honoria that evening, as demure as I knew how, whether it might be possible to beg or borrow or buy an animal that I could ride.

'You will not have time, Arabella,' she said.

Already enough onion-skins had peeled off me, for her to see, aghast, how much work would have to be put in, in order that when I appeared in public I should not cause her to be pitied and derided.

'I think riding is necessary for my health,' I said desperately.

'I do not think your health is under any immediate threat, Arabella,' she said. 'Unlike my own, or my poor Grizelda's.'

I could not tell, so soon, if either Aunt Honoria or Cousin Grizelda was in frail health; but of course she was quite right about me. It may have been the effect of Australia, or simply of my being my father's daughter, but I was most abundantly and obviously healthy. I could not have concealed the high colour of my cheeks, or my disgraceful tendency to run and jump and climb things, any more than I could have concealed a wasting sickness, supposing that I had ever suffered from any sickness. I could not maintain the pretence that I actually needed horseback exercise; I could not maintain, either, the position that I did not need the quantity of education that Aunt Honoria was determined to thrust into me.

I was surprised by the proposition – not quite stated, but made very clear – that a delicate constitution was a badge of gentility, and my own rude health and hearty appetite the mark of a peasant or milkmaid: or, at best, of a colonial. I could imagine my father's comments on such a theory. Perhaps Aunt Honoria was influenced by the genuine frailty of the Duke of Lomond, and the imagined sufferings of the Countess of Crask.

So it came about that I walked down through the park to the river, that afternoon of the mutton-chop-bone outrage. It was a good second-best. It was only a little distance, the turf sloping down among trees, and the noise of the water ever louder as I approached it. The fallow-deer flickered in and out of the patches of sunlight between the trees, and the nesting birds clamoured in the first beginnings of green among the branches. Down here on the low ground there was a feeling of lushness, of incipient, sappy growth; but on the high tops which walled Glengard the snow still shone deep and unbroken.

Homesick for Sydney I may have been: but I felt for the first time the stirring of an opposite feeling. That I had come home. Did that mean that I had two homes, or no true home? The tits piped above me, hurrying through the twigs of the elm-trees. They were my birds, the birds of home. More than the Australian birds, whose strange cries and brilliant plumage my father had taught me to recognise?

I came, confused in mind, out of the trees onto the bare sward that stretched to the bank of the river. The noise of the falls, no longer muffled by foliage, was suddenly loud. This was a place thronged with memories, and with one of the greater disgraces of my childhood. I hoped Aunt Honoria had never heard *that* story.

Three hundred yards upstream, the River Gard flowed smooth and tranquil over a deep bottom. So it flowed three hundred yards downstream. In between it fell steeply, rushing with a great noise among big black rocks. These were the Falls of Gard. When they were in spate, the falls were beautiful and very, very dangerous. A terrifying weight of water came down at dizzying speed, smashing over the rocks, boiling up the granite slabs of the banks, hurling its spray thirty and more feet in the air. As a child I had stood and watched it and watched, with a kind of frightened fascination, struck by the puniness of men faced by such forces of nature.

When the river was low, the waters of the falls were silver. When it was high, the waters had scooped and scraped I know not what, which changed their colour from silver to an amazing tawny yellow, a lion colour. Geoffrey Nicholls said it was the colour of my hair. That was a time when he was in one of his passionately tender moods, which alternated with his cynical moods, and extravagantly generous moods, and violent moods; that was a time when – he being eleven years old and I being eight – he said that he would one day marry me, and not even the waters of the Falls of Gard would stop him.

Geoffrey said, that time and other times, that my eyes were the colour of the summer sky, my cheeks of the wild rose, my lips of the cherry; that I was slender as the bullrush, and graceful as the swallow. Even at the age of eight, I had a notion these comparisons had been made before. In many of the old country songs, the singer used these very phrases to describe his sweetheart. I did not mind that Geoffrey had not thought of them, because I knew very well that he meant them.

Nine years later, I was no longer as slender as the bullrush, in the way of going straight up and down, like a plank; but my hair was still the colour of a lion, and my eyes and cheeks and lips, I supposed, had kept their colours too. But Geoffrey was now a lawyer (so my Aunt Honoria had with slight contempt informed me) and if he were minded to talk about me, he would find different words.

A little upstream from Callo House, but still some hundred yards from the head of the falls, the river divided. It split on the prow of a small island, which, so I had long before been told, was a mass of rock which had been deposited on that spot by a glacier. Perhaps the glacier had grown tired of gouging out Glengard and the bed of the River Gard, and also carrying this lump of granite, and so had dropped the latter, for the future convenience of the Dukes of Lomond. The story was, that that great family had once been, to all intents and purposes, independent kings of the glen and all the country round, and had ruled it with all the greed and ferocity of those ancient tribal times. This had made them

9

bitter enemies, whom they usually succeeded in suppressing, but whom they sometimes had to flee; it pleased me to think of those proud tyrants tucking their tails between their legs and running away from tattered clansmen. Whoever then were lords of Callo (minor lords, faithful feudatories of the great lords) made over to them, as a refuge, this small granite crag rearing its head out of the Falls of Gard. The Dukes had built themselves a miniature castle on the island; because of its position in the midst of the falls, a handful of men could defend it against an army. So, it was explained to me, island and castle still belonged to the Dukes of Lomond, though the river thereabouts, and both its banks, belonged to Callo.

The island could be reached in perfect safety, when the water in the Gard was very low. As children, we had had picnics there, among the stunted whins which had survived successive spates. We had explored the castle. It took about two minutes to do so. It was not a place for living in, but simply a kind of blockhouse where a platoon of soldiers could defend their master. Massively built as it had been, most of it had fallen down (perhaps it had been attacked with gunpowder, which came to the Highlands of Scotland long before peace did). One chamber survived, more or less complete, with a roof and four walls. We all sheltered there once, from a sudden rainstorm; though it was dry, yet it was wet; moss grew inside the walls, and there was an ancient, clammy smell. I once dared Geoffrey Nicholls to spend a night there. He found excuses not to do so. I mocked him loudly, but in truth I did not at all blame him; it was impossible that such a place should not be full of miserable ghosts.

I strolled upstream to the island, with the water snarling below me. Even in the kindly April sunshine, it held a sort of menace. It annoyed me also that there should be this chunk of the Duke of Lomond's own, in the midst of our estate. I knew the reasons; they were perfectly logical; it was not such a very unusual arrangement; and in truth it was nothing to me what Callo owned or did not, as I would never own Callo. *My* reasons were not logical, but as a child they had seemed to me good reasons, and they still seemed good; because it was hereabouts that I had been treacherously betrayed by the heir to the present Duke of Lomond, who had contrived for me to get a whipping. It was the summer I was eight: the summer that Geoffrey Nicholls had first declared that he would marry me. It all made me see, when I was eight, that the world was divided into the people that I loved and the people that I hated; nine years on, I knew that this was a silly and simple-minded view; and, nine years on, I knew that it was still how I felt.

Since we had left for Australia, someone had built a foot-bridge from the bank where I stood to the island. It was made of sturdy planking, resting on iron girders which were let into the rock on either side. It was well clear of the water, out of the reach of any normal spate. The reason was, that a new purpose had been devised for the little tumbledown castle: it was used as a hide for watching the water-birds. I did not know by whom – perhaps visiting scientists, too eminent to get their feet wet. I did not know, either, who had built the bridge; perhaps it was done on the orders of the Duke of Lomond, perhaps by Uncle Ranald with a view to currying favour with the Duke.

As a child, I had identified myself with the ragged High-landers who had sometimes chased their oppressor to this place, as other children are Roundheads or Cavaliers. I still felt so. I remembered how, in my childhood, the shadow of the Duke's authority fell, even from his sickbed, over the whole glen, putting some places out of bounds, forbidding fires in others. It was explained to all of us by our families (perhaps not to Mariota by the Earl and Countess of Crask) that these were wise and necessary rules. We did not think so. We chafed. I chafed still, at the memory. I would not set foot upon a bridge put there by that distant despot in his great four-poster bed.

In any case, I was not dressed for scrambling over rocks and among whins; I was dressed for a demure stroll in a gentleman's park. I wondered if I should ever again wear clothes that allowed me to be active. Not, I thought, while I lived at Callo: and I could live nowhere else until I married, or my family came back from Australia. I contemplated the future with gloom; and I contemplated with despair the music-lesson I was to have at five o'clock.

A voice behind – close behind, so that I jumped – said, 'I shouted and shouted, but I suppose the water drowned my voice.'

I spun round. I saw a girl a year or so older than myself, with a figure much like mine, with clothes as smart and suitable as mine, with chestnut hair most unlike mine, with an excited and joyful smile.

'Mariota!' I screamed, and hurled myself towards her.

We embraced, laughing, babbling nonsense, the years dropped away as though it was the summer that I was eight.

'You are almost grown-up, Bella,' said Mariota, 'and you are not grown-up at all! I was dreading that you had changed.'

And she, as I had supposed, had not changed either; she had grown upwards and outwards, as I had done; her waist was as tiny as ever it was (as, thank Heaven, was mine); and her laughter as much like the warbling of a demented bird.

I said, 'Do you still listen to fairy music, as an excuse for not doing anything?'

'Yes, but of course it is different music. The fairies have grown up too. You are to come to Crask immediately, to have tea with my Mama. She is agog to see you. It is the first time for fifteen years that she has been agog about anything, so you see it is your duty to come.'

'Oh! I should love to! But I am to have a music lesson at five o'clock, and I am supposed to have practised for hours and hours and hours, and I only practised for minutes and minutes and minutes, only they seemed like hours. . . .'

'That is all looked after. I have brought a note from my Mama to your aunt. Did you think my Mama could write a note?'

'Well, no.'

'You were quite right. She dictated it to me. Did you think I could write a note?'

'Only of fairy music.'

'Not even that. So, instead, I have faithfully carried a message, and delivered it, and you are excused your music lesson. The carriage will bring you back in time to change for dinner. So you have no excuse. You are my prisoner. Bella, how well you look! How beautiful you are! Now tell me every single thing that has happened to you since you went away.'

'I want to hear every single thing that has happened to you, since I went away.'

12

'Nothing has happened to me, except the fairies changing their music. I was presented last year. That meant going to Edinburgh. Otherwise I have done absolutely nothing at all.'

'Do you have to stay at home because of your mother?'

'Yes. And my Papa. And my fairies. How could I leave them without an audience?'

'Will you take them with you when you get married?'

'I shall not get married quite yet.'

I thought she blushed. But she would say no more. I wondered which of them it was – Geoffrey Nicholls, or one of the other two. I could not believe her love (and the blush, I thought, had something to do with love) would not come from among that charmed circle of our childhood. I could not believe mine would, either.

We strolled together across the park, towards the house and her waiting carriage. Our arms were about one another's waists, as they last had been six years before. If the snows on the high tops had made me feel that, all homesickness notwithstanding, I was come home, so a thousandfold did Mariota's arm about my waist; so did Mariota's mad birdlike laughter, and the ridiculous remarks that made me laugh exactly as they had, six years before.

It was difficult for me to tell her about my life in Australia, because she interrupted me with so many questions, and because I interrupted myself with so many questions. Her brain was birdlike, as well as her laughter; I do not mean that she was at all stupid, but that her thoughts and questions darted like swallows hunting for gnats over the river on a summer evening.

No, she had not changed. Her beauty had not changed, though now she was a beauty of nearly nineteen, instead of a beauty of thirteen. Her love for me had not changed, nor my love for her. Callo would be made tolerable, for my knowing that she was by. Indeed, I thought I might learn more from her, of all that Aunt Mariota required me to learn, than from all the Callo lessons. She was a year older than I; she was out in society, and, if she did not go out to seek the world, the world would surely come to Crask to seek her. And she was in love, or fancied herself in love, or stood on the margin of love. This was not a subject Aunt Honoria had

13

thought necessary to teach me: but it was one in which I badly wanted instruction.

Aunt Honoria agreed, it seemed, that Mariota could join the regiment of my teachers; anyway, she waved as we departed in the carriage with a warmer smile than I had seen on her face before.

It was not as warm a smile, by miles, as that with which the Earl of Crask greeted me. I had guessed right about him, too – he had not changed by a hair. He was old to be the father of an eighteen-year-old girl, well into his sixties as I judged. In my childhood I had perceived everybody over twenty as immemorially old, without much distinction between them all; now I realised that the Earl must have married very late. I wondered why. He was a most endearing man. He was tall, a little stooped, with thin grey hair, and whiskers which his barber had left a little longer on one side than on the other. He was dressed in old green tweed knickerbockers, in which my Uncle Ranald would never have allowed himself to be seen. He greeted me with most touching warmth, pumping my hand up and down as though I were a machine he was trying to start, or he was a machine he wanted me to start. He asked me a stream of kindly questions about myself, and my Papa and Mama and brothers and sister, and hardly waited for answers, but darted off to new questions, as birdlike as his daughter.

Mariota and I had climbed down out of the carriage to talk to him, and he led us away from the road to the top of a steep bluff of grass and scree. We were still half a mile away from Crask, further up the hill; I was worried that we were keeping the Countess waiting for her tea, but Mariota and her father said that I must see the wonder that was to transform the Crask estate.

The bluff formed one bank of a river, which was a major tributary of the Gard called the Crask Water. The other bank, a hundred yards below us, rose into a similar bluff, so that the river rushed through a kind of gigantic gunsight, before bending and dropping out of sight.

At the jaws, that I have called a gunsight, a gang of men was labouring. I saw blocks of stones being lowered on ropes down the bluff, by men who unloaded them from a cart. I saw on the river bank all manner of sacks that looked like

14

cement and sand. (They had been most familiar sights in Sydney, as the town grew and grew.) There were logs stacked, and great sawn planks. Men with picks and shovels were slicing at the sides of the two bluffs; and, on the far side, I saw that already masons were hoisting blocks into position, and cementing them into the hillside.

· 'We are making history,' said the Earl of Crask. 'We are changing the face of Scotland. We are damming the Crask Water. The benefits will be incalculable. We will be as widely imitated as the Duke of Bridgewater, when he built the first wholly artificial canal to take his coal to Manchester.'

'But you have no coal,' I said stupidly. 'And if Manchester is where I think it is, it is too far away. . . .'

'Down at Callo,' he said, 'your uncle has a fine fishable river. I had many a good day there, in the days when I had time for such frivolities. Our water here is too fast for any fish but the veriest minnows. But, when our dam is built, picture the expanse of water we shall have! Thirty acres! More! we can adjust the level with great exactness, by means of sluice-gates operated by wheels. An artificial loch! A single gigantic stew-pond! From this aspect only, two consequences derive. Stocked with fish from elsewhere, with salmon and Loch Leven trout, Loch Crask when netted with seines will yield a far richer harvest than all my arable acres! We shall put the fish, alive, into casks of water, as they have done for centuries in the Fenlands, and carry them on carts to the market. Not your little provincial markets, but the great hubs of trade! No Glasgow fishmonger's slab, no Edinburgh hotel menu, will be complete without Loch Crask fish! I foresee a gigantic profit. But the commercial use of the net does not preclude the sporting use of rod and line. Callo, I know, lets a few rods fish for nearly a pound a day. In the tranquil and teeming waters of my loch, I shall charge twice that, and be turning sportsman away! They may fish from the shore or from boats. Only the fly will be permitted. I plan a limit of three brace per rod per day, but I am prepared to find, after the experience of a season or two, that our stocks will be so copious as to render this figure niggardly! Then you will not find me closed-minded. I am drawing up also, in the evenings and when my work here permits, schemes for season-tickets, debentures, club-membership. I shall have a resident tackle-

15

maker and fly-dresser. A smokery, of course. None of these facilities will be offered gratis. Callo may bring his salmon to my smokery. I shall allow a discount for neighbours. That is, I think, a sacrifice which friendship obliges me to make.'

'You were saying, Papa,' said Mariota, with an air of encouraging a precocious child, 'that when land is flooded, the water is full of food for the fish. All the things that were crawling in the grass are swimming in the water. I should have thought they would have drowned, but perhaps the fish do not mind that.'

'I would hate to eat a dead fly,' I said dubiously.

'I would rather eat a dead one than a live one,' said Mariota.

The Earl was not listening. He was shouting, in his high voice, to the men below. But the wind plucked his words away, as it had plucked away Mariota's, when she called to me on the banks of the Gard. The Earl began to clamber down the bluff to the workings. I trembled for his safety. He seemed to me too spindly to be adventuring down such a steep slope.

Mariota must have thought the same. 'Be careful, Papa!' she screamed. But of course, in the wind and the noise of the waters, he could not hear her, and slithered perilously on down.

We waited until we saw him safe on the level ground, and then turned back to the carriage.

'There are all sorts of other benefits, besides the fish,' said Mariota. 'Papa has explained them to me. If the land below suffers from a drought, you know, he can let them have water at so much for a thousand gallons.'

'Is there ever a drought in Glengard?' I asked.

'Well, there might be. And then people can bring their yachts.'

'How?'

'And then he can let a little water out of the sluice, and turn a watermill, and grind all the corn. All sorts of things. He had engineers all the way from Edinburgh, to help him design the dam. But he found they were not satisfactory. He had studied the matter more deeply than they had. Also, the way they said it must be built was too expensive.'

This was a very long speech for Mariota to make, without

16

once changing the subject. I knew by this that she was worried about the dam – about the way the Earl had designed it, or perhaps about the whole idea. There had been so many other ideas; and I thought there would, indeed, be more dark patches on the walls of Crask.

There were. I had been there so often in my childhood, that I could remember it almost as clear as Callo. I could remember a big portrait by Raeburn, of a previous Earl, over the fireplace in the hall. That was the first dark patch I saw. And I had guessed right about the chairs with unequal legs, and the servants fewer and more sluttish.

Among these wretched changes, the Countess of Crask was blessedly unchanged.

It was from her father, perhaps, that Mariota had inherited the sweetness of her smile, and the childlike clarity of her grey eyes – as well as the butterfly quality of her conversation, which was only occasionally infuriating. From her mother, without question, came her brilliant chestnut hair, the smallness of her feet, the slimness of her wrists, and the extraordinarily graceful way in which her head was set upon her neck and her neck on her shoulders.

There was a little grey in the Countess's chestnut curls; otherwise I could see no change at all, nor hear one. She lay as she had always lain, in the one sunny room in that almost sunless house. She lay like a high-bred cat, most elegant, her chestnut hair bright against the green velvet of the chaise-longue I so well remembered. There was a book as always open beside her, of poetry, or one of the novels of Jane Austen. Whatever the season there were flowers. The colours of the room had a sort of subdued elegance – the dull green, a dusty pink, the glint of gilt from the frames of little pictures (and only when you looked close did you see how threadbare were the curtains, how tarnished the picture-frames, and how little tables and stools had been placed to try to hide the bare patches in the carpet).

What was least changed, in this unchanged lady, was her welcome to me. I curtsied, as I always had when coming into this room; she stretched out her arms to me, as she always had.

It was another home-coming, no less for being in somebody else's home.

17

'Dear Bella,' she said. 'You bring something into the room with you. Light, that is what you bring. Perhaps it is the Australian sunshine, but I think it is your own sunshine. I want to hear every single one of your adventures, in a place I can only imagine with the greatest difficulty, but I shall treat you like a large box of expensive chocolates. My instinct, you know, is always to gobble and gobble, trying every different flavour, out of a mixture of curiosity and the purest greed. One should eat chocolates one at a time, and at intervals. I shall compel myself to listen to your adventures a little at a time. Then I shall remember so much more, which will be nice, and it will all go on much longer, which will be even nicer. Now tell me first – how did you leave your Mama and the children?'

'Mama was very well, ma'am. She particularly sent her love to you.'

'I hoped she would, but I wasn't going to humiliate myself by asking you if she had.'

I laughed. 'The boys were almost too well, when I left,' I said. 'At least, Archie had had a bump on the head, so he was supposed to be an invalid, but he wasn't like any invalid I ever saw.'

'A bump on the head. Ah – now we shall learn something of Australian life. He was set on by a savage? A monkey threw a coconut?'

'There was a pony they all said nobody could ride. Archie was sure he could ride it. They said it would buck him off. They were quite right.'

'Poor Archie. To be proved wrong and have a bump on the head, all in the same moment. . . . One is supposed to welcome these experiences, because they teach one lessons of wisdom and caution. But the lessons are so disagreeable, that one would rather not learn anything at all. I get glimpses of your life already. How well it must suit your father. And how well it must have suited you. And what a change Callo must be –'

She stopped herself abruptly. I was puzzled for a moment, until I saw that she would on no account allow herself to say anything that even hinted of criticism of Aunt Honoria, not to me, not ever. I was sure that the Countess did not think of Aunt Honoria as nearly as great a friend of hers, as Aunt

Honoria thought of the Countess as hers; and I was sure that the Countess was far too intelligent not to realise this, and the reasons for it. But still they *were* friends, and nothing would have induced the Countess into any disloyalty. In almost anyone else, a malicious remark might have followed that opening; in her, nothing malicious had ever followed any opening. As a child, I had thought that she was the one person I had ever met who was truly incapable of unkindness. Here was something else unchanged. Here was another bit of homecoming.

Well, the Countess did not obey her rules about boxes of chocolates. She gobbled all my stories about Australia, as though they had been crystallised violets, or chocolate truffles. She did not pepper me with distracting questions, as Mariota or her father would have done, but simply prodded me into talking more, and more, and more. She sat smiling and nodding, her eyes fixed on my face, as though it was all even more exciting and fascinating than she had dared hope. From time to time I tried to stop, not in accordance with her theory about glutting herself with bonbons, but because I thought I must be boring and exhausting her. But she would not have me stop, until at last I ground to a halt from sheer exhaustion: and then she was contrite, and exclaimed at her own selfishness; and so I went back to Callo in their carriage, only just in time to dress for dinner.

It was odd to think that my uncle and aunt and cousins had asked only the most perfunctory questions about my Australian days. To them it was an inferior world, to which it was disaster to be exiled.

What they wanted to ask about, at dinner and afterwards, was not Australia but Crask: the house and the Earl and the Countess and Mariota. They wanted the late news. Clearly they were not closely informed, not much up to date, though they did not admit these things.

Lady Crask's refusal to breathe a wisp of criticism of Aunt Honoria became all the more admirable. I knew that my father, like all good soldiers, counted loyalty among the greatest of human virtues. It was good to know that someone who liked me, and who lived nearby, had this steadfast quality. When I ventured on the perilous quicksands of adult social life, I would need all the loyal friends I could find.

I reported on the dam. They had heard about the dam, but not seen it. Uncle Ranald, stocky and square-faced, and speaking in stately periods, applauded the adventurous experiment.

'If the natural leaders of our community do not light the way,' he said, 'the prospect for human progress is faint indeed.'

Uncle Ranald addressed his family as though it were a public meeting. My father often addressed public meetings as though they were his family. Uncle Ranald made an effort to hide his baldness, by brushing his hair very carefully across the bare skin, and glueing it in place with macassar-oil. The effect of this was to make him seem not less bald, but more so. This habit was possibly the least important thing about him: but somehow it seemed the most exactly expressive of his personality.

I did not think the Earl of Crask was the natural leader of anything. He was nicer than that.

'It would be very difficult to predict the ultimate commercial and financial advantages of such an operation,' said Cousin Henry. 'But Crask will have consulted the finest brains.'

Henry was interested in commercial and financial advantages, almost to the exclusion of any other interests. He was even more unlike a future baronet, than Uncle Ranald was unlike a present baronet. He looked like a well-scrubbed cow: not a bull, but a cow. I did not understand how a man of twenty-eight could look more like a cow than a bull, but so it was.

It was possible to imagine the Earl consulting the finest brains, but it was impossible to imagine him taking their advice.

Aunt Honoria was not interested in the dam. She was interested in the effect I had had on the Countess.

'Well,' I said, 'she was as kind today as she always was. She wanted to hear all about Australia.'

'That showed kindness indeed,' put in my Cousin Grizelda.

I knew what she meant, and I knew she was wrong. I thought Grizelda would always be a little wrong about everything. She was thirty-two. She had been presented at Holyroodhouse fourteen years before, and it seemed that her search

20

for a husband had long been abandoned in despair. This had the effect of making her not more realistic, but less so, because to a naturally sour disposition was added the bitterness of failure.

I did not think I had ever been truly disliked, ever before in my life. I found that I was, by Grizelda. She even made pity impossible. She *dressed* to make pity impossible, by grandness; and she spoke to make it impossible, by malice.

'I hope you did not exhaust poor Lady Crask,' said Aunt Honoria, thinking, I supposed, of the effect of my thoughtless crudity on her own future reception there.

'She exhausted me,' I said.

'And was dear Mariota there all the time?'

'Oh yes.'

'With the difference,' said Grizelda, 'that Mariota would not have been listening.'

This was indeed partly true, but, like all Grizelda's remarks, only partly.

'She will not be there much longer,' said Grizelda.

'Have you heard so, dearest?' said Aunt Honoria. 'And so have I, from Lady Nicholls.'

'And I from my maid,' said Grizelda. 'I suppose, Mama, that is the difference between us.'

'Where did *she* get it from?'

'Mariota's maid. A better source than yours, Mama.'

'Yes, although one cannot quite like. . . . It smacks of the back-stairs. . . .'

'I *thought* so,' I said.

'Did Mariota say anything about it, Arabella?' asked Aunt Honoria sharply.

'She refused to say anything about it. But she blushed. So I jumped to conclusions.'

'Instead of over the wall of the sheep-wash,' said Grizelda, 'as you did this morning.'

'Arabella!' said Aunt Honoria in an awful voice.

'I did not tear anything,' I said anxiously, 'or cover myself with mud. . . . Is Mariota. . . . Is it Geoffrey Nicholls?'

'Good gracious no. What an absurd idea. He is to be an advocate, a professional man. He is only a younger son, and only of a knight.'

'Then it must be Peter McCallum or Rupert Fraser.'

'Of course it is not!'

'I don't see how it can be anyone from very far away,' I said, 'as Mariota never goes even a little way away.'

'Not so very far,' said Aunt Honoria mysteriously.

Was there any other unmarried man of marriageable age, of Mariota's class or near it, within twenty miles distance of Crask?

'It must be someone who has come here since I went to Australia,' I said.

'It is someone who was here before you first came here. Before you were born,' said Grizelda.

'Someone,' said Aunt Honoria, in a reverential voice, 'whose family have lived in the glen even longer than we have.'

'That can only be. . .'

Aunt Honoria shot warning glances at the footmen. I understood, but it was perfectly silly: if Mariota's maid had told Grizelda's maid, then the Servants' Halls of every house in the county knew the name.

It could only be. . . . Could it possibly be? . . . It could only be the Most Honourable the Marquess of Gard, son and heir of the Duke of Lomond.

Mariota, to marry the Marquess? Was it possible? Could she bear it?

I was surprised he was still unmarried, if I was guessing right. It seemed more and more likely that I was, to explain the important mysteriousness of the others.

Could Mariota bear it? He was twelve years older at least than she, almost of an age with Grizelda. I remembered him from eight years before, when he was already grown up and I was eleven. I remembered him as hard, proud, ill-tempered, intolerant; I remembered him as vindictive and treacherous.

Could Mariota bear it?

Perhaps she could, if anybody could. She would radiate vague sweetness, and by listening to her fairy music ignore the unpleasantness of her husband. Perhaps life could be lived like that; not mine, but perhaps Mariota's.

I could see why Aunt Honoria was excited. She had known Mariota most of her life; they could hardly shut her out of Glengard Castle, when Mariota was mistress of it.

'Why is it a secret?' I suddenly asked.

22

'You *must* try to understand the polite conventions, Arabella,' said Aunt Honoria, turning a conversation at dinner into a lesson in deportment. 'It is not announced because there is, as yet, nothing official to announce. No firm commitment has yet been made. Do you understand these words? Are they familiar in Australia? We are speaking not of a betrothal but of an understanding. There must be, even in New South Wales, a clear distinction between the two. Any public discussion of the matter would be premature and impertinent.'

'You mean,' I frowned, 'it may *not* be true?'

Aunt Honoria turned away from me with a sigh, to say something to her son. I was not yet fit to talk to, on such delicate and important matters, for more than a minute.

Chapter 2

My father's regiment, the Lennox Highlanders, was sent to India when I was very small. My mother could not take me, because they were to be stationed in a place full of heat and fever. So began my childhood at Callo, with my cheerful and kindly grandparents, and my friendship with Mariota and the others.

I learned to ride and swim and row a boat on the lochans; I was supposed to learn about kings and queens and the books of the Old Testament, but I was not so good at those lessons.

It must have rained; but, years on, I only remembered sunshine. I must have been punished; but I only remembered being indulged, my childish exploits praised, my indifference to my books taken as natural and proper.

One punishment only I did remember. I thought I always would remember it, and the rage it filled me with. That was forced on Grandpapa.

My father's older brother, my Uncle Ranald, then lived with his family in Edinburgh. I thought this choice of home astonished the whole family. I thought, indeed, that Uncle Ranald himself astonished the whole family – certainly two brothers could hardly have been more different. I once heard a grown-up say, not knowing that I was hiding under a sofa, that it was a pity my father was not the eldest. But another person said, that it would have been a pity if my father had been the one to inherit title and estate, because the army would have lost a fine and popular officer. I was so joyful to hear this that I gave myself away, and was dragged out from under the sofa with fluff in my mouth and a cobweb in my hair. I was not punished: and the grown-ups who had spoken were not sorry that I had heard how high they valued my father.

A consequence of Uncle Ranald being in Edinburgh, was that sometimes his children came to Callo for the holidays. I never understood why they came. They took no advantage of river or hill. They brought a gloom which even afflicted my Grandpapa. Grizelda was shocked at my running so wild, and at my being so much in the company of boys older than myself; she wanted me to be a little lady. Henry would have been a bully, but in order to bully people you must first catch them, and he never could run fast enough to catch any of us.

Two days after my visit to Crask, I was once again at liberty in the afternoon. There was a gusty rain, against which I was well protected. Aunt Honoria and Grizelda had gone in a carriage to Lochgrannomhead; Uncle Ranald was being important somewhere; Henry was immersed in his accounts. Nobody was available to improve me; since I was incapable of improving myself, I was allowed to risk catching my death of cold, and getting chapped lips and a red nose.

Instead of descending, I climbed. After a strip of flat pastureland by the river, the ground tilted into a different world, of bracken and stunted thorns, and then of rock and heather. Presently the wind tore gaps in the clouds, so that pale sunlight gleamed on the river below me, and on the wet black slates of the roof of Callo. The bark of a raven, doglike, came down the wind, and the grouse chattered from the higher ground.

I saw that a figure was climbing towards me, taking giant strides over the broken ground. It was a man, a very active man, in tweed knickerbockers and an oilskin coat. He was too far away to recognise, but I was suddenly certain that it was a friend. Which friend?

It was something about the way he moved – impulsive charging up the hill towards me – that told me it was Rupert Fraser. He was a soldier. He had been commissioned, I knew, into my father's regiment of Highlanders (and Papa had had something to do with that, no doubt – he and the Frasers were lifelong friends). He was awaiting his posting. He would join the regiment in India. There he would cover himself with glory and medals, and discover new mountains, and shoot all manner of big game. It was all most improbable. He had been the dreamer of our little tribe. Not with the dreaminess of Mariota and her fairy music, but with a kind of furious poetic dreaminess. Indeed he once wrote me a poem, a thing no one had ever done before, or ever did afterwards. And once, when we were looking at a new moon over the river, hung low in a jade-green sky, I saw tears on his cheek. He commanded me passionately not to laugh, nor to tell. I did not laugh, or tell anyone about his tears. That was the time – that early evening of the new moon – that he said that he had made two decisions about his life. One was that he would be a writer, and the other was that he would marry me. Still I did not laugh, and I did not tell.

Yes, it was Rupert; and I looked at him in astonishment as he bounded up the last few yards to where I stood. He was a little above the average height, lean and weatherbeaten, with untidy dark hair, and a hooky nose that always made him look like a poetical pirate. He was breathing hard after his climb, but his face was creased by a grin that seemed too broad for his face to contain and he stretched out both his hands for both of mine.

'I was calling at Crask,' he said, as soon as he could speak. 'They told me you were here. And they told me at Callo that you were last seen heading for the clouds.'

'I can't believe you're a soldier,' I said stupidly.

'A man has to do something. At least, a younger son has to. Can you picture me in a counting-house?'

'You were going to be a writer.'

'We all talked a lot of rubbish.' He was staring at me. 'And a lot that wasn't rubbish. I shall be here all summer, I think. They send us out in time for the cold weather, so that we don't die of heat-stroke before we're used to the climate.'

'Good!' I cried.

'That I won't die of heat-stroke?'

'That you'll be here all summer.'

'So, unfortunately, will Peter McCallum. So will Geoffrey Nicholls.'

'And so will Mariota.'

We talked of the old days, and of the present days, and of the future. His was mapped out with great exactness, and almost all his active life would probably be spent in India. He seemed content at the prospect. I searched for the poet

26

under the oilskin coat and the cheerful soldier's manner; I
could not see a vestige. Perhaps the poet would show better
when we were off the hill and out of the wind; but I thought
not.

'Down there,' he said, pointing at the river, 'remember
your theatricals?'

'No.'

'When you pretended to be drowning.'

'Oh. Those theatricals. Of course I remember them.'

It had all started as a harmless dare, and developed into
a practical joke, and developed from that into disaster. It was
the summer of Rupert's poem, but it was hard to think of it
as anything but the summer of that disaster. The river was
low and, above the falls, unusually gentle. Rupert and I were
in a boat with an old gillie called Dougal. Rupert and I were
fishing, turn about with the same rod. Rupert got into a good
fish, and Dougal landed him so that he could play it from
the bank. Dougal scrambled out of the boat, too, to gaff the
fish when Rupert had tired it. They had no immediate need
of the boat, so I pushed off and started downstream. I heard
Dougal shout. I ignored him. I knew he knew he had no
cause for worry. There was not enough water in the falls to
make them at all dangerous; I was well used to boats and
oars; and I could swim like a fish. All I had to do was to sit
tight, and be ready to push myself off a rock if the boat got
stuck. It was all something I had wanted to do for months,
because I knew that all three boys had been down the falls,
in low water, in a small boat, and I took very firmly the view
that I could do anything they could do.

In fact the water began to take me faster than I expected,
and to make me wetter than I expected. Still it was not
alarming: or only a very little.

The falls swept me round a bend, and towards the island
with its little tumbledown castle. I saw that a man was fishing
from the island, casting up into the place where the river
divided. I saw that he was tall and dark, grown-up or almost
so. I saw that it was the Marquess of Gard, fishing from the
island which my ancestor had given his ancestor. There was
a gillie behind him. I saw that the Marquess was looking at
me with astonishment: even as I bobbed up and down, and

27

revolved, and bounced off the rocks, I could see the surprise in his face.

I do not seek to excuse what next I did. It was distinctly thoughtless. Simply as a joke, simply to extract enjoyment from a situation that was not in all ways quite as enjoyable as I had expected, simply – since he was bent on staring at me – to give him his money's worth, I began to scream for help. It *was* theatrical. I quailed, and trembled, and flung out my arms, and gave as faithful a performance as I knew how of a female in strong hysterics.

The Marquess dropped his rod, and jumped down into the water. I saw that his rod fell down into the river also. The gillie made no move to follow – the older Highlanders believed that if they got wet they would surely die. The Marquess began to wade across, so as to cut off my boat as it drifted by. He slipped and fell, with a great splash, which was easy to do on those slippery rocks. He was instantly wetter than anybody I had ever seen. He lost his hat. I had an idea that, in falling, he had fallen across his rod. He laboured through the water, which was not much higher than his knees, almost falling again. I picked up my oars, and with two good strokes I sped past the point that he was making for. I was whisked, in almost perfect safety, beside the island, and down towards the lower part of the falls. He fell again, heavily, in three feet of water and I most unfortunately burst out laughing. He was quite near enough to hear my childish shrieks of laughter, even in the noise of the water.

He could be forgiven for being cross; but he could not be forgiven for doing what he afterwards did. The gillie arrived at Callo with a message for my grandfather; it was that I should be whipped, and that, out of my pocket-money, I should pay for a rod to replace the broken rod, and a hat to replace the lost hat.

It took me two minutes to recover from the whipping; it took me two years of saving up my pocket-money, to pay off the loan that Grandpapa made me, to buy a fishing-rod and a hat.

I was truly sorry about the rod, and a little sorry even about the hat – but I did not think I should be blamed for a man dropping his belongings; and I did not think a grown-up man should have made such a desperate to-do about a little water.

'What is he like now?' I asked Rupert. 'Do you see him?'

'Hardly at all. Remember that I have not been here. He has called on my parents, but not often or recently. Of course he is often in Edinburgh and in London. I believe he goes to Crask.'

'Yes,' I said. 'I believe he does.'

'You have already heard that rumour, then.'

'*Is* it true? *Is* it possible?'

'It makes us all very careful what we say in front of Mariota. If his name is mentioned, we change the subject, or say what a good fellow he is.'

'Is he not, then? Is he is . . . as arrogant and treacherous as ever?'

'Arrogant, yes. People do say that about him. Treacherous? In most of his dealings I dare say not, but in some of them, certainly yes. A fellow I knew in the army told me, knowing we were neighbours of Glengard, that his family knew a girl – a young wife, to be exact, whose husband was away abroad – who was driven mad by Gard.'

'How driven mad? Mad for love?'

'Mad to the point of suicide.'

'She actually. . . .'

'No. They stopped her in time. Her life is in ruins.'

'That does not sound like the – the stiff, pompous, disapproving sort of man I thought he was.'

'No. But, if you want to be the kind of man Gard is, what better sort of mask could you find to wear?'

'But that is devilish!'

'I wish you'd promise me one thing. Keep clear of Gard.'

'Nothing on earth is likely to bring me within miles of Gard. Or him within miles of me.'

'Women, I am told, find him very handsome.'

'I won't be in a position to judge. Does Mariota not know, or does she know and not care, or is she expecting to reform him?'

'I've never dared ask. I'm not likely to influence Mariota, and in the meantime I like going to Crask.'

'Well, somebody should warn her. Somebody should tell her about the poor lady he drove demented.'

'If people want to disbelieve something, they can always find reasons for doing so. Mariota and her parents would say that she was half demented already, or that it was some other man, and not Gard at all. How could I or anybody convince Mariota about any of this? I don't even know that poor woman's name.'

'This is very depressing,' I said. 'Let's go and have tea.'

Jean Carmichael was the member of our childhood group who was least a member of the group. She was with us less often, because, it was said, there was 'trouble at home', but we never knew what kind of trouble, and grown-ups would not tell us, and Jean herself would not tell us. When she was with us, she fluttered. She fluttered her eyelashes, and her hands; when she spoke, her voice fluttered. She was as much like a bird as Mariota was, but a different kind of bird. Jean never, it seemed to me, did anything else but flutter. She never climbed things, or jumped over things; I did not remember her ever in a boat, or on horseback. Mariota might spend much of her time dreaming, but when she was awake she was adventurous enough, if great effort was not involved. Not Jean. She never tore her stockings, or got mud or grass-stains on her petticoats. It did not occur to me as a child to wonder why she bothered to join us – that we should all be so often together was the natural order of things – but, years on, I wondered. Perhaps the 'trouble at home' included her loneliness, or made her lonely.

Like me, she went away, and soon after I did. I heard the story from Rupert Fraser, because Aunt Honoria would not discuss it. The 'trouble at home' grew such that Jean's mother went back to her own mother, in Aberdeen, on the other side of Scotland; Jean of course went with her. Then Jean's father went away too, but nobody knew where or why, or what had become of him. What everyone knew was that he left a lot of debts behind. Then, about her twentieth birthday, Jean was married; she had been married for four months when I got back from Australia; she was Jean Hannay; she was Lady Hannay, because her husband was a baronet, like Uncle Ranald. Sir Archibald Hannay bought the Carmichaels' old home, Jean's father's house – a place called Achmore, just over the hill from Glengard. The house was Jean's wedding-gift from her bridegroom. Rupert said that everyone said that this was a most romantic gesture; he also said that everyone said it was the only romantic thing reported of Sir Archibald. The newly-weds were in the process of moving in to Achmore (Jean, of course, in the process of moving back), and very soon Aunt Honoria would call on Jean, who would return the call, so that some very dull afternoons would be spent.

Rupert had seen Jean, though not her husband. He said she still fluttered.

I was surprised that Mariota had said nothing to me of any of this. Perhaps her fairy music had drowned out all the gossip.

Aunt Honoria did call at Achmore; unusually, she took me with her, because Grizelda was suffering from a bilious attack brought on, it seemed to me, by rage at the world. I was pleased to go. I was excited to see Jean again, though we had not been so very close as children (partly, but only partly, because she was nearly three years older than I). I was curious to see Achmore again, which I remembered as a large house, quite new but built in an antique style, though with no land to speak of; I was curious to see Jean being the fluttering mistress of such a place. Rupert had said that marriage had not changed her, but I did not see how marriage could fail to change anybody.

We took the back drive which served Achmore, because this saved us a long way round by road. This meant that we passed the coach-house and stables. The coach-house was as big as a church, and much resembled a church of the most ornate kind. In Jean's father's day it had been almost empty; now it was chock-a-block with gleaming carriages, chariots, phaetons, wagonettes and vehicles I did not know the names of. I remembered the stables as being almost empty, too; now a glossy head poked out over the half-door of every loose-box, and a glossy rump occupied every stall.

I heard Aunt Honoria's sharp intake of breath. Her intakes of breath were not always easy to understand, but this one was. She was realising, as I was realising, one thing about Sir Archibald Hannay: he was rich.

This notion was confirmed as soon as the front door was thrown open to us. The footman was a very splendid footman:

and the butler to whom he consigned us was a splendid butler, accustomed to excellent port. The butler announced us at the door of a small sitting room, where Jean was writing letters. She stood up. Rupert was right; she fluttered. She fluttered as she shook hands with Aunt Honoria, as she embraced me, and as she sent for tea.

I wanted to bombard her with questions, about how she had come to get herself married, and what it was like to be so, and whether she felt odd living in her childhood home, and more intimate matters; but these questions could not be asked in Aunt Honoria's presence; and on such occasions I was supposed to be almost totally silent.

I inspected Jean, instead. She had always been small and slight, and was so still; she looked frail and breakable, like a piece of old French porcelain. She was very pale, as though she never went out of doors. Her hair was black, like Rupert Fraser's; but instead of his nice tousled mop, hers was as smooth and shining as a mute's silk hat. With all this, she seemed quite at home, as mistress of this large and hideous house. She had rapidly grown used to being rich, to having an establishment so different from that of her childhood. Were the rooms, the stairs, the windows, full of the unhappy ghosts of those wretched years? It seemed not; they were overlaid, perhaps, by the fine new furniture and pictures Sir Archibald had moved in.

Jean said she wanted me to tell her all about Australia; but Aunt Honoria did not want me to do this. It was a conflict to which there could only be one outcome; so Jean and Aunt Honoria talked about the wages of kitchen-maids.

Sir Archibald came in just as we were leaving. We learned another thing about him. He was much older than Jean, I thought nearly twenty years older. If he was not approaching forty, he looked as though he were. He was going bald both at the front and at the back, and he made efforts not unlike Uncle Ranald's to conceal the fact, with the same result. He was a small man, which suited with Jean; he was fat, which did not. I was really shocked that my childhood playmate should have found herself a little, old, bald, fat man for a husband; I hoped that this did not show on my face, but I was miserably conscious that it probably did, because everything always did, and that Jean's feelings would be hurt.

He was very friendly to us. He said he had heard much about me, from Jean. Jean herself he treated with what looked like real affection, and Jean treated him with what looked like real affection, so I told myself that I must not judge, and that what would horrify one person may make another quite happy. At least Jean had chosen better than Mariota, if Mariota had woken up enough to do any choosing.

In the carriage on the way home, Aunt Honoria talked about the carriages and pictures and furniture, but not about Sir Archibald's paunch or his pate.

I thought the world was arranged badly. Jean, who never rode or wanted to, had a stable full of horses. I, who had loved riding all my life, had no horse.

I tried to fight down memories of Australia, but they came flooding.

As soon as he was promoted, and posted to Sydney, Papa sent for all of us; but of course the letters took months to arrive. Then there was the fury of packing up, and then the long, long voyage with many strange and exotic stopping places; and then the joy of reunion with Papa, and the joy of finding, from the very first moment, that Australia was a good place to be.

A governess had come out with us; but, if it was hard to do lessons on the boat, it was still harder in New South Wales. Almost my earliest memory of that new life was of escaping from poor Miss Haslam, who had expected to give me a French lesson, and going hunting with Papa. He should not have taken me, of course, on a morning set aside for lessons; but his attitude to lessons was much like mine, and so was his attitude to sport. Hounds and men met quite close to Sydney, in a country where big groves of trees were divided by stony emptiness. I had heard about English foxhunting, though in the West Highlands I had never seen it, and it was immediately obvious that New South Wales kangaroo hunting was a very different thing. Nobody was at all smart; everything was friendly and informal; the pack was a few crossbred, rough-coated greyhounds; and how we galloped! There was not much jumping to be done, because nobody had yet built fences in that part; but there were terrifying sharp turns to be made among the trees, to avoid having one's head knocked off by a branch. During one break, a farmer told me an extraordinary story, which I never forgot. He said that a friend of his one day brought out a terrier, to run with the pack, and a female kangaroo picked up the terrier, and ran with it in her arms, until the hounds caught up with her; then she let the terrier go, and it was perfectly unharmed and cheerful, and ever afterwards wanted the same thing to happen again. The farmer swore the story was true, and by making a great effort I contrived to believe him. Yes, a place where such a thing could happen was a good place to be.

Papa took me racing, too. He liked having a companion, and Mama was busy with the younger ones. I had never been to the races, but I had heard of the smartness and formality and display of places like Ascot and York. I thought I should find as great a difference, from these glorious originals, in the racing as in the hunting. But in Sydney itself, and in Parramatta fourteen miles away, everyone dressed up in their very best for the races, and it was all like a gigantic garden-party. It was also, Papa said, as dishonest as English racing had been fifty years before, but I did not see any sign of that. There were other sorts of races, too, which Papa sometimes went to, and took me to – races in which farmers' boys rode farm horses over strips of stony ground behind taverns. I tried very hard to persuade papa to let me ride in one of those races; he might have done, perhaps, except for all the holes and ditches and boulders which the horses had to gallop over. He never stayed to the end of those afternoons, if I was with him. I found out that it was because everybody went into the taverns and got drunk.

I thought that, perhaps, the two most violently different things I had ever done, were to go to those impromptu Australian races, on one hand, and to sit in Achmore listening to Aunt Honoria talking about kitchen-maids' wages, on the other. It was depressing to think that my life from then on was supposed to consist entirely of that latter thing, and not at all of the former.

We came back to Callo, after that afternoon-call to Achmore, just as the sun was going down behind the big hills to the south-west. We were driving directly into that sunset: so that, when a horseman came out of the gate of the policies, he was against the flare of the sky, and his face was perfectly invisible. I could see only that he was a tall man, in a tall hat, and that he was riding a magnificent horse. He raised his hat and waved it at the carriage, but then turned off the road onto a bridle-path which led away up the glen.

'How infuriating!' cried Aunt Honoria. 'That he should call on the very afternoon that I was out! Oh, I could scream! And poor Grizelda confined to her room! He can have seen nobody but Henry! I wonder he did not stop to talk, for a minute. But I daresay he has a thousand pressing engagements. And I suppose, now, it may be years before he comes here again!'

'But who is he, Aunt Honoria,' I said, 'that you are so very cross to have missed?'

'That was Lord Gard, Arabella. That was our neighbour the Marquess.'

Her rage was explained. I felt almost sorry for her. The local king, or at least Prince Regent, did not come to Callo often.

I felt almost sorry for the Marquess, too, if he had really been obliged to hobnob with Henry. But perhaps he was also interested in accounts, and profit and loss.

What most I felt was relief. If we had trundled towards Callo only two minutes sooner, we would have met him just by the house. We would have talked. I would have been introduced. I would have struggled to hide my revulsion, after hearing Rupert's story of the poor lady the Marquess had driven to try to do away with herself. I would not have been able to hide it. Full in that evening sun, my face would have given my feelings away; and Aunt Honoria would finally have despaired of me.

We found that it had, in fact, been Henry the Marquess had come to see. It was some matter of a cart-road, which Henry had announced he was closing, and the crofters wanted kept open.

Henry pretended, with all his might, that the Marquess was like any other caller come on a matter of farming business.

'He spoke like a reasonable man,' said Henry, trying to keep the tremble of awe out of his voice. 'He understands my position now, and I understand his. I have promised to give the matter my most serious consideration, and let him have my answer in a day or two.'

'But did you offer him refreshment?' cried Aunt Honoria. 'Tea? Or a glass of wine? Did you not press him to stay until my return?'

'He wanted no refreshment. He could not stay.'

'Oh, I could scream!

This I knew to be true, as she had already been screaming.

'Did he speak of Mariota?' she asked. 'Did he mention his plans? Did he speak of his father's health, whether he is stronger in the better weather? Did you not ask?'

The questions poured out, not quite in a scream; and Henry became stiffer and stiffer, and assured his mother that he had said all the correct things, and that he hoped he knew how to conduct a conversation; and Aunt Honoria did not believe him, and lamented again and again that she had been out.

'If he had been entertained as *I* would have entertained him,' she said, 'he would have come back! It might have become a regular thing, that he called in when he was passing on his way to. . . . To any place that he was going to. Now I suppose we shall have to wait until Mariota. . . . Oh that I should have been out! Oh that I did not come back sooner!'

By and by it became Jean's fault, for detaining us longer than she should have done; or Sir Archibald's fault, for delaying our departure by his arrival; or my fault, on grounds which were not explained.

I disgraced myself, in the Buttermarket in Lochgrannomhead. Nobody disgraced themselves in such a manner in Lochgrannomhead, especially in the Buttermarket, where the best shops were, except drunken tinkers. I behaved, said Aunt Honoria, like a drunken tinker. But I did not see how else I could have behaved, without missing Geoffrey Nicholls, and I could not bear to do that. We had finished our shopping, and were starting away up the street. I was glancing backwards, out of our open carriage, because I had an idea we might have run over a kitten. I saw a tall young man come out of a shop. I did not at once recognize him. Then he took off his hat and scratched his ear, not in the manner of a man who has an itching ear, but in the manner of a man who is trying to remember what else he should be buying. Instantly I remembered. Geoffrey had always had that trick, of scratching his ear as an aid to memory. I did not know how it worked, but it must have worked, because he always did it as a schoolboy, and there he was doing it still.

We were being carried away from him, and he was starting to walk away from us. I did what I would have done as a child, in my grandmother's carriage; I did what I would have done in Sydney, in my mother's carriage; I jumped to my feet in the open carriage, and shrieked his name.

'Arabella!' moaned Aunt Honoria, putting a hand to her heart.

'But it is Geoffrey!' I said.

'The whole of Lochgrannonhead knows that you think you have seen Geoffrey.'

'Well, I do not mind them knowing. It need not be a secret.'

I had not yet realised how disgraceful my behaviour had been, or how angry Aunt Honoria was. In any case, my attention was on Geoffrey, who had turned, and stared, and was now running after us.

'Bella! It can't be Bella! It must be Bella! Are you you?'

The coachman had by now stopped, and Geoffrey was able to reach up to shake my hand.

He said, 'Good afternoon, Lady Gordon,' to Aunt Honoria, but while he said it he was still holding my hand.

He was a man now, and a lawyer. He was completely different and just the same. He spoke easily, cheerfully. He had hazel eyes, and thick hair of a pale mouse-brown. He was as tall as Rupert Fraser, but more massively built. He was very neatly and correctly dressed, which had not been his way as a boy...He said that he must hurry away, because his mother was waiting for him at the hotel, but that he would ride over to Callo in the morning.

'Arabella will be occupied with her studies,' said Aunt Honoria in a terrible voice.

Geoffrey looked startled. Probably he did not associate me with any studies. He suggested himself for the afternoon, instead, addressing Aunt Honoria with a solemn correctness which had also not been his way as a boy.

37

She had to allow him to come, because there was no reason on earth why he should not come; but it was obvious to me, as it must have been obvious to Geoffrey, that she was not overjoyed. I could not at all imagine why. Geoffrey was a gentleman, intelligent, sufficiently handsome, already qualified as a professional man though not yet embarked on his career. And he was my lifelong friend. Why should not Aunt Honoria welcome his visit? Why should she have put a hand to her heart when I called out to him?

She did not give me the answers to either of these questions, while the coachman was sitting just in front of us; but she gave me the answers to both in the morning room at Callo, the minute we were back.

Yes, I had behaved like a drunken tinker, like a fishwife, like a backstreet drab coming out of an ale-house. In Scotland, if you saw a long-lost friend disappearing into a crowd, you let him go; you did not stand up in a carriage and shriek. If you did, no decent person would talk to you.

I started to make a remark that would have begun with the word 'But'. It was unwise to make remarks to Aunt Honoria that began with the word 'But'. I bowed my head, and made all kinds of apologies, and used the excuse that I had learned bad habits in Sydney, and the other excuse that I was excited to see Geoffrey Nicholls after so many years.

'It should be no excitement to you, Arabella, to see any member of the Nicholls family. We treat them with civility, as neighbours, but it was excessively tolerant of your grandfather to allow Geoffrey Nicholls to treat Mariota and yourself as equals.'

I looked at her in disbelief. I knew my father had had a warm regard for Sir George Nicholls, Geoffrey's father; so had my grandparents; he had the reputation of being a thoroughly generous and decent man. And Lady Nicholls, I thought, was a friend of Aunt Honoria.

'Sir George has been honoured by Her Majesty,' said Aunt Honoria, 'but we do not forget that his father made a fortune as a Glasgow shopkeeper.'

That was it.

I remembered old Mr Nicholls, Geoffrey's grandfather. I remembered my own grandfather's doubts, shared by the Crasks and the Frasers, when a retired merchant bought the

Invermore estate; but, when Grandpapa got to know Mr Nicholls, he liked him very much, and so did the others; and, when Grandpapa twice a year shot with the Duke of Lomond, Mr Nicholls was there too.

I thought it was funny that the Duke of Lomond should welcome Old Mr Nicholls, and Aunt Honoria should not welcome his grandson.

Any remark I might have attempted on this subject would also have begun with 'But'; so I listened meekly.

Geoffrey had always been a creature of most unpredictable moods. When something made him gloomy, like catching fewer trout than I did, he was gloomier than anybody else in Scotland; when something made him happy, like climbing a tree that nobody else could climb, he almost burst with happiness, so that you expected steam to come up out of his head, as though he were a volcano. When he was excited he was downright dangerous; he might do anything; he risked his life and all our lives. When he had one of his cynical turns, you thought that he believed in nothing, and trusted nobody. And when, just a very few times, he talked about me and about himself, you saw that he had the softest, most loving, most romantic heart in the world.

It had all gone. It was all outgrown. He was placid, even-tempered, adult. He seemed to be much older than Rupert Fraser, although they were exactly the same age. He said he was happy to see me, and I knew it was true, but he kept his happiness in check. He did not leap or shriek from happiness, as once he would have done. I was a little sad, though I had known that it was likely to have happened.

He was serious about his future. He had ideas about going into politics. He had ideas about righting wrongs, and ending injustice. He made me feel young and ignorant, because I knew nothing at all about all the things that were important to him.

I said this, rather dolefully, just as he was leaving; after he had mounted his horse but before he had ridden it away.

'Not quite, Bella,' he said, looking at me very hard. 'You know all about the thing that's most important to me of all. When I got home from Edinburgh, only the day before yesterday, my mother told me you were back. And I was almost frightened to meet you. Anything might have happened to you. You might even not have been beautiul. You might have been dull, or clumsy, or fat. But you are completely glorious, and you are the most important thing to me.'

'Oh,' I said stupidly, not knowing at all how to reply to such an amazing statement.

'I shall be here all summer,' he said, 'and I shall come to your birthday ball. And then. . . .'

He smiled, and it seemed to me he blushed; and suddenly he seemed not so very level-headed or grown-up, but like a bashful schoolboy.

He put his hat on his head, and rode away. He cleared his throat very loudly as he went, as though to undo the effect of his blush, and appear grown-up after all.

After that, both Rupert Fraser and Geoffrey Nicholls came often to Callo. What was curious was, that when one came, the other seemed always to come too. It was as though they had a compact, that neither should ever come alone. Grizelda said that they were both such children, that they needed one another's support in the ordeal of calling on us. It was another thing she got quite wrong.

Like Aunt Honoria, Geoffrey had heard from his mother the rumours about Mariota and the Marquess of Gard. Unlike her, he was aghast. Though he had teased Mariota when we were children, he said that he was deeply fond of her, and I was sure this was true. He had heard the dreadful story that Rupert had told me, from Rupert; he had heard other stories also, from friends in Edinburgh. He said that, as a lawyer, he did not think it proper to repeat them; but he said that they confirmed the tenor of Rupert's story.

'I have wondered what my duty was,' said Geoffrey, 'and I wonder still. I wondered whether to have a word with Mariota, but I'm sure Rupert is right. It would only put her in a rage, and do no good at all. I wondered whether to have a word with her father.'

'That would do even less good,' I said. 'His mind would shoot off onto his wonderful new dam, and he would not take in a word you said. . . . Might not your father talk to Lord Crask, Geoffrey?'

'My father is like your aunt,' he said. 'The Duke was very kind to my grandfather, when some people might have snubbed him, so my father won't hear a word against any member of the family. Feudal attitudes die hard. Confound it, here comes Rupert now. Am I never to have you to myself?'

'No,' said Rupert, grinning at me and scowling at Geoffrey. I thought it ingenious, to grin and scowl at the same moment; I would have thought it impossible, until I watched Rupert doing it.

'You thought to steal a march,' said Rupert to Geoffrey. 'Well, let me tell you I am up to your devices.'

They bickered quite amicably, each accusing the other of unfair stratagems and deceptions, until Aunt Honoria came into the morning room, and the conversation became adult and boring.

It distressed me that Aunt Honoria was so obviously more welcoming to one of my friends than to the other, because Geoffrey's grandfather had been a merchant, and the Frasers had been in Glengard for centuries. This was not simply the effect of the democratic atmosphere of Australia, or the fact that my father never cared a fig who anybody's father was; because Rupert was distressed by the difference too. The person it seemed not to distress at all was Geoffrey. I thought this did both Rupert and Geoffrey the greatest credit, and I thought I was very lucky to have such friends.

As children we had been a tribe of six. Now we were a tribe usually of three, sometimes of four, occasionally of five: for Geoffrey and Rupert and I went sometimes to Crask, where we were always made to inspect the progress of the new dam; and the three of us collected Mariota and went to Achmore, to see Jean Hannay fluttering among the tea-cups. Those visits were, perhaps, more enjoyable when Sir Archibald was not there; this was not because he was unpleasant, or more boring than one could bear, but simply because I could not get over my astonishment at Jean having married him. I knew that Geoffrey and Rupert shared my surprise. I did not know if Mariota did; it was one of the subjects, like the Marquess of Gard, which it seemed better not to discuss.

And then, as spring turned into summer, six was six again, and our circle complete. Peter McCallum had taken his degree the previous year, but had stayed on at his university for some additional diploma. Geoffrey and Rupert both said that they were awed by this academic grandeur. I was, too. It was even harder to imagine Peter covered with such honours, than to picture Rupert winning medals on the Northwest Frontier, or Geoffrey pleading learnedly in the lawcourts. For what Peter had been was the clown of our tribe, the buffoon; I remembered his making me laugh until I was almost sick, and his fooling, more often than anything else, would wake Mariota from her fairy-music dreams, and set her shrieking with the rest of us.

I was sad to think that he had become solemn and bookish: until I met him: and then the relief was gigantic, because unlike the others he was completely unchanged.

He ambushed me in the new plantation of fir-trees, from which my Cousin Henry expected to make an immense profit. From behind an old tree which had been felled, I heard a terrible growling and snarling, which I thought was at least three large dogs having a fight, and then a wail which I was sure was a wolf, except that there had been no wolves in Perthshire for centuries. . . . I picked up a branch that had broken off when the tree came down, in case some great animal came from behind the tree and decided that I was his luncheon: but a man came out, instead, now mewing like a cat – quite a small man, with a mop of sandy hair, and a round, happy face whch I would have known among a million.

I dropped my branch, and ran towards him; and he took both my hands in his, and gave a great bellow of laughter.

'Why are you laughing?' I said. 'Have I got mud on my cheek again?'

'From pure happiness,' said Peter. 'The joy of seeing you, Bella. Let me look at you. Yes! In so far as you have changed, it is only for the better. I was trying to frighten you, you know. I thought I could reduce you to abject terror, and then rescue you. Instead you picked up a cudgel, quite prepared to beat a lion on the head. Your hair is still like a lion's, and mine is still like the stuffing of a mattress. Stand quite still, quite straight. . . . Ah! What a gigantic relief! My growth was stunted, you know, by the shock of your departure to Australia, and I was afraid you might be taller than I am. But no. My cubits barely suffice. I can pursue you without making either of us ridiculous. But another thought has been affording me anguish. I understand from my family that the snake Fraser has been here for weeks, and the snake Nicholls for nearly as long, both undoubtedly attempting by blandishment. . . . They haven't succeeded? Neither? Perhaps they have been cancelling one another out. Perhaps they will continue to do so.'

'Do you always talk as much as this?' I asked.

'No, never. But now I am joyful and excited and frightened.'

'Did you frighten yourself when you howled like a wolf?'

'I am frightened because I know what my heart's desire is, and I might not get it.'

Though he was still laughing, though his face was still pink and happy, I knew what he meant, and that he meant it. It was not so very strange, that he should speak so after a meeting of two minutes; because he had said the same eight years before. Then, as now, in the midst of his clowning, he had spoken his heart; and between his fourteen-year-old heart and his twenty-two-year-old heart there was no difference at all.

I did not think I deserved such devotion; but I was very happy to have it. But in my glee I was sad: because Geoffrey Nicholls and Rupert Fraser had spoken similar words, and I could not bear the thought of causing any of them unhappiness.

Peter, of course, had heard the clash of the glen, the moment he came home to the glen: there was an 'understanding' between Mariota Seaton and the Marquess of Gard. He was as dubious about it as the rest of us, as alarmed for Mariota, as puzzled about where his duty lay. Like the rest of us, he concluded that there would be no profit – and certainly no pleasure – in trying to warn Mariota.

Away in the south of England, hundreds of miles from the

glen, Peter too had heard stories about Gard. If he knew details – names, places, dates – he did not tell me; but it was evident to me that a kind of black cloud of odium hung over Gard. All the time the cloud was increasing, perhaps because people more and more talked to one another, perhaps because he gave them more to talk about. But his humbler neighbours in and about Glengard continued to treat him and to talk about him as a god.

Since there was an 'understanding', it had to be assumed that Mariota went sometimes to Glengard Castle, and Gard to Crask. A courtship, we all agreed, required some meetings; and Gard must have spoken to Lord Crask, and Crask must have spoken to the Duke, if the Duke could still speak. But the only news any of us heard, about any of this, was from servants – Lady Crask's maid to Lady Nicholls's maid, and so to Lady Nicholls and so by devious routes to us: or Mariota's maid to Grizelda's maid, or coachman to coachman, groom to groom, housekeeper to housekeeper. Mariota herself would say not a word to any of us; if, greatly daring, we tried to ask her, she went into one of her trances, and listened to her new fairy music.

We went one day to Achmore – Geoffrey Nicholls, Peter McCallum and I – at Jean Hannay's invitation. The men were to fish, and I was to answer many more questions about Australia, that Jean had not yet had time to ask me. We tried to take Mariota with us, but her father had guests, and it fell to her to entertain them; we tried to take Rupert Fraser, but something kept him at home.

Aunt Honoria permitted the expedition, though it took me away from my attempts to learn to be a lady, because Jean was older than I, married, titled, and for all these reasons liable to have a good influence on me. I could not imagine that Jean could ever have had any influence on anybody; but Aunt Honoria saw things differently.

I would have liked to have ridden; but this was impossible. I would have liked, as a good second best, to have driven myself in a park-phaeton; this was impossible too, though I could not make out why. So I went in the Victoria, with

Wattie the undercoachman, and Geoffrey and Peter on horseback beside us, like outriders.

The resplendent footman handed us to the resplendant, butler, who told us that Her Ladyship could not be disturbed. She already had a visitor, somebody unexpected but important? No, she was alone. Sir Archibald was available? No, he was away all day on business.

This was really most odd. Jean had asked us all, by note, only the previous day; a groom had ridden all up and down the glen, leaving the notes at our various houses. But now she was 'not at home' to her oldest friends. Ill, perhaps? No, Her Ladyship was in her usual excellent health.

It was thoroughly puzzling, and, since we had come all this way, distinctly annoying. Had one of us done something to infuriate Jean, so that she would see none of us? We thought not. Had Sir Archibald forbidden her to receive us? But he had treated all of us, at different times, with great friendship.

Once again, it was a servant who provided what must have been the explanation.

Wattie the undercoachman liked talking as he drove, but he could only do it if I were alone in the carriage. He was having a crack, he said, with wee Johnny Wilkie the groom at Achmore, while we were in the house. Who should have ridden up, an hour before we arrived, but his Lordship, the Marquess of Gard? Hoping to see Sir Archibald on some matter of business, but received instead by Her Ladyship. A footman had told a stillroom-maid, who had told Johnny Wilkie. His Lordship had been with Her Ladyship for near three quarters of an hour. In spite of the footman's best efforts, he had not succeeded in hearing any of the conversation. His Lordship had left Achmore a bare quarter hour before our arrival.

And then Jean was 'not at home'.

It was barely possible that the events were unconnected; something had happened to distress Jean (if distressed was what she was) after the Marquess had gone. No – it was *not* possible to believe that. What could have happened? Did Rupert's story, or the stories the others had heard, suggest a reason?

But Jean had only been married for a few months. . . . And Gard and Mariota had an 'understanding'. . . .

I thought I was learning a lot about Scotland, and I did not like what I was learning. I felt suddenly more homesick for Sydney and for my beloved family, then I had felt for weeks.

Chapter 3

In days gone by, Glengard Castle had been known as the most
hospitable house in Scotland. That was when the Duchess was
alive, and the Duke hale and active. There were balls, and
banquets, and enormous shooting parties, and flocks of people
came all the way from London, and stayed for weeks – all
kinds of people, Grandpapa told me, writers and scientists
and ironmasters, as well as aristocrats and politicians and
sportsmen. But that was before I was born. As far back as I
could remember, Glengard was spoken of as a place under
dustsheets, cold and silent, with an army of servants looking
after one another, and one lonely old man in a four-poster
bed.

It was assumed that the Marquess of Gard could not entertain, without disturbing his father; that he did his entertaining
elsewhere, in private rooms in discreet London restaurants;
or that he had no taste for entertaining, and so abandoned
the happy tradition of his home. So it was that none of our
group except Mariota had ever been inside the castle, and I
had never set foot even in its gardens or park. I had seen it
only from a distance, from a corner of the road which led
from the glen to Lochgrannomhead.

From a distance it appeared ridiculously large, as a home
even for a Duke. It was not a house at all, but a town – it
was one of those walled hilltop towns in Tuscany, of which
there were engravings in a book in the library at Callo,
including a cathedral, a castle, several palaces, and a jumble
of humber dwellings. Like those cities, Glengard dominated
the countryside about; like them, it had an air of pride and
secrecy, and warned impertinent visitors to keep their
distance.

I was mildly curious to know how life was lived in such an
extraordinary place, and how long it would take Mariota

(supposing those rumours were true) even to find her way about. I thought I would never know; though Mariota was not at all snobbish, she would have snobbery forced upon her, and her childhood friends would be her friends no longer. I thought there was no reason I should see the park, or the famous gardens, from any nearer than that bend in the road over the river.

Then one day Geoffrey Nicholls took me to his home, to Invermore, where his mother and father as always made me most welcome; and his mother was on the point of leaving in a carriage for Glengard. She was by no means calling on the Duke; she was not going into the castle; but she had an arrangement with the head gardener, who supplied her with tropical plants for the Invermore conservatory. She asked me to join her, for company on the drive, and because I might like to see the gardens. I was happy to agree – she was excellent company, and I felt a sort of obligation to be especially friendly to the whole family, to compensate for Aunt Honoria.

Geoffrey said that he would not come. This was because his mother hinted that he should not. I did not understand, until we started off, why she should want to talk to me alone. It was some minutes before I did understand, so delicately did she approach the subject.

She wanted to know how I felt about Geoffrey, because she knew how he felt about me. She did not want him unhappy; and she most kindly hinted that she did want me as a daughter-in-law

I truthfully told her that Geoffrey was one of my very closest and dearest friends. I could tell her no more. I knew no more. I had not reached my eighteenth birthday; I was not near ready to commit myself for life.

She talked of Geoffrey – his future, the certainty of his success, his kindness and his popularity. With all this I could heartily agree. Further I could not go, but I was most touched and gratified that she should take this line with me. I wondered if I should have such conversations with Mrs Fraser of Lossie and Mrs McCallum of Miltoun. They also were close to their sons, and cared about them.

I wondered suddenly if I should ever have come back to the glen.

*

From near at hand, the castle was quite as awesome as from a distance. We approached it from below, from the river-bank, the carriage road climbing steeply through a park dappled in light and shade, and alive with fallow deer. We could see from our road almost nothing of the castle, because it was so far above us: only a great cliff of the living granite, and then a wall which seemed to grow out of the cliff, with towers and turrets atop. I could see that, ahead, the road curved round the bald hilltop on which the castle stood; I supposed that it came to a main entrance far away on the other side. Alongside the road, for half a mile, verging the park, was another enormous wall, in which there were one or two great arched gateways, filled with massive iron-studded gates, and many little doorways. By one of these Lady Nicholls stopped the carriage.

We were expected. A boy in muddy gaiters appeared, tugging off his cap. We followed him through the door. I stopped dead, amazed at what lay on the other side of the wall. We were at the bottom of a series of terraces, joined by broad flights of steps as falls join the pools of a river. Far above, and set well back, stood the castle; but from this aspect it was no longer the granite outgrowth of the granite hilltop, but an astonishing palace.

'That's why I brought you this way, Bella,' said Lady Nicholls. 'It is a shock, isn't it, coming from the park into this?'

I nodded, speechless.

I saw, gleaming between trees, what looked like acres of glass: greenhouses, where Lady Nicholls's business lay. I followed her and the boy the length of the lowest terrace, which must have been three hundred yards of perfectly shaven grass, bordered by groups of ancient trees, and by shrubs just coming into flower. As one walked, one saw that the trees had been formed into avenues – unexpected vistas, at the end of one of which was a classical arch, of another a temple, of a third a waterfall.

A man in tweed knickerbockers, very neat, like a grocer on his holidays, emerged from the trees to greet us: this was the head gardener, whom Lady Nicholls greeted as an old friend.

She said to me, 'Mr Blair and I will be half an hour, Bella – would it not amuse you to explore, rather than to listen to

49

us haggling over cuttings? Will that be all right, Mr Blair? Miss Gordon will not trample on any seedlings, or pick any lilies.'

Mr Blair seemed to suffer an internal struggle. It was his pride against his caution. He wanted people to see and admire the miracles he and his men had wrought; he did not want to risk annoying his noble master. Pride won: I was allowed to wander for half an hour.

Lady Nicholls followed Mr Blair toward the greenhouses; I began slowly climbing from terrace to terrace. As I did so, more and more of the castle revealed itself to me; and, when I reached the topmost terrace, I saw it plain at last.

I afterwards learned that an ancient outer wall had been knocked down, so that sunshine and nature could enter right into the castle. They did so. I looked through an archway at a series of archways, and saw that these gave on to a series of open and sunny courtyards, so that the castle was like those colleges of Oxford and Cambridge which Peter McCallum had told me of. I thought the buildings were of many different periods, but blended together so that the effect was of pleasing variety rather than jumble. I thought it was very beautiful. I thought it was grotesquely large to be the dwelling of one elderly and invalid widower, and his single unmarried son.

I looked a little shyly at the tall windows of the southern façade, which faced the topmost of the terraces, and which I faced. Some were shuttered, some curtained, but some stood open. There were no faces in any of the windows. Nobody was watching me. Nobody would rush out, to chase me away. I had twenty minutes still, of my half hour of exploration.

I thought I saw, in the tail of my eye, a face in one of the windows; but when I turned it was gone.

What happened next must be blamed, perhaps, on Australia; or on a little painting my Mama had, which she took with her wherever she went.

At the eastern end of the terrace there stood a huge and ancient beech tree, shading a part of the sward. Under it, there were groups of small wrought-iron chairs and tables, painted white; in the long-gone days when Glengard entertained, people had sat and drunk their tea at those tables, in that grateful shade. One great branch thrust out of the trunk of the tree, some twenty feet above the ground, more or less towards the castle. From the branch hung two chains, a yard apart, and to the chains, a yard from the ground, was fixed a wooden plank.

It was a swing. It was the most perfect swing. Sitting on that swing, one would have the most wonderful view, whichever way one faced – two quite different views, one up the glen and one down; and the views would be better, the higher one swung.

Exploring, with the head gardener's permission, was one thing. To swing on a stranger's swing – a ducal swing – was quite another. For a child to swing on a swing was one thing. For a young lady nearly eighteen, nearly of marriageable age, dressed in fashionable clothes, it was quite another.

There had been a swing in the dusty compound behind our house in Sydney. Often I was called upon to push my brothers and my little sister. Often they were called upon to push me. The very day I embarked on the ship to come back to Scotland, I swung on that swing; almost my last act, before I climbed into the carriage to go to the docks, was to swing on that swing.

And then that picture. It was a copy of a little painting done by a Frenchman called Lancret, a hundred and more years before; it had no great value, being only a copy; but it had been given to my Mama by somebody she loved, and she loved the picture too. I understood, and agreed, for it was full of sunshine and happiness. It showed a swing, a plank of wood on two chains, hanging from the branch of a tree – a swing no different from this swing on the topmost terrace of Glengard. On the swing was a very young lady – a girl – in a grand dress with panniers at the sides, and in a broad-brimmed bonnet laden with flowers. She was being pushed by a young gentleman, in a three-cornered hat and a coat covered in gold lace. He wore a sword. There were people watching, laughing. Another young lady was looking distinctly jealous. (The jealousy of the other young lady was, perhaps, really the subject of the painting; it might have been entitled 'Envy', and been one of a series depicting the Seven Deadly Sins.)

If it was permissible in Sydney, almost in the shadow of Government House – if it was permissible in the formal gardens of Versailles, or wherever Lancret saw the swing he

51

painted – and if nobody was looking, from those tall windows in the southern face of the castle – why, then. . .

I took off my hat, and hung it on a rose-bush. I thought, if I swung on the swing, it would come off. I did not understand how the girl in Lancret's picture contrived to keep her hat on, especially as she was being pushed; perhaps it came off just after he painted her.

I hoisted myself onto the swing, and kicked myself off so that I started swinging. Though it is best to have somebody to push, it is possible by and by to get quite high, by a sort of bending of one's body, and by kicking out one's legs. I was not really dressed for kicking my legs, but nobody was watching, and I thought I was not so very indecent.

Until the plank broke. Of course I tumbled to the grass, and my legs waved in the air, and my petticoats fell about my waist . . . Probably I shrieked, because one would not expect a ducal swing to break. And then I heard another noise, like a snort, like one of the terrifying noises Peter McCallum had made behind the fallen tree. I recovered myself, and covered myself, and turned round. The gardener's boy who had met us at the door in the wall was standing staring. He snorted again. His face was purple. I thought for a moment that he was having a fit, and I was frightened for him. Then I saw that he was trying not to laugh. The struggle in his face was awful. It made me do what I had not expected to do, which was to burst out laughing myself. After that, of course, the poor boy could not restrain his own laughter, so we brayed at one another, like lunatics, he standing with his cap in his hands, and I sitting dishevelled on the grass, in the splintered ruins of the swing-seat.

At last he was able to ask me, between wails, if I were hurt; and I was able to tell him, between wails, that I was not hurt at all – for the falls I had taken off horses in Australia, onto much harder surfaces than this lush Highland turf, had well accustomed me to sudden impact with the ground. I scrambled to my feet, and tried to inspect myself. My laughter did not die away entirely, but it grew suddenly and definitely weaker – for much of the back of my skirt, which had been white, was now bright green. It would not be easy to explain to Lady Nicholls, which did not matter; it would not be easy to explain to Aunt Honoria, which did matter.

I had no kind of shawl or stole or cloak or coat with which to cover up that great shameful area of green.

It would be extremely obvious to anybody who saw it, that I had landed heavily on grass, on that part of me best adapted to landing heavily. It would be extremely obvious to anybody who knew me, that I had been committing some tomboyish folly, to cause the fall.

This thought was in danger of driving away my laughter altogether: but, as I turned, the gardener's boy saw the great green stain for the first time – and it started him off again, which started me off again.

Presently he was once more able to speak; he said that Mr Blair had sent him to find me, as Lady Nicholls's business was concluded, and it was time to go.

I thanked him, and started down the waterfalls of steps which linked each terrace to the next.

A strange thought came to me, as I bashfully approached the greenhouses: that a place in which a gardener's boy could laugh so hard could not be altogether dreadful.

When I rejoined Lady Nicholls and Mr Blair, in the midst of the lowest of the terraces, they must have supposed that I was performing some kind of dance, since I kept turning myself this way and that, and skipping away from them, with the object of keeping my unblemished front always towards them both. I began to hope that I could continue to do so, and to do so when I returned to Callo, until I had had time to change my clothes.

It was a perfectly vain hope. Lady Nicholls shrieked and pointed. Mr Blair struggled not to laugh, and almost succeeded. The coachman struggled not to laugh, and failed utterly. When we got to Invermore, Sir George laughed, and Geoffrey laughed, as soon as he was quite certain that I was not at all hurt.

There was no laughter at Callo.

A bank-draft arrived for Uncle Ranald. It came from my Papa's bankers in Perth, and it came at his orders, which of course had taken weeks to reach them; it was quite a lot of money, and it was to pay for my birthday ball.

I was still quite unready – I was still an uncouth colonial

53

– but suddenly the ball was something that was certain to happen, that even Aunt Honoria could not prevent. So she made a virtue of necessity, and she and Grizelda began drawing up lists of guests. They had rival lists, which were very long; I had a list of my own, which was very short.

It was to be the first really big party they had ever given at Callo, since Grizelda had come out, and Henry reached his majority, before Grandpapa died and Uncle Ranald inherited. Gradually, Aunt Honoria became more and more excited; she was cutting an immense social dash, and all at Papa's expense. There were to be marquees, and hundreds of little gilt chairs, and an orchestra, and a piper or two, and dozens of extra servants, and hampers of food from the hotels and grocers of Lochgrannomhead, and cartloads of champagne . . . And there were to be all the lairds and gentry from miles around, and knights, and baronets, and lords . . . Lords? Oh yes, ever so many lordships and ladyships, every single one with whom Uncle Ranald and Aunt Honoria, and Cousin Grizelda and Cousin Henry, could claim the slightest acquaintance.

The engraved cards of invitation were the first things to arrive, the first proof that all this was actually happening. I offered to help address the envelopes. They said my handwriting was not good enough.

Aunt Honoria and Grizelda were to have new gowns, and I to have my very first grown-up ball-gown. It was on the tip of my tongue to ask if Papa were paying for all three gowns, or only mine. I bit that question back. The atmosphere was becoming tense enough as it was.

Arguments of extraordinary bitterness broke out between Aunt Honoria and Grizelda, about some of the people that should be asked; Uncle Ranald and Henry, if they were by, often joined in too. I never did. As I had met none of the people they were arguing about – because they were people the Gordons themselves barely knew – I did not care if they came to the ball or not. The people that I wanted to come were coming; that was enough for me.

The strangest argument, which caused the greatest bitterness, concerned an invitation to the Marquess of Gard. Still I held my tongue, though it was very hard for me to do so. Aunt Honoria said that it would be a great discourtesy to exclude the Marquess from the list. Grizelda said it would be great presumption and impertinence to include him. For once, I listened to Grizelda talking perfect sense. She pointed out that, since Uncle Ranald had inherited, there had been not one single invitation to any of the family for any entertainment of any kind at Glengard Castle; that she herself had never met the Marquess, and Aunt Honoria had only done so fleetingly, in a huge reception in the Lochgrannomhead Assembly Rooms.

'I, on the other hand,' said Henry, 'have an acquaintance with Gard which perfectly justifies inviting him. He has been with me in this very room, only a week or so ago.'

'Nearly two months ago,' said Grizelda, 'and he came purely on business.'

'As the Hannays and Arabella between them caused the calamity of my being out on the occasion of that call,' said Aunt Honoria, 'it all the more behoves us to show Lord Gard this courtesy.'

'He will not regard it as a courtesy, Mama,' said Grizelda. 'He will regard it as toad-eating.'

This made Aunt Honoria very angry indeed; and she immediately wrote out an envelope addressed to The Most Honourable the Marquess of Gard, Glengard Castle, and put it in a pile with the others.

These excitements and altercations left Aunt Honoria no time for my education; she said that, in any case, the little that could be done had been done, and they must use Australia as an excuse, and hope that their guests would be tolerant.

At least I had been taught to dance reels as a child, and had danced them at Callo and in the houses of all my friends.

To those houses I now went, whenever I could, to get away from all the agonies which seemed to be part of the preparations for a ball. I rejoiced in the good humour and good sense of the Frasers of Lossie, the Nicholls of Invermore, the McCallums of Miltoun. I rejoiced in the affectionate welcome of the Earl and Countess of Crask. I did not go again to Achmore. There had been no word from Jean Hannay, to any of us, by way of explanation or apology for her very odd behaviour. Of course the Hannays were asked to the ball, and had accepted.

Mariota came one day to take me to Crask. She said there was to be an occasion of great importance, and I must be there to witness it. She would not say what it was; she wanted to surprise me.

I thought: the 'understanding' is to become a betrothal. Gard will be there, and we shall drink healths, and Lady Crask will be sweet and funny, and Lord Crask will be thinking of other things, and Mariota will stop for a little listening to her fairy music, and I shall be almost sick.

My heart sank and sank, as the carriage climbed the hill beside the Crask Water. Then Mariota stopped the carriage, and we scrambled out as usual to see the dam. Lord Crask was there, in a state of high excitement, waving his hat.

'Look!' said Mariota.

I saw that the dam was complete, entirely blocking the 'gun-sight' formed by the two steep banks, except for the great iron sluice-gates, which were hauled up on their chains so that the river still ran on uninterrupted. Men stood on top of the dam, by the winches which controlled the sluices. With them was a piper, dressed very fine.

Lord Crask made a speech, which was perfectly inaudible in the noise of the river. The piper struck up; it was a tune I did not know, but it sounded as though it had been composed to celebrate a triumph. To the skirling of that brave music, the men working the winches began to lower the sluice-gates down into the water, and presently to the river-bed.

Immediately the water began to rise, fraction by fraction, up the wall of the dam. The artificial lock was in being; the face of the countryside was changed.

'How long will it take to fill?' I shrieked to Lord Crask.

I did not hear his reply. I thought he had no idea how long it would take to fill.

This was the great event. There was no other. I was overwhelmed with relief. There was still a chance that Mariota might see clear, and avoid that calamitous future.

We went to see Lady Crask, in her sunny shabby boudoir. She was full of curiosity about the ball, and full of regret that her health would prevent her from attending it. But Mariota would be there, and would report on every detail.

I thought Mariota would not report on every detail, because she would not notice any detail.

Rupert Fraser also rescued me from the bristling civil wars of Callo, and took me to luncheon with his family at Lossie.

Of all the folk of the neighbourhood, the Frasers were the family to whom my Papa had been closest. He greatly liked, and had known intimately well, the Crasks, the Nicholls, the McCallums (I thought he had not quite so well known, or quite so well liked, the Carmichaels of Achmore) but the Frasers were his greatest local friends. I thought, now that I was almost grown up, I could at last see why. The families of one's friends, when one is a child, are as much a part of the natural order as the stones of their houses, or the big hills, or the wheel of the seasons. But when you are older – and even if you are an ignorant colonial – you see that they are quite different, one from another, and that they have different excellencies, and that they have faults. Seeing with new eyes, I saw that the Frasers were different not only from the other families, but also from one another. And the differences were interesting, and made them the most interesting of all the folk of the glen.

It was from his mother – and not at all, as might have been supposed, from his father – that Rupert got his vocation to be a soldier, and his cheerful acceptance of all that an army life entailed, and the eagerness with which he looked forward to the adventures of his life in India. And it was from his father – not at all from his mother – that came the poem that he wrote to me when I was eight, and the passionate intensity with which he saw and felt things, and the tears that came to his eyes when he saw a new moon low on a green sky.

It had seemed to me, when first I was reunited with Rupert on the hill above Callo, that the poet had been quite blown away by the years of boarding-school and army; it was a little tender plant that had died, throttled by the lustier growth of the other things that Rupert was. But over the weeks that followed, and in the many, many meetings that we had, I found I questioned this. I found that I fancied I saw little, shy, furtive, momentary glimpses of another creature, peeping out at me between cracks in that cheery, weatherbeaten surface.

I thought that perhaps there was still a poet, hidden inside the soldier. I wondered if this made for a happier soldier, a happier man, or one that was always discontented. I wondered if this made for a spirit more deeply hurt by failure, by disappointment; or whether the poet would console the soldier, by seeing other beauty, and hearing other music. I wondered how I felt, about Rupert and the others: or how I would feel, when I was eighteen years old, and considered old enough to feel.

When I was with Rupert – the two of us, on the hill or by the river, or looking together at the pictures in an old book in his father's library, or from the garden listening to his small sister singing, in a small, sweet, true voice, the old country ballads we all loved – then I was nearly certain that this walking mixture of opposites was what I should like to spend my life with. From my life with Papa in Australia, I knew that that energetic, outdoor sporting life was one in which I thrived; I loved those excitements, and the glorious comradeship in which they were enjoyed. But from Australia I knew also that that life could easily be a half life. Rupert had made me see things inside myself that I had not known were there, and that I could not put a name to. Others had helped to do so too, perhaps, and so had the beauty of the great glen and of that glorious summer: but mostly it was Rupert. There was that in me, Rupert had made me feel, which would not be content with horses and fishing-rods and Highland reels, with bustling cheerfully through life with soldiers and soldiers' wives.

With Rupert I would ride to hounds over the hills of Northern India, and catch the giant Mahseer in turbulent rivers, and live amongst the grandest people in the world. That was good. And Rupert had written me a poem; and Rupert had wept at a baby moon on a summer evening. That was good, too, very good indeed; and every minute that I spent with Rupert it seemed better. And I liked his wind-browned face, and his unruly black hair, and his piratical hooky nose, badge for centuries of his father's family.

What I did not like was feeling beset.

All of them were at me, all that day at Lossie – Rupert allowing the passionate poet to show between the chinks of his military armour, more clearly and more often than at any time since childhood; his mother, aside to me, dilating on Rupert's fine qualities, and his certainty of a glorious future; his father, more skilfully, saying with careful carelessness that there were books and music in India, as well as polo-ponies, and that to see the Himalayas with Rupert would be a most fortunate experience, because of his love of beauty; and his small sister Emily saying – with her mother pretending to try to keep her quiet – that if she were not Rupert's sister, she would want to be his wife. Oh, it was flattering and heart-warming, that they all wanted me for Rupert; it was astonishing; it was impossible to understand; but what they were all doing was trying to push me. The road they were trying to push me down was one, I very well knew, that I might easily choose – that I felt very close to choosing. But my pig-headed character (of which even Papa had complained) made me less likely to choose it, simply because they were pushing me.

Rupert took me for a final stroll, in the early evening, among the syringas, which filled the golden sunlight with a magical perfume.

'You know very well how I feel, Bella,' he said, 'and you know very well how I shall feel until I die. You are the only one. You always were, when you ran like a goat over the hill, and your stockings were in shreds about your ankles, and your lion's mane was full of twigs and moss . . . I shan't say anything now, but be warned. On the night of your birthday . . .'

'I think the carriage is waiting,' I said awkwardly.

I left him among those heavy-scented shrubs. There was a strange expression on his face, which I could not read.

In the carriage on the way home to Callo, it came to me; I recognized the expression on Rupert's face. It was hunger.

Still I was beset.

Geoffrey Nicholls and Peter McCallum called, together, quite early in the morning the next day. A servant had met

59

a servant on the road the previous evening, word had flown to one household and to the other, and they knew I had spent the chief of the day at Lossie. Joking, they condemned Rupert for treachery; joking, they eyed one another with suspicion. I knew they were not altogether joking, and they knew I knew it.

We were to go at once to Miltoun, to fish the McCallums' excellent water, and to have a picnic. Mariota was to join us. Rupert, as a punishment, had been deliberately excluded from the arrangement. (Normally, of course, he would have been there: and normally he would have caught the most fish.)

'We shall catch our luncheon,' said Peter. 'Two little trout each, or one big one. We shall build a fire, like Red Indians, and . . . what do you do to fish? Grill? Bake? Baste? Roast? Boil? Broil? Is 'broil' the same as 'boil'? Or does the 'R' make it into something quite different?'

'Suppose we don't catch any trout?' I said.

'Then we shall send for a jar of bloater paste. We must have fish of some kind.'

Mariota arrived at the McCallums' just after we did, dreamy as ever. She seemed not to know why she was there, or where we were going. But she allowed herself to be packed into a wagonette, with the rest of us, and all our tackle, and things for cooking, and the materials of the picnic.

I thought there would be safety in numbers, and I thought that was what I wanted. But fishing parties break up, one going upstream and one down, and one to a different beat, and the gillie is not forever at your elbow. So it was that I found myself unexpectedly alone, fishing upstream in the pool they called the Saucepan.

To throw a fly is difficult to learn; but, once you have learned, you never forget. I had learned long and long ago, with a little cut-down rod a gillie had made for me; I had learned to tie the necessary knots; I had learned the local theories about what flies to use at different times and places. None of this I had forgotten; none of it would I ever forget. I had had almost no chance to go fishing, that year of my return from Australia, because of Aunt Honoria's attempts to turn me into a lady. Now that she had abandoned those attempts, it was very heaven to be on a river bank on a smiling day, with birds clamouring amongst the grass and heather, and wine-coloured peaty water chuckling among the rocks.

Sometimes I liked solitude, too. At that moment I was happy to be alone, to feel the sun on my cheek, to feel the unforgotten surge as the rod sweeps forward and the line snakes out over the water.

'Beautiful casting, Bella,' said a voice behind me.

I was no longer alone. I turned. To my great surprise Mrs McCallum had joined me, wearing heavy boots and a hat like a cartwheel. It was from her that Peter had inherited his stocky form, his happy round face, and his thatch of straw-coloured hair, though hers was muddy-coloured now. From her, I was sure, he had inherited his clowning, his love of laughter, though now that she was middle-aged she was more apt to laugh than to cause laughter. It was easy to imagine that when she was young she set many a party on a roar. In many ways she was young in heart still, younger in manner and in interests than the other ladies I knew – younger by far, in all ways, than Aunt Honoria. Oddly, only the invalid Lady Crask had any of Mrs McCallum's exuberance of spirit, and with her it was a very gentle exuberance.

'I found they hadn't packed half the picnic,' she said. 'I was about to send someone after you in a dog-cart, but I decided on a day like this to come myself. I won't stay for your lunch – I'm too old to be squatting on peat-hags. I'm glad it's you I happened on, Bella.'

I suddenly knew, for a certainty, that she had not happened on me. She had come to find me. She wanted to talk to me, in the privacy of this wild and empty place. I knew what about. All over again I was flattered and heart-warmed; and all over again I was beset.

Yes, it was Peter. No girl would be dull who married him. And did I realise how fine a brain he kept hidden under all his clowning? And did I see the kindness and generosity?

I said that I did, and it was true. But I tried to speak cautiously; I did not wish to seem to be saying more than I was saying.

There was much in Peter that was not only endearing but also impressive. It was a curious thought, but probably his clowning was the merrier because he had a first-class brain:

probably those fierce and ridiculous imitations he did of the wild dogs were better because of his degrees and diplomas. He was kind, he was funny, he would be eminent; though he was not obviously handsome, his face was thoroughly pleasing; he was just sufficiently taller than I. I was very fond of him, and I was sure I would always be so. More than that I could not say, though more than that Mrs McCallum delicately pressed me to say.

I was sure she was not speaking at Peter's request, or with his knowledge. She wanted me for Peter. Why did she? I was tolerably formed; I had been given reason to suppose that my face was tolerable; I had hair of unusual copiousness, and of an unusual colour which people had admired; I was almost offensively healthy. On the other side of the world I had a very popular father. I was well enough born and connected. I thought I was not excessively stupid, although Aunt Honoria would have disagreed. I was, in sum, a feasible wife for such as Peter McCallum; his family would not cut him off, if he married me, or his future colleagues snub me. But for the life of me I could not see that I was so very special. I could not see why these ladies who had known me all my life should be trying to discover my heart, and trying to influence my heart.

More adroit than Lady Nicholls or Mrs Fraser, Mrs McCallum began talking about my other childhood play-mates. She spoke of them warmly. She said how charming it was that our childish tribe should be reunited, which was so rare a thing. She probed for answers, from me, about Geoffrey and Rupert.

She wanted to know if I were in love with either, if I preferred either to Peter. I did not know. I told her so. She was not quite satisfied, but I could tell her no more.

There was an infinity of goodwill in all this, and it was deeply flattering. But she spoiled my morning's fishing.

'At the ball . . .' said Geoffrey Nicholls, when he had untangled my flies from a whin-bush.

'At the ball . . .' whispered Peter McCallum, when we were leaning together over a pool, trying to tickle a trout.

*

It was horribly ungrateful, but I began to feel persecuted.

I came back to Callo to find Aunt Honoria in transports of delight, Grizelda somehow caught between sneering and singing, and Henry and Uncle Ranald trying to pretend that it was the most ordinary thing in the world – nothing at all to be excited about – simply another guest among so many.

A groom had arrived, with a letter sent by hand. The Marquess of Gard thanked Lady Gordon of Callo for the honour of her kind invitation, and had much pleasure in accepting.

My birthday ball promised to be a most peculiar evening.

'Without wishing to imply the least disparagement of your aunt, Bella,' said Geoffrey Nicholls, 'might we not assume that Gard is coming to your ball because of Mariota? Even at her request?'

I remembered again that curious afternoon at Achmore – Jean, after the Marquess's visit, suddenly 'not at home' to her oldest friends.

'There might be all sorts of reasons,' I said slowly. 'He may like dancing reels. He may have heard that my Cousin Grizelda is getting a new gown.'

'I think he is coming hunting,' said Rupert Fraser. 'I think he is throwing his hounds into a new covert.'

'No no,' said Peter McCallum, 'it is girls who go hunting at dances –'

He did not finish, because I hit him with the thumb-stick I was carrying.

Mariota sent a note to me: her new gown had come, from the dressmaker in Edinburgh, and she wanted to show it to me, and ask my advice about gloves and such. I did not think my advice about gloves would be of any value to Mariota, but I was pleased to be asked. She wanted to see my gown, too, if it was finished and had come.

It had, indeed, brought by a slightly humbler and more local dressmaker from Perth. Aunt Honoria, Grizelda and I had all tried on our finery. They were going to be formidably grand, in satin and strong colours, with complicated and enormous skirts in many hues. I, being a young girl, was to be much more simply dressed, in white as suited my very first entry into Society, except for the glowing colours of the tartan sash.

I looked at myself in a full-length glass, while a maid behind me made cooing noises. I should have been prepared for the sight of myself – I had seen the fashion-plates in the magazines, and I had had fittings – but still I gave myself a shock. The bodice of the dress, as was the fashion of the time, was cut straight across, and was skin-tight; the voluminous skirt was draped over an enormous crinoline. I knew my waist was small, but I did not think it was as tiny as that dress made it look. I thought my bosom was of normal size; I did not think it swelled as proudly as it now seemed to. And what a lot of me was for the very first time visible – shoulders, back, and more of my bosom than I thought quite proper, or quite safe.

Two maids now were staring at me, and cooing. That was definitely encouraging. Grizelda, in her crimson satin, was looking at me with a hatred more open than usual. It is dreadful to admit it, but that was encouraging, too.

We packed up my gown in its bandbox, and I set off in the carriage for Crask.

We paused on the way, as always; if I saw Lord Crask, and he asked what I thought of his new loch, he would be hurt if I had not stopped to look at it. Well, it was growing, growing, creeping up the face of the dam, creeping up the steep banks of the river, spreading backwards over the flatter ground upstream. When it had reached the size they wanted, they would open the sluices again, and it would keep to its new level; and after that they could make it larger or smaller, just as they wished.

Mariota was not listening to fairy music, when she came pirouetting into her mother's boudoir in her new Edinburgh gown. Since she had been 'out' for a year, she could choose what colour she liked; and, since she had that startling chestnut hair, she chose a delicate lime-green. She looked dazzling, superb, irresistible. I thought that, beside her, I in my virginal white would simply disappear.

They pretended they did not think so. They said many kind things. Lady Crask said that it was not possible that a girl like me, quite tall and very active, should have such a small waist – that it was not in nature; although it seemed to me that Mariota's waist was hardly larger. Mariota said that she had not realised that a back could be so beautiful. She had not seen my back before – nobody had – but she had seen many bare backs in many ballrooms, and was in a position to judge.

'I do not know what you had better do, Bella,' she said. 'If you face all the men, they will see that you are the most beautiful girl in the room, and if you turn your back they will see that you are the most beautiful girl in the room. Perhaps you had better spin round and round and round, all evening.'

'I should get dizzy,' I said, laughing.

'So will all the men, so it will be a successful party, and your uncle will not need to pour out so much champagne.'

I could not tell if I thought my own back beautiful, because there was only one looking-glass in Lady Crask's boudoir, and I could not twist round far enough to get a clear view of my shoulder-blades. Once again it was encouraging, as I neared my awesome debut, to be told that I was passable, even though these loving and beloved friends were speaking out of kindness.

The glorious weather broke; the rains came, not continuous, but in heavy and daily showers. Aunt Honoria was distraught, because the party would be ruined. Uncle Ranald was distraught, because the garden would be ruined. I thought it was a pity but not a calamity, because the marquee would be there for the dancing, and the house would be there for the refreshments, and if anybody was determined to wander romantically among the roses, they could take umbrellas.

The weather teased us. The wind swung, and the sun shone; it swung again, and the heavens wept. The river rose a little. A tawny torrent, of moderate ferocity, thundered down the Falls of Gard, and plumes of spray lashed at the little tumbledown castle. The water was many feet below the footbridge, but the planks of the bridge were wet with spray.

'The colour of your hair, Bella,' said Geoffrey Nicholls. 'Do you remember my saying that, years ago?'

'Of course I do.'

'That, and other things. Did you realise that I meant them?'

'Of course I did.'

'I mean them still. Great Scot, here is the infernal McCallum, playing gooseberry. Shall I push him into the falls?'

'I am inclined to dive in, to demonstrate my heroism,' said Peter. 'But I do not think it would be fair on my friends.'

'Oh, we shall manage,' said Geoffrey. 'Don't be deterred on our account. Plunge in, old fellow. Splash about and enjoy yourself.'

'I like to think that you would leap in and save me.'

'At any other time, of course. But these are new trousers, worn to impress Miss Gordon. Do they impress you, Bella?'

'I am never impressed by trousers,' I said.

'By what, then?'

'Only by hats.'

Geoffrey was hatless. Peter wore a straw hat with a very broad brim, round the crown of which he had tied a strip of many-coloured silk.

'A popinjay,' said Geoffrey, 'a miserable fop.'

At this moment, as though by magic, Rupert Fraser joined us; and they all produced that ingenious mixture of smiles and scowls.

'What I want to know, Bella,' said Rupert, 'is this – does your hair imitate the colour of the water in the falls, or is the water in the falls coloured in imitation of your hair?'

'The comparison has already been made,' said Geoffrey. 'It is copyright.'

They felt as they said they felt, all of them; and they knew I knew it. I thought it was truly excellent, in them all, that they should remain such friends. I thought it was truly horrible that I should be hurting at least two of them.

A kind of village of marquee went up, in the courtyard in front of the house; carts brought hundreds of little gilt chairs, which were unloaded in the rain; boxes arrived full of programmes, each with its little gold pencil, which were most

66

scrupulously protected from the rain; cases of wine were stacked up, and a keeper with a shotgun set to guard them. There were endless, furious conferences involving Aunt Honoria, Grizelda, the housekeeper, and the man from the Lochgrannomhead Hotel who was in charge of the extra servants.

I was not needed. I was in the way. Since the rain had come again, I went to my room, and wrote a long letter to Papa and Mama, in which I left a lot of things out.

The weather cleared in the early evening, and a watery sun touched even Callo with magic.

I walked, alone, down to the falls. I looked down at the rushing water, coloured like my hair. The water was in no greater turmoil than my thoughts.

Chapter 4

Of course I should have had Papa to consult; but a letter would take weeks to reach him, and his reply weeks to reach me, and it was not a subject for letters; and Uncle Ranald was no substitute. And I should have had Mama to consult; and Aunt Honoria was no substitute. The kindly neighbouring ladies were no use to consult, because they had all taken sides, and different sides; Lady Crask was no use to consult, because she lived in another world; Mariota was no use to consult, about anything more profound than a choice between bracelets; Jean Hannay was no use to consult, because I would have distrusted her opinion about anything, even bracelets. The idea of consulting my cousins Henry and Grizelda was preposterous. There was no one. I was not quite eighteen. I desperately needed the help and counsel of somebody older and wiser than I, who knew me, whom I trusted and respected, and who would take care to advise what was best for me. There was no one. There was no one within twenty thousand miles, that I could take my problems to.

The ball was to be on Saturday, my birthday. On Friday guests began to arrive, who were staying in the house at Callo. I did not know any of them. I had not heard of any of them. It appeared that they were nearly all relatives of Aunt Honoria; and, hearing this, I found it most easy to believe. There was a general who was much unlike my Papa, and an attorney who was much unlike Geoffrey Nicholls. There were a number of very stiff and frightening ladies, some with daughters. I might have become friends immediately with some of these daughters – it was evidently expected that this would happen – but try as I might, that Friday afternoon and evening, those girls all remained strangers. To be sure, they were all a year or a few years older than myself, but I well knew that that was no bar to friendship; the thing about them, it seemed to me, was that either they too closely imitated their Mamas, so that they were already dragons, or they were frightened of their Mamas, so that they had become mice. I could not make friends easily with either mice or dragons.

Some of the Papas, drinking whisky after dinner, made me elaborate compliments, when their wives were not listening. I was not experienced in dealing with such conversations.

There was heavy, steady rain, all day and all evening; otherwise I would have pretended to go to bed early, and gone instead for a long solitary walk, in order to blow out of my head the dragons, and mice, and heavy compliments.

Other guests were being lodged at Invermore by the Nicholls, at Lossie by the Frasers, at Miltoun by the McCallums, at Achmore by the Hannays, and at other houses within reach. Glengard Castle could have held every one, but of course it held none, because the frail old Duke would have been disturbed by a concourse of strangers; also, even Aunt Honoria would not have dared ask such a favour.

Something woke me in the small hours of the morning. I lay thinking of the night to come – of Geoffrey, and Rupert, and Peter – of Jean, and Mariota, and the Marquess – of all the dreary and alarming people who it seemed were the bulk of the guests. I worked myself into a state of hopeless wakefulness; and lay listening to the steady rain on my window.

The whole gigantic battle, for which all these preparations had been made, and to which all these people had come, was about my birthday. But nobody had any time to mention my birthday. There were one or two hurried, perfunctory remarks at the breakfast-table. I supposed there would be, at some point during the day, some appearances of gifts; and I supposed there would be, at some point during the evening, a toast drunk. But I was not told about these things, and I did not care to ask. 'When am I to receive my many gifts, and who is to propose my health at the ball?' These questions would not have done.

From remarks I overheard, I realised that many of the guests had had no idea it was my birthday; nobody had told them; they thought it was merely my debut, if they were even aware that the dance was (in theory) being given for me. This put them in an embarrassing position, even though it was not their fault. For this reason, I clearly saw, the less talk there was about my birthday the better. But I thought it a little hard. One's eighteenth birthday does not come again.

The principal concern of everybody at Callo, all that day, was to keep out of Aunt Honoria's way. Uncle Ranald was doing it; Henry was doing it; the most dragon-like of her visiting relations were more and more doing it, as the terrible day wore on.

It was difficult to be forever taking evasive action, because of the weather. If it had been fine, we could have dispersed all over the park, like fallen leaves in the autumn winds. But even I was dubious about going out into that steady, chilling downpour.

Then, early in the afternoon, the miracle happened, of which we had all despaired. From somewhere – from Heaven, if our united prayers had been of any use – came a wind, which blew away the rain-clouds, and left a clean, clear sky. It was a sweet wind, a warm and drying wind; it breathed at the earth to such effect that, after tea, I found it was possible to walk on the cropped grass of the park in thin shoes.

That was good. It meant that, if my ball became unbearable, I could slip away and outside, without having to change into heavy boots, which would have been peculiar in my gown. And I thought there was every chance that my ball would be unbearable. And what was so sad was, that the people who would make it unbearable were the three I loved best in the whole of Scotland.

The evil weather of the previous week had made one forget what stage the moon was at. I heard somebody say that the moon that night would be full. One of the heavily-gallant Papas said that I would outshine the full moon, a remark kindly meant but to which I could think of no reply.

I had heard that the full moon did strange things to people.

70

I wondered what strange things it might do to Geoffrey, and Rupert, and Peter – and even, perhaps, Aunt Honoria.

I was sent up early to dress, so that I should be ready in good time to start the evening's programme of interminable curtseying. Aunt Honoria's maid was supposed to do my hair, but the poor woman had her hands full with Aunt Honoria. Grizelda's maid was specifically forbidden, by Grizelda, to do my hair. The girl who finished by doing it was not, perhaps, fully experienced. The result looked well enough; but I was nearly sure that pins would escape from my hair, and my hair from its pins, in the first foursome reel.

From my bedroom window I saw the fiddlers arrive in a closed carriage: four solemn men in black, who looked like mutes at a funeral. Soon one could hear them from the marquee, arguing hotly about the place that had been chosen for them, and then tuning up their violins.

The piper arrived in kilt and bonnet; I hoped he would not also feel obliged to tune his chanters, in competition with the fiddlers.

The weather held. The evening sky was cloudless; it was hard to believe that so much rain had fallen.

Presently I was complete: nobody could think of anything more to do to my appearance. I was encouraged once more by the clucking and cooing of the maids, who sounded like a dovecote full of fancy fantail pigeons, and by the barely-concealed malevolence of Grizelda.

Then we were downstairs, my uncle and aunt and cousins and I, sitting down and standing up and fidgeting, under the eyes of all the extra waiters, and of the fiddlers, who still looked like mutes at a funeral. At long, long last we were joined by the guests who were staying in the house, which made the party both better and worse. And then, at long, long last, others began to arrive, and I started on my programme of curtseying.

Sir George and Lady Nicholls and their party were among the first comers. I had never before seen Geoffrey in full Highland evening dress; he looked splendid. I was about to tell him so, when I saw the way he was looking at me. He had never before seen me in a fashionably low-cut ball-gown.

71

From the way he was goggling, he might never have seen anybody in a ball-gown. He went bright red and, when the others moved off to the marquee where the music was striking up, he stood staring at me, with his mouth open.

The Frasers came, with the party from Lossie. Rupert too looked splendid, in the kilt and in a green velvet coat with Cairngorm buttons that I should have liked for myself. I watched him come in, a little behind the others. The first person he saw was Geoffrey. He looked at him startled, perhaps worried, because Geoffrey did look so very strange. Then Rupert looked round, to see what it was that had turned Geoffrey into a pillar of salt. And so he saw me, and my back and my shoulders and my bosom. His mouth opened wide. I thought he was going to shout; I thought perhaps it was a Fraser custom, to scream a Gaelic greeting on somebody's birthday. But no sound came out. He had not opened his mouth – it had dropped open, and showed no sign of shutting.

The trouble was, that I was obliged to stay exactly where I was, with Uncle Ranald and Aunt Honoria, to greet the guests. I was like the waxworks I had seen as a child, in a travelling exhibition, in Lochgrannomhead – having been placed on that patch of carpet, there I was bound to stay. But I was an animated waxwork, curtseying and shaking hands every few seconds, interminably. Geoffrey and Rupert were waxworks, too, but their clockwork motors had stopped, and they were perfectly motionless.

Of course I was pleased and proud, in part of my mind, that my shoulders should have had such an effect. But the evening promised to be more complicated than ever.

There was no sign yet of the Marquess of Gard. Uncle Ranald and Aunt Honoria exchanged some worried mutterings. They had told a great many of their friends that he was expected.

The younger men guests, as they arrived, and some not young at all, in almost every case asked me for a dance – reel, country dance, or waltz – so that my programme became almost completely full. I left three blanks, together, fifteen and sixteen and seventeen. Though I dreaded dancing with Geoffrey and Rupert and Peter – and dreaded still more sitting out with them – I could not in friendship shut them out of my programme.

The McCallums arrived, with the Miltoun party. Even Peter, who did not in the ordinary way look very impressive, was splendid in Highland dress. He glanced from Geoffrey to Rupert, and from Rupert to me, and I wondered if another waxwork was to litter the Callo hall. But he came, and made his bow, and shook hands. He opened his mouth to speak to me. I waited for his words, some ordinary greeting, perhaps a compliment (every single person who arrived had paid me some kind of compliment, which was doubtless very bad for me), perhaps a request for a dance, or an arrangement to take me into supper. But no sound came out. His face went as red as Geoffrey's, and his mouth was as wide as Rupert's, and a part of me was still proud, and a part was in despair.

I was despatched now into the marquee which was the ballroom. Any guests still to come would be greeted by Aunt Honoria. I was claimed for the opening sixteensome reel by Sir George Nicholls. As we took our places, I saw, in a group by the door, Geoffrey and Rupert and Peter, staring and staring still.

Of course it was only a private party, not one of the great Highland Balls, not so very large and grand even as private parties went. Even so, it was a glorious sight, white shoulders and tartan sashes, the barbaric garishness of the men, the swirl of multicoloured movement, shouts of laughter and excitement over the skirling of the pipes. Dancing with the kind and merry Sir George (and he was an excellent performer), setting, swinging, twirling, I could forget everything except the joy of the moment.

And then, at a moment of rest, my eye was drawn in spite of itself to that silent trio by the door.

Well, I was eighteen. I was launched. I was of marriageable age. I felt no different from the day before. Unadvised, I was far too young to decide about my whole future. I had no experience of love. How should I know if I felt it? How could I choose between the three, as they were trying to make me choose, as their families were trying to make me choose? How could I accept one, knowing that I was right; how could I reject two, knowing that I was right? They must all give me a year, two years, more perhaps.

These thoughts spun through my head, as my body spun through the reel; and I was most unfairly resentful that my admirers were spoiling my fun.

My fears about my hair were thoroughly justified; when Sir George spun me and spun me at the end of the sixteensome, pins fell out of my head like pine-needles in a hurricane, and my hair fell all down my back. There were many renewed compliments – some loud, some very soft – and people begged me to leave my hair loose, because they said they could see the colour better. But I knew that this would not do, and that Aunt Honoria would never permit it. I excused myself, and went indoors for repairs to be made.

I found Mariota, her own bright chestnut hair set off by the pale-green silk. She had an air of one waiting, or of one searching. I knew who she was waiting for, or searching for. I knew he had not come; and it was becoming certain, from the hour, that now he would not come.

Mariota had a right to be aggrieved. The Marquess had sent a note to her at Crask, asking for several dances. She had pencilled those into her programme, so that now for those dances she had no partner. It was a very strange predicament for her to be in; and it was a very shabby thing for him to have done.

I came downstairs, my hair more or less cobbled together at the back of my neck. I was surprised to see an elderly gentleman, magnificently dressed, pacing up and down the hall with an agonised expression. I remembered that he was Lord Ardgarden, and that he was staying at Crask.

When he saw me, he made beseeching noises; I wondered if he wanted to be hit on the back, or shown where he could get a glass of water, or what.

'Been made to promise,' he said miserably, 'to make a speech. What? Propose a toast. Your health. Birthday wishes. What? That's all I can think of to say.'

'I think it is quite good enough, sir,' I said. 'Nobody wants to sit through a long speech in the middle of a party.'

'What? What? Can't be as short as that. Must give better measure.'

'When is this to be?' I asked him: for I had assumed something of the sort would happen, but nobody had said anything to me about it.

'Supper,' he said.

That was after the seventeenth dance – the third of the three I had reserved for Geoffrey, and Rupert, and Peter.

'Better tell me your life story,' said Lord Ardgarden. 'Then I'll have something to talk about.'

But I could not stay, because I was promised for a country dance with Fraser of Lossie, and I would not be uncivil to Papa's old friend.

In the dance we set and swung, and drifted apart and drifted together, and worked our way down the set.

When we were together for a moment, I said, 'Poor Lord Ardgarden is suffering from stage-fright, because he is being made to propose a toast to me.'

'That shouldn't be difficult, Bella.'

'But he can't think of anything to say.'

The dance drove us apart again, and reunited us.

'I hope,' said Mr Fraser, 'there'll be more to announce tonight than just your birthday. Give him his subject matter, my dear, between now and when he has to make his speech.'

He knew I knew what he meant. I felt ennobled by such extreme goodwill. I felt beset.

Peter McCallum was the first to recover the power of speech. He approached me, almost debonair, to ask if there were any spaces left on my programme.

'I kept one for you,' I said, 'in case you were kind enough to ask.'

A huge and amazed grin broke out on his face. I realised that I had put it unfortunately, and raised his hopes.

'I kept spaces for Geoffrey and Rupert, too,' I said, 'in case they were kind enough to ask me. But they haven't, yet.'

'Then I will take their two,' said Peter.

I nearly gave them to him, in a provisional way, because I liked him so very much, and because I did want a partner for those dances. But I would again have seemed to be saying

75

more than I had any notion of saying. I told him I must keep those numbers for his friends.

It was as well I did. Geoffrey and Rupert came up to me together, after I had been waltzing. They spoke at the same moment, producing a garbled discordance, which I was able to interpret. So that, in my programme, Peter had number fifteen, which was a reel, Geoffrey had number sixteen, which was a country dance, and Rupert had number seventeen, which was a polka. Supper came after that. Fraser of Lossie would see me dancing a polka with his son, just before Lord Ardgarden was due to propose the toast. He would be hoping, watching that polka . . .

I was a little nearer understanding, that evening, why these friends treated me with such honour, such generosity, such love. The adults I had met since my return, outside that group, were very few. The ones of whose opinion of me I was aware were the Callo family, and them only. After those months, I was bound in part to look at myself with their eyes, to dismiss myself with their judgement. But that evening was teaching me that even daunting strangers looked at me with approving eyes, and talked to me with evident pleasure, and laughed at things I said. Any doubt I might still have had that I was handsome could not have survived that evening, and probably I looked better and better, from being told so many times that I was beautiful. But it seemed I was other things besides, which I had believed of myself in Australia, and been taught to disbelieve at Callo. It seemed I was congenial, amusing. These people admired me, and very kindly said so; and on top of that they liked me, and some of them said that, too, and many showed it.

With every dance, every conversation, every compliment, I was revising my opinion of myself. I was coming nearer to understanding the feelings of the Nicholls, the Frasers, the McCallums.

By midnight, I was quite certainly the most conceited young female in Scotland.

I danced the number fourteen with Sir Euan Grant, a cheerful gentleman but an extremely small one. For a female I was moderately tall, but no giantess, and I could see over the top

76

of his head. Like many small plump men, Sir Euan was a dancer of most amazing agility; he bounced about on the floor of the marquee like a happy ball. He made everybody laugh; he made me laugh; he made himself laugh loudest of all; so that, although he was almost a midget, and three times my age, he made it the most enjoyable dance of the evening.

I saw that Mariota was sitting out, though in the ballroom; she was talking to two older ladies. This was one of the dances, then, that the Marquess of Gard had asked her to keep for him. Even Sir Euan's joyous clowning could not stop me feeling a brief surge of rage.

I saw three others who were sitting out, though in the ballroom. To the nearest, Peter McCallum, I was promised for the next eightsome reel; there was on his face an expression of the most painful suspense. I was as certain as if he had called out and told me, that he would propose to me during the reel. There would be opportunities, while we waited and others danced. I could not say that I did not know him well enough; I could not say that I did not like him enough. I could not say I was too young, though I knew that I was far too young. I could not say anything except 'No', without giving a reason. It was horribly easy to picture the expression then on Peter's revealing face. I thought that he would not be able to finish the reel, that he would stumble out of the marquee, and leave the field to Geoffrey, to whom the same would happen. I did not want to do that to those dear friends. I did not want over other people the power that I seemed to have.

What does it come to, I thought, this thing that I have that they treasure? Simply, it gives me the capacity to hurt people.

I saw that Geoffrey and Rupert were looking from Peter to me. They knew he had the next dance with me. They knew what use he would make of it. Their faces told their feelings. I wished myself in Australia.

Seeing whatever my own face was showing, Sir Euan pranced higher and faster and more comically, but now I had to force myself to laugh at him.

The dance ended. We clapped the fiddlers, and I curtseyed to Sir Euan. He laughed, and took both my hands – and proposed to me! Oh, how I wished that all proposals should be jokes from endearing little fat men. How I dreaded the number fifteen, and the number sixteen, and the number seventeen.

We were behing a knot of people who, having been dancing, had drawn together into a clump to talk to one another. We were out of sight of Peter and of Rupert, though I thought Geoffrey could see me.

There was beside us a join in the canvas of the marquee – two great sails, overlapping by an inch. Normally this would have been held together by short pieces of tape stitched to the canvas, but they had been untied. Probably it was one of the hired waiters, wanting to take a short cut. It did not matter, on such a fine and warm and windless night, the tapes having been untied.

It was my escape-route. I gestured silence to Sir Euan, putting my finger to my lips, and squeezed my crinoline through the gap.

I stood on the edge of the courtyard, breathing deep the delicious air. The moon was indeed full, and full overhead. Everything that it touched was as visible as by day; but the shadows were as black as soot, and nothing had any colour.

I heard a shout from inside the marquee, from very near where I stood. It was Peter's voice that should have been my partner in a few seconds. I started to speed away: but after a dozen paces I stopped, spun round, and sped towards the house. In this moonlight, my white dress would shine like another moon. I ran into the house by a side door, and along a passage to the hall. Somebody had left a shawl, dark-coloured, filmy, over the back of a chair.

'I'll bring it back,' I said out loud to nobody, which shows the turmoil my mind was in.

The music had not started, for number fifteen. A buzz of voices came from various directions, punctuated by laughter, punctuated by cries I thought were Peter's, and Geoffrey's, and Rupert's.

The hall was no place to be. The park was the place to be, with trees and the shadows of trees. I wrapped the shawl round me, wishing that it was three times the size, and slipped out through another side door into the garden.

But that little pause while I put on the shawl was just too long. One of the three – I could not tell which – had come

78

into the hall another way, and glimpsed me as I slipped out of doors. I heard what sounded like a hunting cry. It would bring the others. Were they hunting as a pack?

Slippers worn for dancing reels did well, I found, for running. A crinoline six feet across did not. I found it was awkward to run while holding a shawl about my shoulders.

Roses and lavender were silvered by the moonlight, and after the rain the air of the garden was heavy with the scent of summer flowers.

There was a door in the garden wall, bolted inside. The bolt was stiff, fatally stiff. I was still struggling with it, when I heard another hunting cry. Though my pursuer was far off at the end of the garden, the part of my white skirt that I could not cover had given me away.

Then I was through the door – having been seen, for certain, going through the door. I sped across the springy turf of the park towards the nearest clump of elm trees. Glancing back as I ran, I saw a kilted figure in the door in the wall, lit, by the moon, as though by the footlights of a theatre. He saw me, and started after me, this time with no hunting cry. He was better dressed than I for running, but I thought I was as fast a runner as any of the three.

I reached the deep shadow of the elm trees, and looked back again from behind a shaggy trunk. He was pelting towards me. I thought it was Rupert. Another figure and then another appeared in the garden doorway. They started running.

I sped out of the elm-copse, keeping it between myself and the pursuit. I crouched behind a clump of furze. I thought they would seach the corpse, as best they could, thinking that I would choose to hide in that deep blackness, thinking that I would grow tired of running. When they found I was gone, they would not know which way.

This was the most ridiculous situation – a mad outdoor game of hide-and-seek, at midnight, under a full moon, hunters and hunted all dressed up for a ball. It was supremely ridiculous that, in the middle of a ball given for my birthday and my debut, I should be spending my time crouched behind a furze-bush in my uncle's park.

I thought that the hunters would not hunt me as a pack, but take their own lines. I thought each would hope to be alone if he caught me. I thought that whichever caught me, if any did, would hope to have caught me indeed. There was more to this chase than the excitement of the chase. We were all behaving like young children, like ourselves ten years before, but in our minds and hearts it was a different game. I had not wanted to be caught, when I was chased then by those boys that had become men. I did not now want to be caught.

They were hunting each for himself, not as a pack? That improved my chances of escape. Each would be jealous of any glimpse he had, any clue: he would not share it with the others. I thought Rupert would be the fastest runner, that Geoffrey would have the sharpest eyes, that Peter would have the quickest brain.

I sped away again. That sweet grass made a perfect surface for running, and the hem of my crinoline brushed it with a tiny whisper.

One saw me, and pounded after. I fled into another dense patch of shade. In a moment footsteps were crashing round me in the dark, crunching dead leaves and twigs, and I heard heavy breathing. Two of the three, or all three, were in the spinney with me.

Number fifteen, number sixteen, number seventeen – reel and country dance and polka – and the dancers were playing hide-and-seek in a spinney. I almost burst out laughing.

I fled away from them, and downhill towards the river, using what cover there was. I was not at all tired. I felt I could have run and run for ever.

I thought that soon I must turn back. I must rejoin my own party. This return to a madcap childhood must not go on too long. After number fifteen, and number sixteen, and number seventeen there was to be supper, and then Lord Ardgarden would rise, suffering, to propose the toast. I must be present then. I had never had my health drunk since, I suppose, my baptism; I had never had a speech made about me; and there were Lord Ardgarden's feelings to consider. My programme after supper was full to the end of the ball, so that I was safe from pleas and proposals, except as jokes.

I had shaken off pursuit, it seemed. I could not hear or see any sign of my kilted hunters. I allowed myself to relax. I looked forward to the small hours of the morning, in which

I should have nothing to do but enjoy the dancing, and listen in silly vanity to the compliments.

I walked downstream by the river, towards the falls and the island and the castle. The river was moderately high, after the rain, but not in full spate. Its chuckle grew to a rumble as it crashed among the rocks of the falls. It was beautiful in the moonlight, the water no longer the lion colour of my hair, but a rush of molten silver.

I was entirely astonished to see a light on the island. Were other people playing midnight hide-and-seek? Was some guest so bored with the ball, that he decided to explore instead? I saw that the light came from the window of the one habitable room in the tumbledown fortress. Poachers? Never, in the midst of the falls – if men were to net the river, they would try the long smooth pools above and below. A vagrant? No tramp or tinker I had ever seen carried a lantern. Ghosts? We had always believed the castle to be haunted. I did not think any ghost had a lantern, either.

Full of curiosity, I approached the footbridge. It was damp from spray, as I could see from the reflected gleam of the moonlight. It would be slippery. The water below thundered black and silver among the rocks. If I was to cross, I must go careful. Cross? Would I? Was I frightened of what might be in the castle? But I *was* full of curiosity. I was not accustomed to feeling frightened – at least, not very, or very often. And no one in the castle need see me, peeping into the light from the dark outside.

I crossed the footbridge, holding tight to the handrail, my crinoline most awkward. I crept towards the lighted window. Of course there was no glass in the window, which was not much more than a slit in the massive old wall. Beside the window was the little doorway into the single room. The door was closed.

The first thing I saw was the lantern, on a hook in the wall on the far side of the room. Then I saw the people in the room, one standing, one kneeling. One I knew very well. One I knew only by sight. A tall man, in Highland evening dress, was standing with his arms folded. A young woman in a resplendent ballgown was on her knees before him. She was clutching at his legs. Her face was turned towards me. It was bathed in tears. She was saying something, sobbing and at

81

the same time desperately talking, talking. She was pleading. She was in despair. I could not hear what she said over the noise of the falls.

The man was the Marquess of Gard. The woman was Jean Hannay.

I should immediately have gone away, back over the footbridge, back to my ball. But I watched them play that dreadful scene in dumb-show, with horrified fascination. It was awful to me to see a woman, a girl, a young wife, my friend, so utterly without shame or pride. It was awful to see anyone in such naked misery, such agony of spirit.

The Marquess looked magnificent. I could not read his face. If he broke into the torrent of her words, I could not hear his voice.

She looked up at his face. Her own was streaming with tears. He said something. She seemed to collapse, as though she no longer had strength even to kneel. He leaned down, and took her by one arm above the elbow. He made to try to pull her to her feet. She was completely limp – she could not or would not stand.

I remembered that, after the Marquess had been for a time alone with Jean, she had locked herself away from friends she had invited.

I remembered that another young wife had only just been saved from a suicide to which the Marquess had driven her.

I looked with disgust at pure evil, and at the misery caused by evil.

I would now have gone away, sickened, shocked, deeply embarrassed to have seen what I should not have seen. I would have gone away, but that I was worried for Jean. I was worried about what she might do to herself, in the madness of despair.

At last the Marquess contrived to pull Jean to her feet. She was a crumpled, deplorable sight, her raven hair half unpinned, her face puddled still with tears. She seemed to throw herself upon him, to try to embrace him. He held her off. I thought there was anger and contempt on his face. His mouth moved. He was speaking sharply, commanding her.

The story of this disgraceful meeting told itself. Every part of the situation was as screamingly obvious as though it had been spelled out in letters of fire on the mossy walls of the room. The Marquess had amused himself with Jean, and now he was tired of her. Her life was in ruins, tatters; he wanted to get on with his, forgetting her.

She seemed to make a gigantic effort to be mistress of herself. She stood unaided. She spoke. She stretched out her hands to him. He shook his head, and answered her. Still I could hear no word, over the crash of the falls.

She turned away from him. She picked up a shawl that had fallen to the stone floor. She was still weeping. She moved away from him, so that she was out of my sight. Suddenly the door was open, and she was beside me. She saw me, a yard away and full in the moonlight. She screamed, the first sound I had heard over the noise of the waters. The Marquess was behind her in the doorway. He saw me. His face looked thunderstruck in the moonlight.

Jean scrambled, more active than I had ever seen her, down the rocks to the footbridge. I was in a sudden terror that she would throw herself into the falls. But she crossed the footbridge, slowly, as though she was frightened. She hurried away over the moon-silvered grass, towards the lights of the house.

The Marquess gestured to me to follow him into the room. I shook my head. I made to follow Jean. I found my arm grasped, urgently, and I was pulled into the room. He shut the door behind us. Though the room was still full of the shouting of the falls, it was possible to talk.

'What are you doing here?' he said, his face full of anger.

'I saw a light.'

'So you came to pry, to eavesdrop.'

'I came because I could not understand why there should be a light here.'

'To stand watching that distasteful and very private scene was an act of the most extreme vulgarity.'

'But I did not know what I should see!'

'One glance, and you should have gone immediately away.'

'I was frightened for Jean Hannay. I have heard of another lady . . .'

'There was no need to be frightened for Lady Hannay. She threatened to destroy herself, but she did not mean it. However, with that threat she compelled me to meet her here.'

'Jean? She said she would kill herself, if you did not . . .'

'An hour ago. I was on my way into the house, into Callo. She stepped out of a shadow. She had been waiting for me.'

'But if you knew she did not mean it . . .'

'I could not then be quite sure she did not mean it. I could not take the risk. She blackmailed me into coming here. Once here, she blackmailed me into hearing her out, with the same threat. I am telling you this simply so that you will not misunderstand what you have just seen.'

'I am quite sure,' I said, 'that I do not in any way misunderstand it.'

'Who are you?'

'I am Arabella Gordon.'

'I think I remember you. You have been in Australia? I wish you were still there.'

'So do I.'

'Why in God's name were you wandering in the park at midnight, during a ball being given for yourself?'

'I had excellent reasons.'

'Enumerate them.'

'Why?'

'Because I tell you to. I have unnecessarily explained to you, Miss Gordon, the reason for my being here. I require the same courtesy from you.'

'Well, I was escaping.'

'From unwelcome attentions?'

'Too many, and too . . . fierce.'

'You are a friend of Lady Hannay?'

'We were friends as children.'

'Then you will wish, for her sake, to forget what you have just seen.'

'I could never possibly forget it. I have never seen anyone so unhappy.'

'At least you will say nothing to a living soul.'

This was not a request, but a command. Though I was a soldier's daughter, I did not care to be given commands, and least of all by somebody who had caused such grief.

'I shall be guided by my conscience,' I said hotly, 'and not by your orders.'

He looked angry. He said, 'You would destroy your friend's reputation? Her marriage?'

'I leave that to you, My Lord,' I said.

At this moment, and even as I spoke, there was a change of tone in the thunder of the falls, muffled as it was by the granite which encased us. It rose in pitch, and in volume.

'My God,' said the Marquess.

He strode to the door, opened it, and stepped out. I followed him. There was no doubt of it – the river was higher, fiercer, throwing up more streamers of spray into the moonlight.

Then came such a thing as I had never seen before, and have never seen since, awesome, terrifying, somehow beautiful. A wall of water came round the bend in the river, at unbelievable speed – a tidal wave, a sudden and appalling flood.

The Marquess pulled me violently indoors, shut the door, and stood with his back to it. even as he did so, the tidal wave struck the island. I could hear the crashing of the waters on the rocks and on the stones of the castle. A plume of water flew in by the little window, and water came in under the door and flooded half of the stones of the floor.

The worst passed. The Marquess opened the door again, and looked out, I with him. The river was higher than I had ever seen it. It raced like a beast each side of the island. Had we not shut the door on it, we would have been drenched within seconds by the spray.

I saw something else, in the brief glimpse I had of the falls. The big wave had carried away the footbridge.

'Crask,' said the Marquess. 'The old fool's dam. He was told he was building it far too flimsy, too cheaply. But he knew better, as he always does.'

I hated the sneering tone the Marquess used about dear Lord Crask. But it was obvious that he was right about the cause of the flood. The heavy rain of the previous week had built up such a weight of water in the artificial loch, that the dam had burst.

'At least,' said the Marquess, 'the water will be down by morning.'

'Then how –?' I said. 'Then what are we –?'

'You must resign yourself to staying here, Miss Gordon, until I can get ashore and send somebody to get you ashore.'

'But the ball – Lord Ardgarden – the toast – Aunt Honoria . . .'

'You should have thought of all those things before you came trespassing here.'

'I could not have foreseen this flood,' I said angrily, 'any more than you could.'

'We should all have foreseen it. That old lunatic should be put under restraint.'

'I cannot spend the whole night alone with you in this room!'

'The prospect is quite as odious for myself as it is for you,' he said. 'But if you decide to try swimming ashore I shall make no attempt to stop you.'

I looked round the little room, in absolute dismay. It was about twelve feet by ten, with the single unglazed slit of window. The rough walls were clammy to the touch, and more moss grew on them than I remembered. Half the floor was awash with the spray that had come in under the door and through the window. There was no furniture of any kind, not so much as a rock.

If I sat or lay down, I should ruin my gown, my first ball-gown, the most expensive thing I had ever had. I was not at all sure that Aunt Honoria would get me another. If I tried to stand up all night, I should presently fall down from sheer fatigue.

'At least you have escaped, Miss Gordon,' said the Marquess, in that sneering tone which I particularly disliked, 'from those unwelcome advances from which you were fleeing.'

That was true, indeed. I was in no kind of danger from the Marquess. Though others might be desperate to catch me, he would have been thankful to be rid of me. He looked at me seldom, and then, I thought, as though I were a beetle. Jean Hannay was – or, rather, had been – the kind of female who caught his fancy. Since I was her opposite in every respect, he must find me repellent. Very evidently, he did find me repellent. It was curious, to find oneself thankful and relieved that one repelled a handsome nobleman.

He repelled me, too, not by the way he looked but by what I knew of his life and character. Knowing what I knew, I could see hints of it all in his face. His lips were thin and his eyes hard. All his life, he would have been accustomed to obsequiousness, to getting his own way instantly in everything. He would have grown used to treating other people as tools or toys, to be used or enjoyed for a little, then broken up and thrown away. I had just seen that happening. Horrible as it had been to see, it was no bad thing I had seen it. I had already been sufficiently forewarned; now the warnings had been made real, by the sight of Jean's misery.

I would have sat on a rock outside the castle, but for being soaked to the skin by the spray.

The lantern went out, through lack of oil.

I tried lying down, on one of the drier parts of the floor. But you cannot lie down in a crinoline, and the floor was too hard and rough. If I used that lacy black shawl as a pillow, the stones hurt my bare shoulders; if I did not, they hurt my face. I sat, leaning against the clammy wall. There was no hope of sleeping. The floor felt harder and harder, through the silk of my skirt.

The Marquess did not speak. I did not know if he slept. The moon went down. It seemed to me that the noise of the falls became, little by little, lower in pitch and less loud.

That night was the longest and most wretched I ever spent.

Suddenly I was aware of movement, and a little pale light in the window. I had at last fallen asleep, and it was dawn. I was stiff and sore, cramped and cold. I struggled to my feet, and to the door.

The Marquess was outside, looking at the water. His hair was a little tousled; otherwise he might just have finished dressing. The same, I knew, could not be said of me.

The paling sky touched the rushing waters with little dim arrows of light. It was down to the level it had had, before the bursting of the dam. There was no question of anybody venturing into it.

The Marquess glanced at me. He said nothing. There would have been no purpose in his speaking, because I would not have heard him unless he bellowed in my ear.

He looked at the sky, and at his watch. He frowned, and tapped his jaw with his fingertips. I thought I understood. It was imperative that he should get ashore without being seen, which meant that he must go as soon as possible. But he must wait until the river went down further, and he must

87

wait as long as possible. I hoped he would decide soon, very soon, that he could safely cross the falls. I did not want him to drown, precisely, but I did not want him on the island.

He looked at me again, and with his chin gestured towards the door. His manners did not improve on better acquaintance. He followed me in.

'You have been marooned alone on the island, Miss Gordon, having come here for any reason you care to invent just before the flood. You have not seen me. I have not been near Callo. I have not left Glengard, because of some anxiety about my father's condition. I shall write to Lady Gordon, with my apologies, to that effect.'

'Will you write to Lady Hannay with your apologies?'

This was, perhaps, not a clever remark to have made. He did not reply to it.

He went out. I stood, stupid with fatigue. It struck me suddenly that he had spoken because he was now leaving. It was unthinkable that he should trust himself to the terrifying power of that water; but he was about to do so.

There was no rope nor stick, and he should have had both. He should have been wearing hobnailed boots, instead of dancing pumps. The water was still far too high. But second by second the sky brightened, and he could delay no longer.

I wondered how he would go about it. I went outside to see. I was frightened of what I might see – a man pounded to death on rocks, or knocked out and so drowned.

He nodded to me curtly. He went to the downstream end of the island, where a little cliff dropped sheer into the water. The water there swirled in a great eddy, caused by the meeting of the two divided halves of the river. I was astonished that he was proposing to enter the water at that point. He climbed down the little cliff, and let himself drop into the water. Immediately he was plucked away downstream. His head disappeared and reappeared. He was swimming strongly when he could, with the current, making no attempt that I could see to reach the bank. I understood. His plan was to reach, undrowned and if possible undamaged, the untroubled water below the falls. There he could swim ashore, although he would be carried a long way down stream before he reached the bank. I saw that this was the only way it could have been done.

I lost sight of him, as the falls swept round a bend. I had no way of knowing if he was alive or dead. It might be days before I knew, unless I asked questions I must not ask.

Long and long after, when the sun had risen, I saw a horse and cart coming down the hill towards the river. There were half a dozen men, of whom one was Uncle Ranald. They stopped where the end of the footbridge had been. They waved and apparently shouted to me. I waved back. One of the men produced from the cart a coil of thin cord, like a clothesline. He mimed that he would throw it to me, and that I should catch it. I did so, just. I could not imagine what use there could be in a clothesline across the water. Then they got a much thicker and heavier rope from the cart. They tied it to the clothesline. They tied to it also a small anchor. They gestured that I was to pull the larger rope across, by means of the smaller one. They helped me as much as possible, but it was heavy work, with the weight of the anchor as well as the rope, and the effort of keeping it all out of the water. At last the anchor was in my hands; I found a crevice in a rock, and jammed one fluke of the anchor in until I was sure it was safe.

Then from behind the cart came a boy I had not realised was there. I knew him well by sight; he worked for one of the tenants. He was called Malcolm McVicar, but he was always known as 'Monkey' because he was astonishingly agile, and could climb up or down anything – he was called for all up and down the glen, when a cat got stuck in a treetop. 'Monkey' McVicar wrapped his legs round the rope, and hung from it by his arms, and joined me on the island, grinning, in a matter of seconds. I shook his hand, of which Uncle Ranald probably did not approve.

After that, all was straightforward. They tied a loop of rope about the big rope, and in it put one end of a great plank, to which was tied another rope. This other rope was thrown across to 'Monkey', and he and I were able to pull the plank across. Now there was a bridge, and a kind of handrail. I went across, feeling ridiculous in my crinoline. I thanked them all, and told my story for the first of very many times.

'It sounds ungrateful and even cowardly, Aunt Honoria,' I

said, 'but I could not face being proposed to during the fifteenth, and sixteenth, and seventeenth dances, and I knew I was going to be, and I did not want to hurt any of them, so I ran away and hid on the island. I was going to come back in time for supper, truly I was, because I knew Lord Ardgarden was going to make a speech, and by that time I would have other partners, who I thought would not be proposing to me . . .'

I had decided that the exact truth, with one omission, was best. Scores of people knew about Geoffrey, and Rupert, and Peter – their families, this family, and everybody at the dance who had eyes. People must know about the chase, from Sir Euan Grant, and from hearing the hunting cries, and from seeing the boys returning exhausted and empty-handed.

'It is what we have come to call,' said Aunt Honoria, 'Australian behaviour.'

'I could not,' I said (as I had said, on the island, nine hours before), 'have known that Lord Crask's dam would burst.'

'Australian,' repeated Aunt Honoria, making the word sound like the most frightful insult.

Later in the morning, I was summoned to Uncle Ranald's study. I stood, at his command, in front of his desk. I felt like a child at school, though I had never been a child at school.

'A shepherd called Francis Grey,' he said to me, 'crossed the park at first light this morning, which, though he is not in my employ, he has my permission to do. His way took him near the falls. He was astonished to see a man, on the island, and then in the water. He recognized the man as the Marquess of Gard, for whose father the Duke his uncle works. Grey thought it extremely strange, but no business of his. He then heard, as the whole glen has by now heard, of your rescue by myself from the island. It was as obvious to Grey as it will be to everybody else that Lord Gard could not have crossed to the island after the sudden flood, and that you could not have done so, either. That, in sum, you and Lord Gard were alone together, in one room, far from anybody else and unknown to anybody else, for most of last night. Well?'

'We were the victims of a natural disaster, Uncle Ranald. There was nothing whatever we could do about it. He treated me with perfect correctness. As a matter of fact I think he finds me repellent.'

'That is unfortunate,' said Uncle Ranald, 'since you are about to marry him.'

Chapter 5

I was unable to speak or to think. The words I had heard
held no meaning. I could *not* have heard what I had heard.
It would have been something to laugh at, except that it was
not something to laugh at.

It did not matter that I could not speak. Uncle Ranald
was in a mood to speak.

'We received a message from Lord Gard, brought by the
hand of a messenger, this morning,' he said. 'He wrote, cour-
teously enough, that he apologised for not honouring his
acceptance of our invitation, and pleaded that a sudden
apparent deterioration in his father's health had compelled
him to stay at home. He wrote that he had not left Glengard,
and did not imminently contemplate leaving it, owing to his
father's state. When this letter came into our hands, we had
already been apprised by Francis Gray that Lord Gard had
been, beyond any possibility of doubt, on that island for most
of the night. His letter was a lie. I do not place undue
emphasis on that. At such a time, under such circumstances,
it could be argued that to conceal or distort the truth was a
necessary act of chivalry. His motives in seeking to mislead
us are, in any case, irrelevant, since he has failed to do so.
We know that he was on the island, on which there is one
building, in which there is one room, from soon after midnight
until an hour after dawn. We know that you were also there.
We have had no intelligence as to his reasons for being there.
We have had from you a reason for your being there which
your aunt and I find wholly incredible. We are bound to
assume that you had an assignation with Lord Gard.'

I opened my mouth to deny such a preposterous idea, but
Uncle Ranald did not give me time to speak. He swept on,
as though I were a public meeting all of whose members he
detested.

'Since he could come freely to a house to which he was an invited guest, and could there have such converse with you as he wished, we are bound to conclude that the assignation was made for an illicit, an immoral purpose.'

I made a sort of croaking noise, of absolute outrage. He ignored my croak.

He said, 'Scores of people know by now that you and Lord Gard spent the best part of a night together, alone, in one room. By nightfall hundreds will know. By the week's end, thousands will know. You will be branded as a trollop, Lord Gard as a rake. Your father is a gallant soldier and a respected public servant. Your mother is a lady of aristocratic connection and impeccable reputation. I am not without honour in my own country. Your lady aunt is a pillar of rectitude, respectability, and Christian conduct. You have cousins. You have younger brothers and a sister. It is not tolerable, it is not thinkable, that the grossness of your indiscretion should not be at once redeemed by marriage. I have written to His Grace the Duke of Lomond to this effect.'

'What?' I squeaked. It was the first intelligible word I had uttered since I went into the study.

'Naturally,' said Uncle Ranald, 'he will agree. He will be obliged to agree. Even if he were inclined to ignore the intolerable dishonour done to this family, this ancient name, he could not ignore the implications for his son. The inheritor of so great a name and title, to sully, irremediably, without reparation, the reputation of a lady of gentle birth, a child barely out of the schoolroom? His Grace will not countenance such blackguardly cynicism. If he does, he will have me to contend with. Old and frail as he is, I shall beard him in his very bedchamber. Right shall be done, and be seen to be done.'

'Wrong,' I squeaked: because it seemed that I could only squeak.

'When you and your paramour made this assignation,' said Uncle Ranald, 'the most recent of we know not how many, you not only failed to reck of conscience, morality, Christian duty, maidenly virtue, all that raises us above the level of the beasts and of the savages, black and white, of barbarous lands. You failed to reck also of the duty of example to the humble which is forced, willy nilly, on those whom Providence has placed in positions of social eminence. Were this scandalous episode to be brushed under the carpet of well-bred oblivion, what of the consequent behaviour of grooms and maidservants?'

It was at this point that I realised how carefully rehearsed was Uncle Ranald's speech. I was still not in the way of believing a single word I was hearing.

He went on and on. Probably I was the most attentive and obedient audience he had ever had. He made many points, most of them several times. It came always back to his honour and reputation, and Aunt Honoria's. They refused utterly to be besmirched by the immoral folly of a niece for whom they were, for the time, morally responsible. Their faces would be blackened. They would be derided, despised, ostracised.

He slowed at last, and came to a halt. By this time I had received the power of speech.

'I am sorry, Uncle Ranald,' I said, 'that Lord Crask's dam burst, which is all you are really complaining about. I will not marry Lord Gard. I would rather die.'

'If you do not marry Lord Gard,' said Uncle Ranald, 'you will be as good as dead.'

For the next three days, I was a leper among the family, and a sensation among the servants.

I offered to swear, upon as many Bibles as they liked, that Lord Gard had not touched me. (Although my arm was bruised, where he had touched me.) But I was made to see that this was not the point. It was not of the slightest consequence, what had happened or not happened; it was not of the slightest consequence that we had been trapped by the flood. Though they were bound to assume that we had an assignation (and I came to see that this did look probable, to anyone not knowing about Jean Hannay), it was not of the slightest consequence that we had met by the purest chance. It did not signify that we had hardly touched one another, that we disliked one another, that we had exchanged very few words, and most of those rancorous. *All* that mattered, at that time, in that society, to those people, was that the Marquess and I had spent those hours of the night alone together.

Aunt Honoria dabbed ceaselessly at her eyes with a lace handkerchief, but I did not know why, because as far as I could see she was not crying. Grizelda left any room I entered. One of the young maids winked at me, and I winked back. It was only afterwards that I realised that that wink would be reported, by the amazing telegraphy of servants' halls, to scores and hundreds, and that it amounted to a plea of guilty.

I could not stand up against the outraged morality of the Gordons of Callo, which was carrying me irresistibly, like an express train, towards the altar. But Uncle Ranald's notion was still evidently preposterous. The Marquess of Gard would not be bullied into marrying me. The Duke would not be bullied into commanding it. To them Uncle Ranald, though a laird and a baronet, was not much more than a nobody. They would ignore his yapping. His letter to the Duke would have been torn up and dropped in a fire. I might suffer all kinds of agonies, because of the bursting of the dam, but betrothal to Lord Gard was not one of them.

I was quite wrong.

Uncle Ranald was expecting hourly an invitation from the Duke. He was *in loco parentis* (as he often said, and I knew what he meant after I had looked it up), and it would be normal, in such a case, for the two to meet.

But when a card arrived from Glengard, written by a secretary at the Duke's dictation, it was to summon me to meet the Duke.

Aunt Honoria said that she would come with me; but the note said that I was to come alone. 'His Grace must deny himself, on the strictest medical instructions, the pleasure of entertaining other members of Miss Gordon's family, though he hopes in due course to be sufficiently recovered to do so.' Those were lines, I thought, between which it was extremely easy to read. Grizelda certainly read between them, and laughed outright at her mother.

During those three days, other notes flooded inevitably into Callo – little stiff messages of thanks to Aunt Honoria for a charming party.

There were no messages for me – not from Geoffrey Nicholls, or Rupert Fraser, or Peter McCallum; not from Mariota, or Jean Hannay. I might not just have had an eighteenth birthday; I might not have had any friends.

All of them knew by now that I had spent hours of that night alone with the Marquess of Gard. All of them (except perhaps Mariota) knew the Marquess's reputation. They knew that I was free in my ways and in my speech, having lived all those years in Australia; they might hope that I was strictly virtuous, but they could not know it, and might guess otherwise.

I might not have had any friends? It seemed I did not have any friends.

It was on the Thursday, the fifth day after the ball, that I was summoned to the Duke. I could not refuse to go. I did not want to refuse to go. I was curious to see the insides of those courtyards, those collegiate quadrangles. I was curious to see the Duke, who had been a kind of distant legend even when I was a child. I did not suppose I would see the Marquess. I supposed I would be asked to tell my story of the night of the ball; it would be exactly the same as the Marquess's story, with the same omissions about Jean Hannay. It would reassure the Duke, if he needed reassurance, that this preposterous notion of Uncle Ranald's could be ignored.

I had a notion that it might be sensible to look as hideous as I could. I thought I might borrow from one of the maidservants a gown she wore when she scrubbed the kitchen floor; great clumping boots from another; an old, old bonnet from a third. I could purposely make myself cross-eyed (a trick I had learned from my younger brother Archie), though I could not do it for very long without giving myself a headache. I could talk with an adenoidal voice, having heard a good many of them in Australia. I could make myself awkward, pigeon-toed, knock-kneed; I could make myself unable to go through a doorway without bumping into one doorpost or the other. I could make myself so horrible a sight that the Duke, the very moment he saw me, would tear up Uncle Ranald's letter if he had not already done so.

It was a game I had played, to amuse the children. Sometimes I had to stop, because it made my little sister scream.

I was sorely tempted; but I saw that it would not do. Aunt Honoria would inspect me more rigorously than ever, before I set off for Glengard. Probably she would come with me in the carriage; they would not let her in, it seemed, but she would go as far in as they would let her, so I would be in the custody of Glengard servants before I was out of her sight.

There was another factor. The Duke had known my father and my grandfather. I did not care in the least what the Duke thought of Uncle Ranald; but I did not want to betray the memory of my grandfather, and I did not want to lower the esteem in which I knew my father was held. For their sake, I must behave myself, and act as much like a lady as I could.

And so I did a turnabout: I dressed with as much care for that call as I had for my ball five days before. This time, Aunt Honoria's maid was free to do my hair. I wore my very best watered-silk afternoon dress, and a hat with a feather that stuck straight up in the air. I practised a new way of walking, the intention of which was to signify dignity. I was a general's daughter; I would hold myself like a general. I practised a new voice, lower than my usual voice, the intention of which was to signify maturity. I interrupted my own rehearsal with a fit of giggling which must have been hysterical. I had nothing whatever to giggle about.

I was not very afraid of fire or flood, having experienced the one in Australia, the other in Scotland. But I had to face the miserable truth about myself: I was afraid of my coming interview with the Duke of Lomond.

Aunt Honoria did indeed inspect me. I stood in the middle of the morning-room, slowly revolving on her orders. I tried to revolve as a general would have revolved, though perhaps generals do not much revolve.

'Miss Arabella is the bonniest young leddy in Scotland,' said the housekeeper, to my great surprise.

And to my even greater surprise, to my absolute amazement, Grizelda nodded.

Aunt Honoria cleared her throat, as though about to make a pronouncement; but she merely nodded, and said that it was time to go.

On the way to Glengard, I thought that this could not be happening to me.

We came again to the outcrop of granite, from which the castle grew like an extension of the hill. This time we went on and round, to the part I had not seen. It was completely unlike those sunny, open courtyards I had glimpsed from the garden – it was a frowning, warlike place, a castle in truth, not a peaceful college, with battlements and towers which I would have supposed a recent imitation, some coal-owner's grandiose folly, except that I knew they were ancient.

Aunt Honoria had been silent during the drive; she was silent still. I was sure she was quite as abashed as I was.

We went over a bridge into a courtyard where moss grew between the flag-stones. The courtyard had very high, battlemented walls, interrupted by towers; it faced the north; I thought the sun had never struck those flagstones. I thought the cushions of bright green moss showed that very few wheels came into that courtyard.

The carriage stopped by a short, broad flight of shallow steps, which led up to a door like that of a cathedral. Half the double door was open. What I could see of the interior was as dark as night. A footman came out of the door and down the steps, with a magnificent lady whom I took to be some kind of upper servant: but I would not have had any idea what her position was called, or how she would spend her time.

She spent it now in intercepting Aunt Honoria, and saying that His Grace was grieved not to be able to receive her. She took Aunt Honoria away, not through the great door, but by a side door twenty yards away.

I followed the footman. He was a pleasant-looking young man, very solemn, in a sort of half-livery. I supposed he dressed up grander in the evening, or when he was attending

98

the Duke himself. He was not nearly so impressive as Sir Archibald Hannay's footman at Achmore.

I found I was forgetting to walk like a general. I reminded myself to do so.

Nobody was going to torture me, execute me, throw me into a dungeon, or condemn me to bread and water. Nobody, I was very sure, was going to make me marry the Marquess of Gard. I told myself I had nothing to be frightened of. I found myself most unconvincing.

The great hall was not quite as large as the fields on which my brothers played football, nor quite as dark as the Callo coal-cellars.

And then we were in a broad, high corridor, with tall windows and many pictures. The sun reappeared. I was pleased to see it. It gave me courage. And then we travelled I could not think how far, or round how many corners; and we came at last to a door which stood open; and in the doorway stood a clergyman.

For a moment I was astonished. A clergyman was the last thing I had expected to see. Then I realised that, of course, a house this size would have a resident chaplain.

Then two thoughts hit me, at exactly the same moment. One was that the Duke had died. The other was that I was to be married, immediately, by this parson, to the Marquess of Gard.

'Miss Gordon,' murmured the footman.

'Thank you, James,' said the parson, who had a low, soft, soothing voice even in using three words to dismiss a footman.

The clergyman was about sixty, very pink and scrubbed, with little bright black eyes like the Aborigine children of New South Wales.

'I am Doctor Pericles Davidson,' he said, 'His Grace's chaplain. I am to welcome you to Glengard, Miss Gordon.'

I curtseyed, and we shook hands. He did not look a man whose master has just died; I did not know if he looked like a man who was about to perform a marriage ceremony.

'I must explain to you the, ah, unusual circumstances in which we all find ourselves today, Miss Gordon. His Grace is not expecting us for another minute or two, so let us take this opportunity. There is a small sitting room here. Will you be so good . . .?'

Blinking, not at all understanding what was happening, I went through the door. I blinked again, because it was the most beautiful room I had ever seen, perfectly circular, with a domed ceiling covered in delicate plasterwork of flowers and foliage and fruit, and walls hung with silk, and painted medallions; and it was not at all overpowering – it gave no sense of lavishness – but most welcoming. There was not much furniture; I could not judge, but I guessed that what there was was priceless.

I exclaimed at the room. I revolved, as I had revolved in the morning-room at Callo, so as to see every part of it.

'This is known as the Tambour Room, Miss Gordon,' said Dr Davidson, 'both from its shape and from the richness of its decoration. It was designed and made in 1736, for the third Duke, and is perfectly unaltered from its original appearance.'

'It is the most beautiful room I have ever seen,' I said.

He nodded. His little black eyes never left my face. He was not quite smiling, but he was certainly not grim.

We sat down, although I wondered if chairs made in 1736 should have been sat on. I remembered to sit like a general (although my father, when he was off parade, was apt to loll back and put one leg over the arm of his chair).

'His Grace,' said Dr Davidson, 'is suffering at the moment from a condition of the throat which effectively prevents him from speaking. His hearing and eyesight are, I should tell you, quite unimpaired – remarkable in a man of his age. His brain I can only describe as formidable. You can probably imagine the frustration of seeing, hearing, feeling, thinking, deciding, and being unable to communicate, except by the wearisome expedient of writing on a piece of paper. Fortunately there are some of us in the household whose association with His Grace is of such long standing that we can in many cases anticipate his wishes – can even, it sometimes seems to us, read his thoughts. Fortunately also there are moments when, for a few minutes at a time, his throat clears and he can speak without discomfort. There was such a moment earlier today. It was possible for us to discuss your coming interview with His Grace. It was possible for me to hear from him what questions he wishes asked. So it will be a strange conversation, Miss Gordon – the questions will come from me, but the answers will be for His Grace.'

'I am sorry about His Grace's throat,' I said. 'I hope it will be better soon.'

After his long speech, all delivered in that smooth, soothing voice, Dr Davidson seemed to have run out of anything to say. At any rate he said nothing, but simply sat staring at me. Of course he knew why I was there – he knew where I had spent Saturday night, and with whom. Every soul in Glengard Castle, for a certainty, knew these things. He might in consequences have stared at me appraisingly, or with disapproval, or with open horror. But he did not. He simply stared. There was no expression on his face at all. I became restless under this scrutiny. Not alarmed or unnerved, not by this little elderly clergyman, but bored. I tried staring back (staring like a general) but I found that did not relieve my boredom.

At last I stood up, and went to look at the painted medallions in the walls. In the back of my neck I could still feel his eyes on me. I did my best to ignore them, and to concentrate on the paintings.

I found it peculiar that the two of us should be together in this room, in total silence. Aunt Honoria would have said that politeness required conversation. I saw that, for once, she was right. Well, if Dr Davidson would not make conversation, then I would.

I said, 'These paintings are French, are they not? They remind me of one my mother has, which she takes with her wherever she goes. It is by Lancret. That is to say, it is a copy of a Lancret. These are wonderfully delicate, like the whole room. They seem to be all on the subject of enjoyment. They are all full of sunshine. It is strange that men wore swords, when they were strolling in gardens in the company of ladies. Did they expect to be attacked by robbers? Or might they suddenly find themselves fighting a duel? All these trees seem to be the same trees that we have in Scotland. Of course the trees in Australia are quite different . . .'

I came lamely to a halt, aware that I was in danger of beginning to babble nonsense. An oppressive silence invaded the room again. I had by now completed a circuit of the room, and was back where I had started. But, since looking at the pictures was better than looking at Dr Davidson, I began to make a second circuit. And indeed all the paintings were worth looking at twice.

I began to talk again, driven by the knowledge that Aunt Honoria would have required it, driven by the feeling that this dead silence was unnatural and uncivilized.

I talked about the pictures, since they were what I was looking at – about the girls' hats and gowns, and what could be seen of the gardens; and I began to imagine conversations between the people. It occurred to me that I was becoming childish – that I was talking to Dr Davidson as I might have talked to my younger brothers, inventing such conversations to amuse them. But I preferred being childish to being a silent waxwork.

I realised that I was not talking like a general. I realised that I had forgotten to use my new, mature voice, and my new, dignified posture. I did not think it greatly mattered what Dr Davidson thought of me.

The door opened, admitting a different footman. He nodded his head to Dr Davidson, who immediately rose to his feet. He nodded to me, and indicated that I should follow the footman. I nodded back; it seemed that this was a time for nodding. I followed the footman; Dr Davidson followed me; and we proceeded in single file down another great corridor, so thickly carpeted that we might have been walking through two inches of snow.

We went through what seemed to me a kind of ante-chamber, in which one could imagine people waiting for audiences; and then the footman threw open a door onto a blaze of sunshine so bright that I thought it must be an outside door – that we were going out onto a terrace.

But it was a room, of moderate size but with huge south-facing widows. It was another room to startle you, not by the beauty of its decoration but by the beauty of the prospect out of the windows. One glance was all I could spare for the huge sweep of the glen below, and the curtain of the big hills in the far distance; politeness obliged me, after that one glance, to look at the Duke; curiosity did, too.

He was sitting in a deep armchair by one of the windows, and wearing a brocade dressing-gown. From his position, he was half in the brilliant sunshine which flooded into the room, and half in shade. Though he was sitting, it was possible to see that he was very tall; though he was wrapped in the voluminous brocade, it was possible to see that he was very thin. The skin of his face was stretched tight over his jaw and cheekbones. His nose was high-bridged, and his mouth thin. He was clean-shaven; his hair was thick, white, and worn long. His eyes were deeply sunken, with dark shadows about them; this was the only obvious sign, apart from his extreme thinness, of the long illness from which he had suffered.

'Miss Gordon, your Grace,' said Dr Davidson.

I curtseyed. The Duke gave a faint nod. Dr Davidson indicated where I was to sit, on a chair close to the Duke's, and facing the window. In walking towards it, I remembered to move like a general. I held my chin high and, when I sat down, I kept my back straight.

Dr Davidson stationed himself beside the Duke's chair. He stood perfectly still. The Duke sat perfectly still. I sat perfectly still. The footman had left the room. Silence re-entered, and lay over the three of us like a blanket. I made a deliberate effort to keep my chin high and my back straight; but it was an effort. Dr Davidson's eyes, small and black and bright, were fixed on my face. The Duke's eyes, of a colour I could not see because of the sun in my own eyes, were fixed on my face. I had been warned that the interview would be strange; I had not expected anything as strange as this. I thought things were becoming ridiculous.

I cleared my throat, making a much louder noise than I expected, in that dense silence. I said, 'I suppose you want to know what happened on Saturday night. Sunday morning, I should say. Nothing happened. I imagine Lord Gard has told you so, if you discussed it with him. That place is not comfortable enough for anything to have happened, of the kind which, er, I suppose my Uncle Ranald hinted at in his letter to you. There might have been a hundred people there, for all the difference it would have made, except I would have preferred it if there had been a hundred people there, only I don't know where so many people would have gone, to keep out of the wet . . . We were like people in a station waiting-room, you see, but instead of waiting for a train we were waiting for the river to go down. Nobody is obliged to get married, because they have been together in a station waiting-room.'

103

I looked at the Duke, to see if he agreed with me. I could not tell if he agreed with me. If there was any expression on that white, bony old face, I could not read it. It was hard to see his face as one face, because half of it was brilliantly lit by the sun, and half in shadow. I glanced also at Dr Davidson. His mouth was pursed, as though he found improper any mention of station waiting-rooms.

Silence fell again. I waited for one of the questions which Dr Davidson had said he had been told to ask. He seemed to have forgotten to ask questions. The Duke did not seem to expect him to ask any questions. It was up to me once more, to save the whole situation from becoming absurd.

I raised my chin, and straightened my back, and said, 'Of course it was Lord Crask's fault, for thinking he knew better than the engineers from Edinburgh. I am sorry to be saying that, because I like him very much, and they have both always been very kind to me. But if anybody ought to be punished for Saturday night, by being made to get married, then it is Lord Crask, only of course he is married already . . .'

Into a new silence, Dr Davidson, soothing as ever, suddenly said, 'His Grace wishes to hear about your life in Australia, Miss Gordon.'

'It was sometimes quite hot,' I said, much surprised. 'We had beautiful horses. We hunted kangaroos.'

They both stared at me, waiting. Obviously I had not given a sufficient account of Australia.

Well, I thought, if they want a lecture on Australia, they shall have one. I embarked on descriptions of Sydney, the raw new nearby townships, the remoter estates and great houses of the squatters, the outback and the Aborigines, the smart races and the humble, impromptu tavern races, some of the criminals who became famous and some of the politicians who became infamous . . . I came to a halt, embarrassed, knowing that Aunt Honoria would say I had been talking far too much. They stared, waiting. They wanted more? It was hardly to be believed, but it seemed they were anxious to hear about Australia. I started again, and went doggedly on; and, when I could think of nothing else to say about the country and the people, I talked about the birds and the trees; and, when I had exhausted my knowledge of them, I talked about my own family.

'I am sorry, your Grace,' I said at last. 'I think the subject is exhausted. I think I am too.'

After a moment, the Duke and his chaplain exchanged a look. They did not gesture, or speak.

Dr Davidson turned back to me. He said, 'His Grace thanks you for your courtesy in coming to visit him, Miss Gordon. He now begs you to excuse him. It is time he rested.'

I nodded. I rose. I stood as tall as I could, like a general. I curtseyed, as I thought a general would have curtseyed. Dr Davidson made a gesture towards the door. I turned, and saw that it was open, and that a footman stood beside it. I did not understand how he had been called; perhaps he had been there for a long time. I went to the door. Having reached it, I turned and curtseyed again. The Duke made no sign, that I could see. I went out of the room, and the footman closed the door behind me.

The footman led me back to the lovely place they called the Tambour Room. It seemed I was to wait there; I did not know for what. I fell to inspecting the pictures again, although I knew them all by heart.

Dr Davidson came in, and asked me to sit down. I expected again the bright, beady inspection of my face: but he looked away, towards a window.

He said, 'His Grace accepts, Miss Gordon, your account of the events of last Saturday night – or more properly, as you yourself said, Sunday morning – which confirms, and is confirmed by, the account previously given His Grace by his Lordship. His Grace has also pondered the contents of the letter with which he was favoured by Sir Ranald Gordon of Callo, and has discussed the matter with myself, in regard to morality, the teaching of the Church, the duty of his family and yours to set an impeccable example to the humble, the future usefulness in high government office of the Marquess of Gard . . . and, in sum, his Grace has formed the clear conclusion – with which, I may say, I am in total if reluctant agreement – that your worthy uncle is right. There must be an immediate marriage between yourself and the Marquess of Gard."

I looked at him, stupefied. I was more surprised than I had been by Uncle Ranald.

He droned on, his voice no longer soothing, although I

thought it was meant to be. Really he repeated all Uncle Ranald's arguments, about Papa's reputation in the army, and the Gordons' reputation in the glen, and so forth, and added a lot of Christian morality as well; and he made it clear that under no circumstances could the Marquess or I escape.

At last I followed a footman the weary way to the front courtyard, and I moved not like a general but like a sleepwalker.

I was completely puzzled by that silent and inscrutable Duke. As far as I had seen, his face had shown no expression, of any kind, at any moment. He had simply sat and listened, and listened, and listened, as I had babbled on, and on, and on. He and his chaplain must have decided, long before that strange interview, that I must marry Lord Gard. The chaplain's arguments – Uncle Ranald's arguments – were right if they were right, and they were not affected one jot by my monologue. Then why the interview? Why so ridiculous an interview? What purpose was served by a sick old man condemning himself to listening to an interminable account of kangaroo hunting in Australia?

Aunt Honoria was waiting for me by the carriage. She was almost smiling. She had the look of someone fighting down a triumphant grin, under an attempted expression of moral outrage.

She already knew, somehow, what the Duke had decided.

On the way back to Callo, she examined me minutely about the conversation. She was as surprised as I had been, that I was made to talk so much about Australia. She thought I must have bored the Duke, which I thought also. She could not make out why my going kangaroo hunting when I was fifteen had anything to do with my being compromised when I was eighteen; and nor could I.

'You will be married there, I daresay,' said Aunt Honoria. 'In the private chapel, by the Duke's chaplain. I imagine it will be a private occasion, immediate family only. Grizelda and I will both need new gowns. I wonder how the chaplain will view the idea of your being married in white? How surprised your dear parents will be – but I am thankful your mother has been spared the . . . At least the promptness and decision with which both families have reacted is a reassuring affirmation of old-fashioned virtue. Your uncle never doubted that the Duke would be exactly of his mind. Of course he had no choice – none of us had. Duty still rules us. We shall have played our part – we shall hold our heads high. And here we are. Change at once out of that gown, Arabella, before you ruin it with some tomboy frolic. You will have to mend your ways at Glengard. There will be no jumping over walls there. I must at once find your uncle and tell him the news, though it is only what he confidently expected.'

That was an aspect, obvious as it was, that I had not properly faced. I had thought only of the Marquess, as a person. I had not thought of his way of life. I had thought of being shackled to that person. I had not thought of being tied to a ducal treadmill, living in public, always on my best behaviour, with a thousand eyes watching for mistakes, or vulgarities, or 'Australian behaviour'. I would have thought of all this, perhaps, if any of it had seemed possible at all.

I had not taken Uncle Ranald seriously. I would not take the Duke seriously, either. I did not think it would be easy to defy the two of them, and the majesty of the Episcopalian Church; but the Marquess of Gard could.

I was helped out of my lovely dress, and into an unlovely one. I sat at the writing-table in my bedroom, and thought, and thought, and thought.

After many false starts, and much wasted paper, I produced this letter, not much blotched or ink-spattered:

My Lord,

The accidental events of last week are to have consequences, it seems, as odious to me as I am well aware they must be to you. I find myself helpless, since my own family are on the other side of the world, and there is nobody here I can turn to. I appeal to you to extract us both from this Awful Predicament. I am confident that you will use your best efforts, and that they will be successful.

Believe me, my Lord, your most obedient servant but your most reluctant Betrothed,

Arabella Gordon

I was extremely pleased with this letter, especially the end, although I was not sure that it was quite correct to put capital letters to 'Awful Predicament'. Somehow, the words seemed to ask for them.

I was pleased with more than the letter; I was pleased with an idea which I was sure would work.

I gave the letter to one of the grooms who had known me as a child. Seeing the direction on the envelope, he gave an excited, conspiratorial grin. He thought I was entrusting him with a love-letter to my sweetheart.

'No,' said the Marquess of Gard.

He had replied to my note not with a note but with a visit.

I was returning from one of my many, many solitary walks in the park – they were more frequent, and went on longer, since I had become the leper of Callo. I was wearing clothes for scrambling, and boots for crossing rough ground, because I was still free to do these things. As I came up the hill from the river, I saw a horseman approaching the house. He was a long way off, but I saw that it was a tall man on a tall bay horse. His style of riding was very unlike my Cousin Henry's. I knew immediately who it was, and why he had come.

Aunt Honoria would think he had come to call on her.

A few minutes later, I was crossing the hall of the house. I heard voices from the drawing room. What I should have done, was hurry upstairs to change. What I did do, was tiptoe to the drawing room door, most curious as to what Aunt Honoria and the Marquess would find to say to one another.

She was offering him his choice of the entire larder, still-room and wine-cellar of Callo House. He was declining. I would not have supposed that a conversation on these lines could have lasted very long, but this one promised to go on for ever.

The door opened suddenly, and Grizelda came out. I had not realised she was in the room; she had not contributed to the conversation. She swept past me, with barely a glance, and crossed the hall towards the back parts of the house.

Aunt Honoria and the Marquess were sitting in upright chairs, not very close together. They both looked towards the door. They saw me. The Marquess rose.

'I was just on my way to change my clothes,' I said. 'I am not fit to be seen.'

'That is true, Arabella,' said Aunt Honoria.

'Do not change on my account,' said the Marquess.

His tone said clearly: you repel me as much in your richest finery as in those tattie-bogle garments you are wearing.

He turned to Aunt Honoria, and said, 'I beg you will excuse me, Lady Gordon. I am pressed for time, but it is urgent that I have a few words with Miss Gordon.'

Miss Gordon. Not the way, I thought, that a man refers to his betrothed. I am not his betrothed, then. He is contriving as I knew he would contrive.

Aunt Honoria made a last attempt to press refreshment on him, of all the kinds that he had already refused. He continued to refuse, politely enough.

To me he said, 'I suggest we stroll in the garden, Miss Gordon, unless you are already exhausted.'

The suggestion that I should be exhausted after a mere half-hour of walking was absurd, and made me cross. Then I thought that, after all, I might have been walking for three hours, for all he knew. I nodded. I was agog to know how he had extricated us, how he had won over the Duke and the chaplain.

'No,' he said, in the middle of the formal rose-garden.

I looked at him dumbly.

'I know that the prospect of being joined to me is odious to you,' he said 'and I know why.'

He knew, then, that the truth about him had got out, and that I was aware of it.

'Knowing that,' I said, 'how can you be a – a party to forcing this on me? On both of us?'

'I am quite as reluctant as you,' he said, 'for different reasons.'

Yes, different reasons. He disliked and despised me. He bracketed me, naturally, with Aunt Honoria's pretentious snobbery, which was unfair; he saw in me an uncouth colonial, which was fair, although it did not seem to repel my friends or their families.

'The person I must consider above all others,' he said, 'is my father. Not only is it my duty to obey his command, but also it is my duty to protect him in any way I can from pain or distress. He has concluded that, after the calamitous events of that night, his honour as well as mine requires this marriage. The reputation of your family as well as yourself requires it. I have tried to budge him from this position, but he will not be budged. I have pleaded your detestation of the prospect, with your reasons, which are excellent, and which I believe I fully understand.'

So he should understand them, indeed.

'I pleaded my own reluctance, with reasons with which I thought he was bound to sympathise.'

I would have thought so, too – a *mésalliance*, a descent, if not to the gutter, then at least a long way down from Glengard.

'I pleaded,' said the Marquess, 'the certainty of the most wretched unhappiness for you. I pleaded that certainty for myself. I pleaded in vain. I had not realised the granite strength of his religious and moral convictions, or his jealousy of the honour of his name. Brought face to face with these, I dare not defy him.'

For fear of being disinherited, I thought.

'It is dangerous for him to become excited,' said the Marquess. 'The last time he flew into a passion of rage, he very nearly died of the paroxysms that the rage brought on. The doctors warned me – warned the whole household – that he must never be crossed in such a way again. In defying him now, I would be murdering him.'

'I am to be sacrificed to your father's health,' I said flatly.

'I understand that you met my father, Miss Gordon. Would you make yourself responsible for his death?'

Still Miss Gordon. He might be resigned to marrying me, but he did not speak as though he were. This kept a tiny hope alive.

At this very moment he killed it. 'I think I must ask your permission to address you as Arabella,' he said. 'Whatever your feelings or mine . . .'

'Since appearances seem to be what we are concerned with,' I said, more elaborately than I had intended, 'let us have regard for appearances. I suppose engaged couples had better use one anothers' Christian names.'

'Mine is Charles.'

For the sake of appearances, the Marquess and I were

110

suddenly on Christian-name terms. Not for the first time, the preposterousness of the situation tipped me into a helpless snort of laughter.

'My name amuses you?' he said. 'I have always thought it a decent enough name, if rather ordinary.'

'We are being pushed into intimacy,' I said, 'like a brother and sister, or lovers, or school-friends, just so as to seem an ordinary couple . . .'

'I am glad you can laugh at the situation,' he said.

'I can't,' I said; and indeed my laughter was dead, gone as quickly as it had come, and I did not think I would ever laugh again.

The next shock was the arrival, only three days later, of my wedding dress. Aunt Honoria lifted it out of the hamper in which it had been delivered; Grizelda stood up and walked out of the room.

The dressmaker in Perth had my measurements, which had not changed. Aunt Honoria had consulted pictures of the latest modes, and had chosen what she regarded as suitable. Bridal gown for a leper – what would be suitable? Something, it seemed, on the demure side. It was not the dress I would have chosen. Uncle Ranald would settle the reckoning; he would send the account to my Papa, to whom, meanwhile, as he said, he was lending the money without interest.

It was not what I would have chosen, but it was what I would wear, in the chapel at Glengard, the following Thursday, just twelve days after the flood in the Falls of Gard.

This was the new shock – the greatest shock. It was a message from the Duke's man of business to Uncle Ranald, written on the Duke's instructions. The date was, for various reasons, the most convenient. The Duke hoped it was convenient for Sir Ranald and Lady Gordon. He did not say that, if the date was inconvenient for them, it would be changed; the implication was, that if they did not come they did not. On that date I was to be produced and to be married. Henry and Grizelda were invited also. Henry said that he would go, out of politeness, simply out of civility to a neighbour. Grizelda said she would not go, even out of politeness.

I was not asked to Glengard again, before the day of the wedding. The Marquess (I had not got into the way of thinking of him as Charles) did not call at Callo again, and I did not see him again, there or anywhere.

I did not see Mariota or the Crasks; or Geoffrey or the Nicholls family; or Rupert or the Fraser family; or Peter or the McCallum family; or Jean Hannay or Sir Archibald.

I tried on my wedding dress. I did not want to, but I had to, in case it needed pins or stitches. I would not look at myself, in the pier-glass in my bedroom. I was draped in the veil which would cover my face until we were pronounced man and wife. Round my head was placed the fillet which, on my wedding day, would carry a wreath of white blossom.

None of this was happening to me. None of this was possible.

On Wednesday, the eve of my wedding, I found I was suffering from toothache, and backache, and shooting pains in my legs. I had never suffered from any of these things before. I was not suffering from them then. The trouble was all in my mind and in my heart.

I thought that I was truly facing, for the first time, what was coming to me on the morrow.

At ten o'clock in the evening, I wondered where I should be in twenty-four hours' time, and what I should be doing.

At one o'clock in the morning, sleepless, I wondered still.

Thursday dawned grey; by mid-morning the sky had become a sort of dirty brown; by noon it was raining, a steady drizzle.

The atmosphere at Callo had been strange ever since the dance; that morning it took on a sort of lunacy. I was still a moral leper – at no moment was I allowed to forget that. But I was also a bride, shortly to be helped into the gown which

I should wear this once in my life, to be bedecked and garlanded for the happiest day of my life.

I felt like one of those Inca virgins, dressed up as smart as could be to be sacrificed on a stone altar, with a stone knife.

I must have spoken the responses. I must have promised to love, honour and obey. I did so as though in my sleep, and I could not afterwards remember having done so. I found that a ring was on my finger. My bridegroom must have put it there. I did not remember him doing so, nor what words went with that.

The chapel was large, dark and almost empty. There was no music. The chaplain's voice was as smooth and soothing as I remembered; perhaps that was why I seemed to be asleep.

Through my head, like a litany, went those words again: none of this is happening to me – none of this is possible.

Chapter 6

The chaplain made a sign to me that I was to lift my veil from my face. I woke up sufficiently to do so. My bridegroom stared at me and I at him, as though we were strangers meeting for the first time. There was no expression on his face. I did not know what expression was on my face – perhaps misery, perhaps rage, perhaps stupefaction, perhaps a kind of numbed stupidity, for these were what I was feeling.

The chapel had a vestry, like a full-sized church, which I had not expected. We trooped into it, to sign the register, as the law required – the Marquess, myself, the chaplain, and as witnesses Uncle Ranald and Aunt Honoria, and my husband's groomsman, a somewhat older man, whom I discovered to be a cousin of the Duke, and to be called Lord Crieff.

I remembered weddings in Australia, mostly of officers on my Papa's staff. I remembered seeing the newly married couple, with their families or friends, going into the vestry, and then hearing the happy and excited laughter, as people kissed one another, audible over the noise of choir and organ. Our ceremony of signing was as different as could be. We hardly spoke, any of us, and when we spoke it was hardly above a whisper. The atmosphere was exactly that of a funeral. The only festive note was struck by Aunt Honoria's gown. In the Marquess's face (I could still not think of him as Charles) there was now an expression to be read. It was despair.

We walked arm in arm down the aisle of the chapel, passing the two or three upper servants who constituted the congregation. Husband and wife we slowly proceeded, giving an imitation of a married couple. I remembered to walk like a general, and to keep my chin high. I tried to smile, but the muscles of my face would not obey my brain.

We came out of the west door of the chapel, into a court-yard. It was still drizzling. No bells rang. Somebody opened an umbrella just behind me, with a great rattle. It was a footman; he held the umbrella over my head as we crossed the courtyard. The flagstones of the courtyard glistened with the wet. No weather could more perfectly have suited that day of misery.

We went through an archway, into the great corridor which I had seen before, with pictures and tall windows. Rain ran in dribbles down the glass of the windows. Servants lined the corridor, men and women, shoulder to shoulder, all its length. As we passed, the men bowed and the women curtseyed, every one. They all stared at me. Very few of them had seen me before. Every single one knew exactly why I was there. Every single one thought I was a trollop, who had entrapped the Marquess. I wondered if I should acknowledge the bows and curtseys. I wondered how to. Should I nod? Wave? Smile? I did not think I should nod or wave; I knew very well that I could not smile. I stared straight ahead, walking very slow on the arm of my husband, my chin so high that I was like to get a crick in the neck.

We were bowed into the room where I had had that strange interview with the Duke. I was to have another, even stranger. We were followed into the room by Uncle Ranald and Aunt Honoria, my cousin Henry, Lord Crieff, and the chaplain. That was the nuptial party: that was the joyous crowd gathered to drink our health.

Crossing the room, I spared a glance for the glorious view from the windows. But the air of the glen was full of mist and drizzle, and the big hills were invisible in the murk.

The Duke was deep in the same chair, and in the same brocade dressing-gown. A servant was with him, I thought a valet, who poured something from a carafe into a glass. I supposed it was medicine; it was certainly not champagne.

His voice still failed him. He was entirely silent. We were all entirely silent. Uncle Ranald and Cousin Henry made deep bows; Aunt Honoria made a deep curtsey. They had resolved, it seemed, not to speak until they were spoken to; and nobody was going to speak to them.

Champagne was poured. Lord Crieff proposed the health of the 'happy pair' in what must have been the shortest speech

115

in all the history of weddings. They all drank, the others champagne and the Duke his medicine.

Aunt Honoria made a remark about the weather to Lord Crieff; at the same moment Uncle Ranald made a remark about the weather to the chaplain. Finding themselves talking at the same time, they apologised to one another, fell silent, and did not attempt any more remarks.

The Duke stared and stared at me. I could see his face better this time, because there was not the same glare of sunshine. His eyes were very bright; they looked hot, feverish; I could not tell if they were grey or green. I looked back at him, not intending defiance, but not intending to be stared down, either.

The chaplain gestured that I should go to the Duke. I went to his chair. He stretched out a hand for mine. I put my hand in his, which felt very thin and frail. He held it for a moment, looking into my eyes. Looking into his, I saw that they were both grey and green, the colour of the sea under a cloudy sky. He let my hand go, and suddenly we were all to leave; the chaplain's gestures ended the drabbest and most miserable party I ever was at.

A maid led me to a room that was to be my room. I tried to remember the way as we went. Some of my clothes had been sent ahead from Callo. I changed into the dress in which I was to go away; the other things I was taking were already packed. The maids were deft, respectful, and almost silent. That is to say, they contrived to pretend to be respectful.

The wedding trip was to be very brief. There had to be one, because in all things we had to be exactly conventional, owing to the scandal of the island in the falls. It had to be brief, because the Duke's state did not allow his son to be away for more than a very few days. This also was the reason why the Marquess did not have an establishment of his own, which at his age might have been expected, in one of the Duke's many other properties. It was the reason why, when we came to live as man and wife, it would be at Glengard that we should live.

I realised with a shock that I was now, in name, mistress of this gigantic place. It was not a role I had the slightest idea how to play. From the very little I had seen, everything ran like an enormous, perfect and completely silent machine.

Probably there was no need for me to interfere in any part of it; probably there was great need for me not to interfere. I wondered whatever I should do with my time.

I was led downstairs at last by a kind of beadle, who carried a long wand of office, while a retinue of footmen came silently behind with my bags. The Marquess was in the great hall, saying goodbye in the semi-darkness to my family. Uncle Ranald and Aunt Honoria both embraced me, which they were not in the way of doing.

We climbed into a travelling carriage soon after the Gallo party had left. We were to spend four days in a shooting-box in the north of the county, near Pitlochry. I wondered if, by the end of that time, we would have found anything to say to one another. We had not found anything yet.

We curved round the north and east sides of the castle, and started down the hill towards the river. The rain was harder. To my surprise I saw a horse tethered to one of a clump of trees; it was half hidden, but the rain was making it fretful, so that it was tossing its head and so drawing attention to itself. I wondered who would leave a horse tethered in such unpleasant weather, and I thought how wet his saddle would be when he remounted.

A head poked out of a drift of bracken, only a few yards from the side of the carriage drive. It was a young man, hatless, his hair plastered to his head with the rain. It was Peter McCallum, and he was looking at the carriage and at me as though at his own death.

I did not think my husband had seen.

At the bottom of the drive there was a charming pair of lodges, built in the manner of Sir Christopher Wren (I was indebted to Cousin Henry for my knowledge of the manner they were built in). I imagined visiting those lodges, enquiring after the health of the folk's children, and accepting cups of dark-brown tea. But perhaps, if the folk were strict Wee Frees, they would not let me into their dwellings, owing to bringing a moral contagion with me.

There was a small closed carriage drawn up close to one of the lodges. The coachman was on his box, swathed in oilskins. He waved a greeting to our coachman; he looked full of self-pity, and I did not at all blame him. There was a passenger in the carriage, looking out from behind the half-closed curtains. There was no mistaking that pale, pointed, rather beautiful face. It was Jean Hannay, and she was looking at the carriage and at us as though at her torturer.

My husband saw. I had no doubt that he saw and recognized Jean. He said nothing. I did not know if he knew that I had seen her.

It was a very bad start.

We arrived at the shooting-box well before dark, for though autumn was approaching the Highland nights were still very short. The skies were weeping, and there was no wind to blow the clouds away.

I had had an idea that we would be almost camping in this remote place, in this squat unpretentious house. I was quite wrong. There were footmen and maids and cooks and a comfortable housekeeper, and because of the damp there was a fire in a sitting room and one in my bedroom.

My bedroom? Yes – my husband had a dressing room next door, with a bed in it and all that he required. He would leave me at the door of my room, and rejoin me for breakfast in the dining room, unless I preferred to breakfast upstairs. He told me this briefly, knowing that it was the only tolerable arrangement for either of us.

A life of play-acting. Less than half a life. I thought it was a waste of myself.

We had made no effort in the carriage, because none was called for. Dinner tête-à-tête, with servants often in the room, was another matter. We could not sit in a hostile or indifferent silence. Our performances began, mine and his. I called him Charles, for the first time, after a dreadful moment when I thought I had forgotten his name. We spoke about the weather, and were able to agree, without any difficulty, that we both hoped it would improve for the remainder of our stay. We spoke about the food they were setting before us, which Aunt Honoria had told me was a thing no lady did; the food was excellent, much better than any I had ever had at Callo, and I found to my surprise that I was very hungry. Charles drank little wine, I less. We talked about the solid way the shooting-box was built, so that it was proof against the wild Grampian weather. We agreed, most serious, that thick walls and solid doors were better, in a house in such a place, than thin walls and flimsy doors. We were quite rational. We set ourselves to make conversation, and we made it.

It was quite unlike any other evening I had ever spent. It was the most boring evening I had ever spent. I looked forward to a lifetime of such evenings with a sort of numb disbelief. It was still impossible that any of this was happening to me.

In one part of my mind I accepted the undoubted fact. I was the Marchioness of Gard, and in four days' time I should be mistress of Glengard Castle. In another part of my mind I was young Bella Gordon, the colonial tomboy, certain one day to marry Geoffrey Nicholls, or Rupert Fraser, or Peter McCallum.

We smiled when we spoke to the servants. I think we did not smile at one another. I probably smiled too much at the servants, to make up for the lack of married smiles.

After dinner, in the sitting room of the house, there was a shelf of books to talk about — which of them we had read, which we had enjoyed — and then, when that subject was exhausted, there were the pictures on the walls, to be compared to other pictures on other walls.

I agreed that I was tired, after the hectic excitements of my magical bridal day.

A maid was waiting for me in my bedroom. There was something both motherly and mischievous in her manner; of course; this was my wedding night.

I did not hear Charles go to bed.

Fine weather would have made the next days tolerable, because the country round about was wild and beautiful. I could have covered miles of it without anyone being aware that my bridegroom and I were not together; and there were trout to be caught in the burns, and birds to be spied on the hillsides. But the persistent rain continued, day after dismal day. We did go out for brief walks, starting together and returning together with a briskly cheerful air, but separate as soon as we were out of sight of the house. I would have gone

119

mad without that exercise, that solitude, that relief from my continuous performance of being a happy little bride.

Often and often two pictures came back into my head. Peter McCallum, his unruly sandy hair plastered down and darkened with the wet, waiting and waiting in the rain, and then staring in misery. And Jean Hannay, huddled in her carriage, peeping out from behind curtains, waiting for a glimpse of the man for love of whom she had threatened suicide.

Charles did not mention either Jean or Peter. I did not mention them.

I supposed that Charles would go on as he had, using assumed names and discreet rendezvous, using the padded private rooms of expensive restaurants, using his rank and wealth, using his commanding height, his masterful arrogance, what must have been seen, by Jean and all those others, as his handsomeness. I could not prevent any of this. I would not, if I could. I wanted to make no claims on him that would give him claims on me.

It was a half life. It was a waste of myself. It could have no end.

By an irony, the weather cleared just in time for our return to Glengard. A warm wind from the south-east ran through a new-washed world. I caught a glimpse of the castle, from that bend in the road above the river; in a few minutes, according to all the rules, I would take my position as mistress of it.

I did not want to be daunted; but I was. I did not want to be frightened of my own servants; but I was.

In the north courtyard, Charles himself handed me down out of the carriage. All about stood a kind of guard of honour of servants. Charles's performance was expressive of kindness, consideration, affection, respect; he was acting a man just returned from a magical honeymoon who, however, did not wear his heart on his sleeve, who did not forget his dignity in front of servants. I tried to match his performance with my own. I was a general descending from the carriage, a happy general, with a smile pinned to my face for the guard of honour.

Excusing himself, most punctilious, Charles went at once to see his father. I was taken again to the room which was my room; it was assumed that I should want to rest after the fatigues of the journey.

I wanted not to rest but to change into thick boots and walk ten miles. I thought that I must feel my way, before I did any such thing. I was not sure if Marchionesses went for long solitary walks. I was not sure how to fill the rest of the day. I was not sure about anything.

Part of the rest of the day was filled for me, in a way that grew no less strange with each renewal. I was summoned to the Duke, and handed like a parcel from one footman to another until I stood again in that silent, sunny room.

In the clear early evening, the view was as magificent as when first I glimpsed it. I paused a moment as I crossed the room – only a moment – to look out at that huge sunlit prospect. I thought a daughter-in-law might be entitled to do so much.

It was as though the Duke had not moved, since the first and second times I had seen him. The same chair, the same brocade dressing-gown, the same silence, and the same chaplain, standing by to interpret the silence into questions.

I curtseyed. He took my hand in his paper-white and paper-thin one. He held it a moment, then pointed to the chair which faced the window. I sat like a general; I returned his stare like a general.

The Duke nodded to the chaplain, who bowed to me. He said, smiling, 'Your Ladyship will see that I am dismissed. His Grace your father-in-law requests that you will give him the pleasure of talking to him.'

'Well,' I said, 'of course I assumed I was brought here for that reason. What would my father-in-law like me to talk about?'

The chaplain shrugged, blinked his bright button eyes very

121

rapidly a number of times, bowed to the Duke and to myself, and went as softly as a cat out of the room.

The Duke stared at me. He was waiting for me to speak.

I cleared my throat, and said, 'I can report a safe journey to and from Pitlochry, sir. That carriage is very well sprung, and fortunately it keeps the rain out. I was sorry we could not see the country that we passed through better, as I had never been there before. But I do not believe that even at the very top of the Cairngorms there can be a finer view than this one out of your window. I should find it dreadful to be confined, like you, sir, to a chair, but it would not be quite so dreadful with that out of the window. I have noticed that the colour of the big hills changes every moment of the day, as the sun goes up and down. If I were a painter, I should paint those hills once an hour, on the hour, to show how their colour was changing . . .'

I thought he did not want to hear about the colour of the hills outside his window.

I cleared my throat again. 'We continued unfortunate in the weather. I do not mind getting wet, but it is depressing to be soaked every time you put your nose out of doors. Of course, with all that rain, all the burns were in spate, dark brown and almost over their banks. A worm would have been the only way to catch a trout. I used to catch trout with worms, when I stayed at Callo as a child, in my grandfather's time. But, as soon as I learned to cast a fly, I swore I would never use a worm again, and I never have . . .'

I fell awkwardly silent, aware that I was doing no better. He nodded to me. I thought I saw a faint smile. He made a gesture, raising the palm of his hand in his lap.

I was to go on. Manfully I went on. I said the first things that came into my head, because, if I had stopped to think what to say, I would not have been able to think of anything.

Perhaps this got me onto dangerous ground. I said, 'I do not at all know how to go about being mistress of a house as big as this. Of course I will do my best to learn, but I despair of ever learning it all. I have never been considered very good at learning things, except about horses and birds and fishing and so forth. I think I must steer a difficult course. I shall be expected to do my duty here, but people will not be pleased if they think I am interfering. I think my best plan is to start

122

by simply asking questions. Then the worst I shall be doing is wasting everybody's time. I expect I shall find that almost everything is being done in the best possible way. But supposing I found that somebody was being cruel to a little kitchen-maid? Or that a boy in the garden was being made to do work that was too heavy for him? Then I must try not to fly into a rage. Or, at least, I must try to hide the rage that I probably will fly into. I only twice in my life saw my Papa in a really thundering rage. Once was when he saw some labourers beating a mule that had broken its leg. He beat them, with his riding whip. He had to shoot the mule. Once was when some drummer-boys were doing punishment drill, running and running and running, with full equipment, at midday in midsummer. They were dropping like flies all over the barrack-square. I think they had been caught smoking. Of course I do not expect that those precise things are so very probable here. I doubt if you have mules, for one thing, although they would be very useful on the hills. If you had punishment drill for the footmen, who would command the parade? I suppose the butler. And the chaplain could be by, in case of accidents . . .'

I was with the Duke for almost an hour, talking, talking, just to fill the silence. I did not think his eyes ever left my face. Mine strayed from time to time to the window, to see the big hills changing colour as the sun went down.

Again I asked myself: what was the Duke about? Why did he inflict on himself the babbling monologue of an ignorant colonial? I could understand the purpose of the last interview no more than I could understand the purpose of the first. He sat in silence, staring at me, with no emotion, no expression, no reaction. What was he about?

Charles and I had rooms not quite adjoining – there was a sort of lobby in between, to which both our rooms had doors. My room was very large – larger than any room in the whole of Callo. I did not know if Charles's was the same size.

He said that we should both keep the communicating doors

unlocked. He said that he would not enter my room, and that I would not enter his.

I wondered if he would smuggle some other person into his. I wondered if, in the despair of utter loneliness, I would smuggle some other person into mine. I thought not, though the sin was no greater than the one I was supposed to have committed. There was no other way in which I could save the utter waste of myself.

I had no experience of the formal manners used on great occasions. There was no formality in my Papa's family life, and not much, that I ever saw, in his official life either. Indeed, although so many things were imported from Britain to Australia, formality was not one of them. At Callo, there were certainly attempts at formality: but there were no great occasions, and when Uncle Ranald or Cousin Henry stood in front of the fire and made orations, it was to the family.

In one evening at Glengard, I made up for a lifetime of informality. Though Charles and I dined alone (the chaplain would join us two or three times a week) it was the stateliest occasion I ever was at. That two people – one barely eighteen years old – should have so many candles, and so many servants, and so much silver, and so many courses, seemed to me ridiculous. I did not say so. I tried to pretend that it was precisely what I was used to, what I had a right to expect.

Charles's manner to me had always been formal – aloof, cold, unsmiling. Now it was as though he was adding a performance as a feudal Archduke, to his performance as a loving husband. He asked me in stately periods if I were quite comfortable, if the lights were placed as I liked them, if the various courses of dinner were to my taste. I thought I was obliged to adjust my performance also; I tried to be a feudal Archduchess.

We were, to be sure, dressed as though for a banquet. I saw that I was going to need a great many new clothes.

I came down to breakfast – my second meal at Glengard – wondering if I should be battling with the same awesome

124

atmosphere. I was shown the way to the breakfast saloon, which was full of morning sunshine and of the smell of coffee and fried bacon. I was to breakfast alone. Charles had come down an hour earlier, and was already out.

A footman waited beside the sideboard, and another behind a chair. I decided that I did not need two footmen; I did not need one footman; I would establish a new rule, in defiance of whatever had been the old rule.

I said, 'I prefer to help myself. Please let me have breakfast alone. I will ring when I have finished.'

'As your leddyship wishes,' said the older of the footmen. They bowed themselves out. I wondered whether to make a new rule immediately, that footmen leaving a room simply left the room. But I thought I had better confine myself to one audacious breach with precedent.

I helped myself to bacon and eggs and coffee, without any difficulty, and then to oatcakes and honey.

After breakfast, I asked to be taken to the housekeeper's room. I found her surrounded by pretty chintzes, drinking a pot of tea. She was in her middle fifties, dressed in black, with a bunch of keys at her waist. Her face was carved out of grey wood; she did not look as though she ever smiled, or could smile.

She was called Mrs Murray, and she was very cross at being disturbed.

I said that I wanted to be shown everything below stairs – kitchens, larders, sculleries, still-rooms, laundries, creameries, whatever there was. I said that, if she was busy, I could be guided by another servant. But she would not hear of that.

My tour with Mrs Murray exhausted us both, and left me utterly bewildered. Dozens of servants were presented to me; I knew that there was no chance of my remembering any of their names. I asked Mrs Murray for a list of all the indoor servants in the castle, with their ages and positions. This seemed to me very sensible; it was what my father did, whenever he was appointed to a new command. Mrs Murray thought it was the most extraordinary request she had ever heard. I was already making a thorough nuisance of myself.

I realised during the morning that, as time went on, I was

going to make more of a nuisance of myself. I saw that the laundry was stupidly arranged, with the little laundrymaids having to carry piles of wet linen twenty yards from the coppers to the mangles. I saw that, in the great larder, things in daily use were out of reach except with a ladder, and things rarely used were on the lower shelves. I saw that this was a household ruled by habit, where things were done in certain ways, or put in certain places, simply because it had always been so. I knew that Papa thought carefully before he made changes, but that having thought he was not afraid to turn everything upside down. I would watch, and learn, and think, and talk to people, and then one by one I would turn things upside down.

I had a solitary luncheon, too, Simpson the whiskered butler booming at me that his Lordship sent his apologies, since he was detained on business.

Afterwards I saw a tray being carried out of a room in another part of the castle. The door was closed behind the footman. It was the door of Charles's business room. The tray had been laid for one person. He chose to eat alone. He found making conversation to me as exhausting and depressing as I found making conversation to him.

The footman who told me what door it was showed a trace of embarrassment. He knew. They all knew more than I had realized. They would make it more difficult for me to turn things upside down; and they would be more resentful when I did so.

Papa had never been frightened of taking an unpopular decision, if he had come to be certain he was right. I knew that those mangles should be moved, and that the larder should be differently arranged. Papa said that, if he had not the courage to make small-minded people resentful, he had no business to be a general. I thought that if I had not that courage, I had no business to be a Marchioness.

Of course I knew very well, myself, that I had no business to be a Marchioness; but I was not prepared to let anybody else think so.

I thought I should give the servants a rest that afternoon. I

126

did not want to give myself a rest. I wanted fresh air; I wanted to explore the gardens, as a step to exploring the stables and coach-house, the steading of the home farm, the park, and the hills above the park.

The fair weather held. I put on a hat, because I thought I should; I would have preferred to go bareheaded. I went down the waterfall of terraces, descending from the top instead of, as before, ascending from below. It was so very short a time before, when Lady Nicholls was bargaining for hot-house plants with the head gardener of the castle. I wondered what I would have said, if some visitant from the future had told me then that, such a little time later, I would be walking down, instead of up, from the castle that was my home. . .

I was down to the third terrace, where the grass was mown as smooth as a billiard table, and set about with ornamental trees whose names I did not know. There was a young boy working among the trees, raking away dead leaves and twigs and loading them into a barrow. The boy wore leather gaiters, a shirt open at the neck, and an old tweed cap perched on top of a head of unruly red hair. I recognised him. At the same moment, he looked up from his work and recognised me. He burst out laughing – he could not help it. He was the boy who had been sent to tell me that Lady Nicholls was ready to go: the boy who had seen me fall and sprawl when I broke the swing on the top terrace.

I remembered I had thought at the time, that a place was not altogether dreadful where a gardener's boy could laugh like that. I thought the same still.

We stood laughing at one another; I pointed to where the skirt I had had that day was covered with a great green strain. He was doubled up. He was an ugly little boy, but I thought he was my favourite person at Glengard; and it came to me that I was laughing for the very first time since the flood in the falls of the river.

Another figure came through the belt of trees that bordered the terrace, brought by the sound of our laughter: a neat, sturdy middle-aged man in tweed knickerbockers. It was the head gardener; I remembered his face, and, by great good luck, his name.

Seeing him, the boy stopped laughing as sudden as the

127

snuffing of a candle. He bent with furious energy to raking the dead leaves.

The head gardener tugged off his billycock hat, and bowed as though he was not at all accustomed to bowing.

'Your leddyship wull forgi'e the laddie,' he said. 'He didna ken wha ye waur.'

'Of course I forgive him, Mr Blair,' I said.

Mr Blair himself suddenly grinned, and then stopped grinning, all as quick as a dark-lantern opened and shut with one flick of the wrist. I realised he was pleased that I had remembered his name. I was pleased that I had.

I asked Mr Blair to show me the gardens, if he could spare the time. He twisted himself into knots with apologies – he was expecting, at that very minute, a shipment of exotic plants from the botanical gardens of one of the universities, coming by express, to be planted out immediately in various special kinds of compost. I saw that for him these plants were much more important than I was; I thought he was quite right. He said the boy would show me the gardens, if I permitted; the boy's name was Geordie Gault; he had known the gardens all his life, since his father had been an under-gardener, and the family lived in the midst of them. The father had been killed the year before, when a beech-tree came down in a gale. The boy was a good boy, said Mr Blair, only given to laughing too much.

Geordie Gault was quite agreeable to abandoning the dead leaves, and instead spending the afternoon strolling and showing off his knowledge. Indeed, what he knew was impressive – the name of every plant that I asked him about, and when it was pruned, and how much water it needed. He pointed out to me the cottage, just visible among trees from the top terrace, where he lived with his mother and sisters. He expected to live there all his life, and to spend his life in the gardens of Glengard.

The swing had been repaired – I wondered on whose behalf. Geordie glanced from me to the swing, suddenly grinning expectantly. I laughed, and shook my head. The swing was added to the list of things I thought I could not allow myself. But it was hard, because he was there to have pushed me; and then I could have pushed him.

*

128

We were joined for dinner by the chaplain, by the Reverend Pericles Davidson. He was voluble, and I quite warmed to him. Since he had pronounced my life-sentence, which had for me the face of a death-sentence, I had felt an unreasonable bitterness towards him. He had agreed with the sentence; he had agreed with the Duke; he told me so. But, after all, he was only a messenger. I thought I could think of him as a friend, because I had great need of friends.

His volubility had a curious effect, which was that there were two conversations, alternately, all through dinner. The chaplain talked to Charles, about local matters, and politics, and a notorious feud between two professors at Edinburgh; and I took no part in that conversation at all. And he talked to me about the army, and Australia, and affairs in India (he had a brother there); and Charles took no part in that. Charles and I were relieved of the necessity of any conversation between us. Having seen that tray come out of his business room . . .

To the chaplain, Charles was serious rather than solemn. He smiled occasionally. It seemed to me that I had never seen him smile before, except in brief recognition of something a servant had done for him. He had not smiled at me. He did not look at me, when I was talking to the chaplain. He looked at the chaplain, or at his plate, or at the ceiling. I thought I was looking my very best; but still he preferred not to look at me.

I went to bed early. I left them together, poring over a folio in the library.

At dinner next evening the chaplain did not join us. We were obliged to talk to one another. We were feudal Archduke and Archduchess again.

I said, in a manner unlike my usual manner, 'Is it possible that there might be a horse in the stable that would suit me, and that I would be permitted to ride?'

'I will send word to the head groom,' said Charles, 'to expect you at whatever time you appoint.'

He was not going to discuss his horses with me; he was simply going to send me to the head groom.

*

129

As so often, the stables were a different world. Instead of pale, scrubbed footmen gliding like cats through deep pile carpets, here were ruddy-faced men in riding boots stamping on cobbles. Instead of a solemnity that seemed almost like tragedy, here were broad grins, a welcome, and a great deal of cheerful talk. They were visibly glad that I wanted to ride. They chuckled, and chattered, and punched one another on the arm. They began bringing horses out of stalls and loose-boxes, and leading them round the stable yard, as though they were trying to sell them to me.

My eye was taken by a roan mare, a little under sixteen hands, who if not thoroughbred was nearly so. They saw me looking at her. They nodded and grinned. It was the one they had intended me to have, from the beginning; they had been testing my judgement.

She was called Marmalade. They said this was from her colour, although I had never seen marmalade the colour of a roan horse. There was a side-saddle that would fit both Marmalade and me, which had belonged to the late Duchess, who was just of my height. Marmalade would be brought to the front courtyard at eleven next morning. A groom would go with me. There was no question of my riding alone.

I thought I might shortly be making another new rule.

Charles did not ask me whether I had found a horse that suited me. He had put the whole matter out of his mind. It was a matter of indifference to him whether I rode, what horse I rode, where I went.

I could almost have said that he did not care whether I lived or died. That would not have been true. He would much have preferred me dead.

I might not yet be allowed to ride alone, but nobody could stop me walking alone. I saw some astonished faces, when I set off in unbeautiful boots. I raised my chin, and stared at the servants who were staring at me with an arrogance I did not quite feel.

I said to myself that a solitary tramp might not, once upon a time, have been considered Marchioness-like behaviour.

But now it was, because I was the Marchioness, and I was doing it.

I walked all the way down to the river. I stared at the water with mixed feelings. It was high, after nearly a week of rain; it was tawny coloured, lion coloured, the colour of my hair. I had always loved it, and it had repaid me by destroying me.

I grew very hot, climbing up through the park to the castle. I felt my face growing scarlet, and my hair struggling out of its pins. I wanted to go straight to my room (which I could now find with hardly any hesitation or wrong turnings) but I was intercepted by Simpson the butler. His Grace begged the favour of my company in his room.

'I am in no fit state to be seen by his Grace,' I said. 'I must change my clothes, and somebody must do something about my hair. Please to tell his Grace that I shall be pleased to join him in half an hour.'

But his Grace particularly wished me to come immediately. His Grace understood that I had been walking. He would not expect me to be wearing a silk afternoon dress or elegant slippers.

We had another of those eerie hours. I was more than usually self-conscious, because of my boots and my old skirt, and perhaps for this reason I talked even more than usual. I talked about my walk, and the birds and flowers I had seen. I talked about Marmalade, and Geordie Gault, whose poor father had been killed by the beech-tree, and who already knew so much about the gardens. I found myself talking, to my own slight horror, about the foolishness of the position of the mangles in the laundry, and the foolishness of the position of the foodstuffs in the larder. Desperate, filling the silence, I talked about my Papa's refusal to be put off a decision which he knew to be right, because it would be unpopular. I talked until I was hoarse, and the Duke stared at me in silence.

Marmalade was in the front courtyard as the clock in the tower struck eleven. I was there at the same moment. With Marmalade was the groom who was to ride with me, with a big cobby horse. The groom was Malcolm Menzies, a big young man with a round red face. He was very smart in a

131

green coat and white neckcloth, as though he had been going hare-hunting. He was much smarter than I, though I wore my best habit; it had been made in Sydney, and it was somewhat the worse for kangaroo hunting. I had not had another made, because of there being no horses to ride at Callo. I had not then predicted Marmalade, or Malcolm Menzies, or the need to look like a Marchioness.

We went a beautiful way, which I asked Malcolm to choose, because he knew the country and I did not. We walked while I got used to Marmalade's mouth and manners and stride; we trotted; we cantered; and then I let Marmalade out on a great smooth swell of grass with sheep folded in a corner. The grass seemed to end in a belt of fir-trees, but there was a gap between the trees, and Marmalade went happily through and onto more grass beyond. Malcolm Menzies came pounding along behind on his powerful horse, which did not have the legs of my lovely Marmalade. When he pulled up, his face was redder than ever, and he was grinning from ear to ear.

He complimented me on my riding, very warmly. He was not in the least obsequious in this; he was an expert, and he spoke as an expert. His praise was worth having, and I was most happy to have it.

He showed me a different way back, which went by a croft under a wood. As we neared the croft, which was a very poor place, three children ran out of it, calling to Malcolm by name. He grinned to me, and said that they were friends of his.

'Yon's grand bairns, your Leddyship,' he said. 'Misheevous wi'oot malice, as ye might say. This yin's Peggy, the laddie's Jaikie, an' yon's wee Morag.'

They were barefooted. Their clothes were patched but clean. They were skinny children, but I thought that was because they were active, not because they were starved – I had been a skinny child myself. In a shrill chorus they asked us into the croft for a glass of their mother's barley-water.

A glass of barley-water suddenly seemed an extremely good idea – it was a hot midday, and I was having my first ride for months. I glanced at Malcolm Menzies. It was quite evident that he would be *very* glad of some barley-water. I prepared to dismount, unwrapping my right leg from the pommel and making ready to jump unaided to the ground, as I had so often done in Australia. Malcolm Menzies looked scandalised. I remembered that ladies were always assisted to mount and dismount, for reasons of propriety. Even a hearty personality like Malcolm, and even in this remote place, would be greatly shocked if I jumped.

He dismounted, and helped me to dismount, and I shook hands with the children.

He told them who I was. I expected saucer eyes and curt-seys. I got no such thing. They screeched with laughter, most infectious; they did not believe a word that Malcolm said – they thought he was joking. And, when I laughed at their laughter, they were sure of it.

Their father was called Tam Urquhart. He farmed very few acres – too few. He was away to market in Lochgrannom-head. He was a tenant of the Duke of Lomond, which was to say, as things were, of the Marquess of Gard. This was a landlord who did not look after his own.

There were more changes to be made, when I was ready to make changes – every day revealed more, and more, and more.

After a solitary breakfast, I spent another hour with Mrs Murray the housekeeper. I saw things I had not seen before, and which she did not wish to show me. I saw a scandalous waste of good food. I saw a dormitory, half underground, where a dozen kitchenmaids and scullerymaids slept; the walls were sweating with damp.

After my subterranean journeyings, I was most anxious for fresh air and sunlight. My boots were no more beautiful; perhaps the servants were getting used to them. I went in a new direction, east of the castle, where I had not explored. There was another drive, which ran through a considerable wood. I followed it through the wood, glad of the shade of the trees. I saw ahead of me a gate, and one lodge. Beyond the gate on the road, stood a small carriage, which I thought I recognised. Inside the gate, hidden from the carriage by the lodge, a man stood at the head of a horse. I knew the horse; I knew the man. With him was a woman, slight and dark. I knew the woman.

Jean Hannay held my husband's free hand. They were talking to one another earnestly, passionately. He had been married for less than two weeks.

Chapter 7

I shrank back into the cover of the wood. They were far too engrossed to have seen me. I crept away.

It was as I had expected, and not as I had expected. Knowing how Charles had lived, I had not expected him suddenly to become a saint, a hermit. It seemed he had always had women; obviously he would go on having them. So far there was no cause for surprise, as there was no cause for any other feeling. But it had been so very obvious, what that scene was between them on the island in the Falls of Gard. Jean on her knees, Jean weeping, Jean in despair; Jean rejected, Jean done with, Jean cast aside with contemptuous distaste. And now Jean returned, back in Charles's life, clutching his hand, the two of them deep in earnest and passionate talk.

He had decided that he still wanted her, after all. It must be so. It was all one to me. I thought it bad manners, simply, that they should meet so close to his doorstep, to my doorstep. There was something crass about that, something brutal and uncaring. I had thought Charles would have been more discreet: I had thought Jean would, too.

I walked back to the castle at great speed, much muddled in my mind, angry at the discourtesy I thought had been shown me, angry with Jean for her shamelessness, her immorality, her betrayal of her decent husband, angry with myself for being angry. I should have felt a bland indifference. I thought, instead, with anger, that Charles might have waited a month after his wedding.

I went to find Mr Blair in the gardens, and to be shown the new exotic plants from the university. I found young Geordie Gault instead, with his muddy gaiters and the tweed cap crammed on top of his wild red hair. In his cheerful company I began to feel better, and the plants and trees he showed me ministered to my spirit.

Calmer, I went indoors to change for luncheon, for which, though I ate it alone, I must be properly dressed. In an upstairs passage, three housemaids were taking pictures down to dust the backs and polish the glass; two of them I knew by sight, one I thought I had not seen.

I had been studying the list Mrs Murray had given me, and adding notes to help me, such as 'Mole on right cheek', or 'Very pale curly hair'. Thus I was able to greet by name the maids whose faces I knew. Startled smiles came and went on their faces, exactly as on Mr Blair's face. I blessed, as so often, the lesson I had learned from Papa. I asked the other maid's name, and looked at her closely so that I would be sure to remember name and face together.

They might believe me an adventuress; at least they would know me an adventuress with good manners.

One might have expected Charles's face, across the dinner table and under the golden glare of dozens of candles, to have shown something as a result of his meeting with his mistress – perturbation, glee, triumph, guilt. Of course it showed nothing. For the benefit of the servants, he recounted the events of his day, and the problems he was having with one of the tenant farms. For all I knew, some of what he was telling me might have been the truth.

Cards were brought to me on a salver: Sir Ranald Gordon of Callo; Lady Gordon of Callo; Mr Henry Gordon, Younger of Callo.

My first callers. I had to be 'at home' to them. The prospect of seeing them filled me with weariness. I said I would receive them in the yellow saloon, and that we should want tea.

Aunt Honoria embraced me, very gingerly, as though it was an audacious thing to do, from which she might contract a contagious disease. Uncle Ranald and Cousin Henry bowed, and then stood waiting to be asked to sit down. They all spoke in low voices. They asked reverentially about my father-in-law's health. I supposed they were speaking softly so as not to disturb the Duke, which was ridiculous, as he was at the other end of the castle. That subject exhausted, Aunt Honoria began to admire, at great length, the decorations of the yellow saloon, which I myself did not admire at all. Uncle Ranald and Cousin Henry echoed her, with passionate if muted enthusiasm. Answering Aunt Honoria's questions, I told them about the roan mare Marmalade, and the exotic plants which had arrived from a university, and my explorations of the nether parts of the castle. To my astonishment, they followed everything I said with the most minute attention, which none of them had ever done before. They were agog, it seemed, to hear about the laundry and the larder; they were agog to know how many candles were set upon our dinner table, and whether we drank wine every night, and what callers had come. Tea arrived, to provide a diversion. The Meissen cups, I knew, were very valuable and very beautiful; the silver teapot was very valuable and very ugly. When I gave them cups of tea, they accepted them as though they were crocks of gold. Uncle Ranald's cup shook a little in his saucer. Cousin Henry dropped a piece of cake. He tried to apologise but, as he had just taken a bite, his mouth was full. Scarlet, he fell to his knees to gather up the crumbs. Aunt Honoria looked at him in fury. They said it was the best tea they had ever drunk, and the best cake they had ever tasted.

And suddenly I saw what these people were. They were toad-eaters. I was no longer a moral leper, because I was a Marchioness, and would one day be Duchess of Lomond. My infamous night was forgotten, because I could now wear a coronet.

I suddenly burst out laughing, at the folly and dishonesty of my relations. They laughed, too. I had the conviction that, if I had started dancing, they would have danced, and if I had thrown my teacup into the fireplace, they would have done that.

Charles came in, in riding boots, into the midst of senseless hoots of laughter. They stopped laughing, and jumped up like marionettes out of their chairs. Charles was polite to them, and politely accepted a cup of tea from me. This time my hand shook, rattling the cup in the saucer, because I was still foolishly giggling.

They left soon afterwards. It seemed natural to me to see them to their carriage; to them it seemed an honour they had not dared to hope for.

'His Grace understands,' said the Reverend Pericles Davidson, 'that you and your family were convulsed with laughter at tea-time. He hopes he may share the joke. I also am to be permitted to stay, to hear what so greatly amused you all.'

'Nothing amused them, Doctor,' I said. 'Nothing ever has amused them. If I tell you why they were laughing, you will accuse me of uncharitableness.'

They both looked at me, eyes equally bright, their faces asking questions.

'Well,' I said, 'I do not wish to sound ill-natured, or ungrateful to people who took me in, but I am afraid they were laughing because, hum, they thought that in that room, at that moment, laughing was the correct thing to do. They were laughing because I was laughing. They did not know what I was laughing at. They never will know, because it would be cruel to tell them. They used to despise me, you know, because I was uncouth and ignorant. And now . . . If I *was* ignorant, I still am. All I have learned is how to find my way about Glengard, and the names of some of the servants, and the names of some plants in the garden. I am exactly the same person as I was. I hope I will not always be, because there is great room for improvement, but just now I am. If they did despise me, they should still do so. I know that nobody need be quite consistent. I am not, myself. I used to like sugar in my coffee, and now I prefer it without. But I do not believe in a complete change of opinion about a person, in just two weeks, during which they have not seen me. Oh dear, I *am* being uncharitable. But I feel a duty to answer your questions as honestly as I can.'

The chaplain nodded and blinked, many times. Perhaps he was disappointed, not to have heard repeated some hilarious story told at tea-time by Uncle Ranald. He excused himself, and left me alone with the Duke.

I was to talk. I had a whole new subject to talk about: I

138

talked about the stables, and the grooms, and Marmalade, and the ride I had done and the rides I intended to do.

Perhaps word sped about the glen that I could be visited without risk of infection; I had other callers, all of whom, for different reasons, I was a little frightened to talk to.

The first to come were the Earl of Crask and Mariota. The Countess, of course, was (or thought she was) too frail to attempt even so short a journey.

Dear Lord Crask seemed to have no idea why I had been married at such speed and in such strange secrecy; or, if he knew, he did not mind. He treated me exactly as he always had, with the warmest friendliness, and the assumption that anything that caught his interest was the most fascinating subject in the world, to everybody. If he had been grieved by the destruction of his dam, he had entirely got over his grief, and his mind was busy with new projects for regaining the fortune he had squandered. Certainly he did not blame himself for the flood; and, if he knew the one astonishing consequence of the flood, he did not know that it was calamitous.

Mariota looked as beautiful as I had ever seen her, with her bright chestnut curls and her untroubled grey eyes. Her fairy music would not have kept from her ears the events of the night of the ball, and the result of the events of that night. If she envied me a fate that she had wanted, she bore me no grudge at all. If she compared Glengard with Crask, she seemed content with her home. If she thought I had cynically entrapped my husband, she did not let that affect our friendship. She was as loving as she had ever been. I was sure that, if she was disappointed, her heart was not broken. She had not been deeply in love with Charles. She would not have knelt and wept and clutched, as Jean had done. I was deeply thankful. I had friends besides grooms, and gardener's boys, and crofter children.

I had friends indeed, and they were very much more like Mariota and her father than like the Gordons of Callo.

The Frasers of Lossie came. They apologised for not bringing Rupert; they said he had an engagement he could not break. I knew the real reason he had not come, and I

139

was very sorry. The Frasers were a little reproachful, not because I had entrapped Charles, but because I had not been entrapped by Rupert. In spite of all that had happened, I was still the daughter-in-law they would have chosen, and not only because that would have saved Rupert unhappiness. I was moved almost to tears by this goodwill.

Lady Nicholls of Invermore came, combining a morning call with another session of bargaining in the conservatories. I showed her the Tambour Room, which I knew she had the taste to appreciate.

When she left she said, 'You know quite well, dear, that we hoped you would choose our Geoffrey. But I can see now that it was foolish. Lodgings in Edinburgh would be an unthinkable frame for a glorious creature like you, whereas, in a castle like this, you look supremely at home. You were born to be a Duchess. It is not often that accidents have such utterly satisfactory results.'

She meant what she was saying. I was stunned. I could think of no reply at all.

The McCallums of Miltoun came. They thought Peter had been to visit me, and were surprised when I told them he had not. He had, they said, set off in the direction of Glengard.

I remembered – I would never forget – that rain-wet hair, that look of death. I was appalled to think that Peter had come to Glengard, had hidden in the park or the gardens, and waited for a sight of me. I did not want or deserve such adoration, now less than ever. So that, although the McCallums were most kind and friendly, their visit threw me into the deepest gloom.

Jean Hannay did not come. That is to say, she did not call on me. My cousin Grizelda did not come, which had the odd effect of raising my opinion of her.

Mariota came again, on her own. She said it was because she had nothing in the world else to do. I might have been offended by this, if I had thought Mariota had thought about what she was saying. But as I knew she had never thought about what she was saying, and never would, I could not be offended; I was simply happy to see her.

She might not have envied me Glengard, but she certainly

envied me the horses. Since we were the friends we we
did not have to make with dainty teacups indoors. We c
stroll and even stride. We strode to the stables. She had
them, but not thoroughly; she had met one or two o
grooms, but not got to know them. We put that right.
unassuming friendliness – perhaps her beauty too – mad
an immediate favourite in that cheerful world. We pass
happy afternoon.

I was beginning to see that happy times were possil
Glengard – with my friends, in the gardens, on Marma
I was beginning to think that a half-life could be livabl

My fears were realised: Peter McCallum was seen sku
in the park near the gardens, with his horse tethered
hundred yards off. He was seen by a keeper who knew
who was himself in hiding because he was trying to
pigeons. The keeper knew him because he had worke
the McCallums at Miltoun; he had come into the serv
Glengard because he had married the daughter of the
keeper.

All this I knew from Geordie Gault, my friend
gardener's boy; by which I realised that everybody o
estate knew it, and everybody in the castle knew it.
Glengard servants knew the Miltoun servants; the Mi
servants knew poor Peter's feelings (I do not know how
it is quite certain that they did); all the Glengard serv
then, knew why Peter was hiding behind furze-bushes i
Glengard park.

Nobody except Geordie Gault, said anything to me
it. Charles most certainly heard the news; he said nothi
me about it.

In the manner of a prelate, Charles said at dinner, 'I
that I am compelled to go away on business for a few
I am able to do so because the doctors have pronounce
father in a stable condition. There are no immediate anx
concerning his state. I do not expect to be gone more t
week.'

141

'Where are you going?' I asked, not because I cared, but because it was something new to talk about.

'I shall be in Edinburgh for part of the time,' he said.

That was all. We had been married for less than a month. He did not say where he would be in Edinburgh. He did not say where else he would be. He did not say what his business was. I thought it a pity – these matters would have sustained a feasible conversation for a quarter of an hour.

He had left before I came down to breakfast the following morning.

I was completely astonished, that very afternoon, to be brought, on a salver, the card of Sir Archibald Hannay of Achmore.

I sent a message by the footman asking Sir Archibald to join me in the garden, where I was proposing to have tea on those pleasant wrought-iron seats under the tree. (I was not proposing to swing on the nearby swing, though it was hard – it was hard.)

When the footman had gone, and before Sir Archibald was brought, I was suddenly not astonished at all. But I deeply dreaded the conversation I thought we should be having.

It was much worse than I expected.

Sir Archibald was dressed up very fine for an afternoon call on a weekday. He wore a frock-coat, and tight white trousers, and a most gloomy silk hat. His face was pink in the heat. He was sweating a little; his hand was damp when I shook it. I thought he had lost weight, in the few weeks since I had first met him. There was something haggard about his look, and a pouchiness about his face. He looked an unhappy man. He had enough to be unhappy about.

'We are alone, Lady Gard?' he said. 'We shall not be disturbed? We shall not be overheard?'

'I hope somebody will bring us some tea,' I said. 'Otherwise nobody will come near us unless I tell them to.'

I realised that I was talking like a Marchioness, very confident and haughty. I would have laughed at myself, but Sir Archibald's misery set me far from laughing.

And immediately my arrogance was rebuked – young Geordie Gault came trotting up, like a puppy wanting a

142

game. Although he knew who I was, he was in no more awe of me than the Urquhart children, who did not know who I was. I managed a smile for him, and sent him away.

'This is intensely painful for me,' said Sir Archibald. 'I am afraid it will be so for you. So much so, that I would have preferred to keep you in ignorance. Or, at least, that your knowledge should have come from some other source. I have kept silent, until now, in some agony of conscience as to whether I was right to do so — as to whether I *had* the right to do so. But there is a new development, which I am absolutely obliged to bring to your notice, since it concerns your own safety. A new development which dates, we must suppose, from your Ladyship's marriage to the Marquess of Gard, and about which I have only in the last days discovered.'

'My safety?' I said. 'I am safe. I am surrounded by an army. I wish I was allowed to live more dangerously than I do.'

'Whatever perils you faced in Australia,' he said, 'are as nothing to those which surround you now. Please forgive me for the pain I am certain to be about to give you. Please believe that only the utmost necessity obliges me to speak. Please believe that I myself am as deeply wounded as you are sure to be. Now — as you may know, Jean my wife left this neighbourhood with her mother when she was hardly more than a child. It was, I think, soon after your own departure for Australia. If while she was here she knew the Marquess of Gard, it can only have been very slightly. She was still in the schoolroom, he was already adult. And her father's affairs were, I understand, in so embarrassed a state that the Achmore family would scarcely have met the Glengard family on easy and equal terms. Consequently, when I brought Jean back into this neighbourhood, she met the Marquess for what was, to all intents and purposes, the first time. And he was meeting her as an adult for the first time.'

'I had not thought of it quite like that,' I said, 'but of course it is quite true.'

'I was astonished,' he said, 'that a beautiful young woman like Jean should consent to the entreaties of an older, a much older man like myself. A man never blessed with a face or figure which had cut a dash in ballrooms. A man with a reasonable understanding, but without that gift of wit which I have so much envied in others. I do not wish to sound . . . unpleasantly over-humble, Lady Gard. I do not wish to abase myself. But I *was* astonished when Jean took me, and I could not fail to be aware that my astonishment was widely shared. I hazard the guess that you shared it youself, when you came to my house with your aunt?'

I could not answer this. I made a kind of gesture. I think he could not have known what my gesture meant, because I did not know myself. This decent and deeply unhappy man deserved better than a lie. He deserved better than the truth, too.

'I loved her very deeply,' he said. 'I was encouraged to think, entitled to think, that she loved me also.'

'Do you love her still?' I asked.

'I ask myself the same question,' he said. 'The extreme difficulty of answering it will come clear, I think, if you bear with me. Jean and the Marquess met very soon after we removed from Aberdeenshire, very soon after we took possession of her father's one-time house. It was inevitable that they should do so, and I thought nothing of it. He paid her no particular attentions, that I saw. Her manner to me was unchanged; her love for me, her happiness in our marriage, were as far as I knew unchanged. I did not know when their liaison started. I do not know now exactly when it became – irrevocably wrong. But it was not many weeks after we came here and not many months after we were married.'

'I am sorry,' I said, not knowing what else to say.

He burst out, with agony in his voice, 'The horned husband is the last to know, always, always! It is a subject of coarse jokes, of ribaldry in smoking-rooms! A man who looks like me, a man of forty, deserves to be treated so, for his folly in marrying a beautiful and penniless young wife. That is what everybody says, laughing behind their hands, and I am coming to see that they are right.'

'I am not laughing behind my hand,' I said, distressed almost to tears by the pain in his face and voice.

'I thanked God,' he said, 'for the news of your marriage. I thought it would save my own. I thought it would save me. I thought it would save Jean. I thought there was no future for her in that relationship, except misery and humiliation and disgrace. But there were things I did not understand – things I had not reckoned on. I had underestimated her passionate obsession with your husband. She had never been truly in love. She had imagined herself in love with me – oh yes, I am satisfied as to that. I was kind to her, you understand, and life had not been kind to her. I was mature, well travelled, not ill informed. I was adequately wealthy – I could and would and did give her things that had never come her way before – jewellery, silks, a house like Achmore, furnished as you have seen it, horses and carriages . . . I am not suggesting that Jean was entirely mercenary when she accepted my offer – simply that she confused love with gratitude – that her yearning for things she had never had clouded her young mind, her immature judgement . . . She could think herself happy, content, loving and loved. Until we came here, and she met the Marquess. I was sick with misery and with anger, but still I did not fully understand. She was and is besotted, mindless with passion. She would murder to get that man. She will try to do so.'

'She will try to murder you?'

'No, because she knows I will release her.'

'Who, then?'

'She will try to murder you.'

'Oh no,' I said. 'Oh no. We were friends all our childhood. I do not think Jean would harm anybody, and I am quite sure she would not harm me.'

'You are quite wrong, Lady Gard, with respect. She would and will harm you, unless you take enormous and unremitting care. You have not understood, as for weeks and months I did not understand. There is this about it, also.' He paused. 'I have said that I acquitted Jean of being entirely mercenary when she married me – but that my moderate fortune did not have the effect of making me repulsive. I acquit her of being entirely mercenary in her infatuation with Gard. But could a woman brought up as she was brought up be indifferent to – this?'

He waved a hand at the castle and the gardens – that great wall of tall, sun-flooded windows, that sequence of smiling courtyards, this waterfall of lovely terraces, and the great glen below us and about us.

145

'I do not think,' he said, 'you need be frightened of her in a physical sense. There is nothing intrepid or violent in her character. She might lure you to some lonely spot, on some ingenious pretext; but it would not be her finger on the trigger.'

'Whose, then?'

'Why, your husband's. Who else?'

'Oh,' I said, trying to come to terms with this amazing remark.

Sir Archibald might be talking nonsense, but he did not think he was. There was no doubt about his sincerity, as there was none about his misery. He was doing what he saw as his duty, to give me a most solemn warning; he was concerned about me; he was frightened for me.

Was it, after all, so very unlikely?

He had been forced, as much as I had, into a marriage that was odious to him. Why was it so very odious, unless he were deep in love with somebody else? I had been in the way of being told that I was beautiful, but he looked at me with repulsion. Why would he do so, unless the woman he loved was completely different?

Once again I compared us, Jean and myself. I tall, she tiny. I strong and active, though mercifully slim, she frail and sedentary. I direct and free-spoken to the point of brashness, she soft-voiced and fluttering. I with a mane of lion-coloured hair, she with that smooth jet-black. . .

But you did not murder somebody, I thought, because of the colour of their hair. You murdered somebody because you very badly wanted somebody else. In the castle in the Falls of Gard, Charles had not wanted Jean.

'I thought Charles had tired of Jean,' I said. 'I had reason to think so.'

'I thought so, too,' he said. 'I too had reason. We were both right, but not quite right. I am not, in this matter – ' he gave a wretched little laugh – 'in my wife's confidence, but I am positive I know what happened. She wanted an open, immediate breach with me, a scandal which would compel a divorce and an immediate remarriage. He was determined to go more slow, more careful, more – if you will – respectable about it. His concern with his father would in part explain that, and his concern for himself would assist

146

the explanation. I think he did not, as I had supposed, actually reject her. I think he grew angry and impatient with her importunity. I think this caused a brief rift between them, which their love for one another has since entirely healed. I am turning knives in my own heart by saying this. I am appalled to think that I am turning knives in your heart too.'

'I would rather have knives in my heart,' I said, 'than bullets in my back.'

'Would you so?' He said. 'I am not sure that I would.'

We stared at one another. I had to look away, because I thought he was about to weep.

He now looked away, so that I could not see his face.

He said huskily, 'I have to tell you, Lady Gard, that your husband is as besotted about my wife as she about him.'

I said, 'How *can* you know that? I do not doubt you, Sir Archibald,' I added quickly, 'but I wonder how you know?'

'How can you be married, live intimately with another person, and not know such a thing?' he said. 'Not at once. In my case, not at once. I accuse myself of thick-headedness, insensitivity, complacency. But over days, weeks, how *could* you live as man and wife, and not be aware that your wife was desperately loved, and not be aware by whom?'

I was silent. 'Living as man and wife' took different forms.

I faced the truth. Charles was in love with Jean, as Jean with him. He had been a rake, a heart-breaker. Probably he would be so again. But now he was in love with Jean. He might not remain so, but now he was. He might not truly be so, but he thought he was. It all came to the same.

Sir Archibald was to be believed. No one could have disbelieved him. Jean was prepared to kill (to help to kill) to get the man that she wanted, and the castle that she wanted. Charles, it seemed, was prepared to kill to get the woman he wanted.

It was depressing. It was frightening.

'Having at last learned the full state of affairs,' said Sir Archibald, 'I have been desperately asking myself what action to take that would save you. There is none, except to warn you. As far as I can see, there is nothing else I can do. Am I to accuse my own wife, to the County Police, of plotting something so appalling, so unthinkable? I should be laughed at. I have no evidence that would convince a jury. No lawyer would state my case. How can there be evidence, objectively convincing, of what is going on in a person's mind? More by token, how can I accuse Lord Gard? I could not accuse a tinker, with the hard evidence available to me, let alone a man of his wealth and rank. *All* I can do is tell you the truth, and to give you the most urgent warning.'

'Well, I am safe for a few days,' I said. 'My husband has gone away.'

'I know. That is why I came today, and not yesterday, praying that I was not too late.'

'How did you know he was going away? He only told me yesterday.'

'By Jean's misery. She will not see him for a week or more.'

'I suppose there might be some other instrument,' I said, 'somebody in their pay.'

'I think not. I am certain of it. Would they put themselves in the power of a hired assassin?'

I nodded. This was sense. Someone who did such a thing, for money, would be able to ask what he chose, and get it again and again and again. I was safe until Charles came back. By that time I hoped I would have made a plan.

I remained sitting on the terrace, after Sir Archibald had left me. My world had turned inside out. Now it was upside down too. That plump little man, pink, balding, slightly ridiculous, was distraught with grief and with worry for my safety. I could not have failed to believe him. I could not have failed to be certain that I was in deadly danger, the moment my husband came back.

I felt the glorious sunshine, and looked out over the glorious view, and between them they made changes inside my head. That warmth, that beauty, brought commonsense back. Sir Archibald *was* distraught. I believed him that Jean was besotted with Charles; after what I had seen on the island, I could not have believed that she was not. He, newly married to a much younger wife, was struck to the heart by that. And so his judgement was tilted, and his imagination inflamed, and these nightmares came out of his troubled heart, these fears of peril and murder.

Since some of what he had said I knew to be true, I took it that it was all true. I was suddenly certain now that half of it was the fevered imagination of a deeply unhappy man.

148

I could not look across the great glen, at the big hills, and believe in the danger of violence and murder. I could not look back at the calm and smiling vastness of the castle, and believe in the kind of ruthless cruelty of which Sir Archibald had spoken. In the back alleys of cities, perhaps, cut-throats murdered for shillings. In desert strongholds in Africa, perhaps, Moorish princes had their unfaithful wives garotted with bowstrings. Even here, centuries since, in the barbarous tribal times, deeds of treachery and violence stained the flagstones with blood. But immediate danger to me, here, today, was the purest fantasy.

I risked an indifferent dislike that would almost have amounted to cruelty, had I not rather welcomed it. I risked a husband who was already, and would always be, unfaithful. I risked a half-life, all my life. I did not risk a bullet, or a bowstring, or a knife between the ribs.

I looked down and down the lovely waterfall of terraces. I saw one of the undergardeners on a step-ladder, pruning a tree. At the foot of the ladder, busy as a terrier, Geordie Gault was picking up the fallen prunings. I heard the gardener's laughter and Geordie's, carried up to me on the warm south wind. All nightmare fears blew away like fallen leaves, in the face of that peace and sanity.

I sent a message to the stables that I would ride next morning. The message came back that Marmalade, and Malcolm Menzies, would be in the courtyard at eleven.

To have sent and received those messages was perfectly unnecessary. But sometimes, it seemed to me, it was wise that I should behave like a Marchioness, the more so because I felt so very unlike one.

A message had come to Malcolm Menzies, so he told me – by hand of a shepherd, I think – that something was amiss in the Urquhart family, in the croft under the wood. Did her ladyship mind if we went that way?

Of course her ladyship did not mind. It was a beautiful way, and included a superb natural galloping-ground. And we must find out at once what trouble the Urquharts had.

Marmalade seemed pleased to see me. She was affectionate, as mares often are. I thought she had enjoyed our first ride together, and was looking forward to this one as much as I was.

Malcolm Menzies shot me up into the saddle, I arranged my habit-skirt and my reins, and we walked our horses over the bridge and out. Malcolm's notion was to ride behind me, but I signalled to him to come up alongside. I might behave like a Marchioness in the matter of sending messages, but I was not going to carry it to the length of riding in silence. Though young, he was very knowledgeable and interesting about everything to do with horses, and, because many things were done differently in Australia, I thought I interested him, too. We could learn from one another, and have a cheerful time as we did so, which is what makes for the very best kind of conversation, and did so that morning.

We came to the sweep of grass where Marmalade and I had enjoyed our gallop; Malcolm grinned, rightly assuming we should gallop again. At the moment of his grin, there was a scream from within or just beyond the belt of trees – a scream of pain or of terror, the scream of an animal or a child.

'Ma Goad,' said Malcolm.

The same thought, I was sure, jumped into his head as it jumped into mine. It was one of the Urquhart children, and their trouble was serious.

I kicked Marmalade into a gallop, and we flew over the springy turf towards the gap in the trees. The scream was repeated, louder than before because nearer, a high shriek over the pounding of our horses' feet and the rush of air past my ears. It was human, not animal. It was one of those children, caught in a gin-trap, or being threatened or tortured by a tinker. . .

I screamed myself, for no reason I can think of. I whipped Marmalade to her utmost speed, and she responded gallantly. I knew I would be leaving Malcolm Menzies far behind; but it was comforting to know that he was there, and that whatever needed doing he would help to do.

I tore into the gap between the trees. And, as I was in the midst of the trees, there was suddenly nothing in front of my saddle – Marmalade had no head, no neck, no withers. She

150

stopped completely dead, in her tracks. I have a memory of flying through the air, and then rolling, and then coming to rest, painfully, against the trunk of a tree. I have a memory of lying feeling battered, winded, a little sick, utterly puzzled, and enraged that for the moment I could do nothing about the child who had screamed.

Malcolm Menzies thundered up on his big cob. He reined in, and stopped just by the place where we had been brought down. Marmalade was up on her feet. I could not tell how badly she was injured; I could not tell how badly I was.

By the time Malcolm reached me, I was struggling to my knees, sobbing for the breath that had been knocked out of me. It was already evident to me that I had not cracked my skull, nor broken my back, either or both of which I could have done if I had not been miraculously lucky – either or both of which I would probably have done if I had been thrown against a tree instead of onto springy grass – either or both of which could have killed me outright.

Malcolm helped me to my feet, very gentle for so powerful a man; I found that without his help I could not stand; I had somehow twisted my ankle, by landing awkwardly; but that was all I had done.

Speaking with difficulty, I said, 'I am hardly damaged. I have had much worse falls than that, kangaroo-hunting in Australia. But what about Marmalade? And what about the child?'

He protested that I must not stand, or walk, or do anything at all until he had fetched help.

'We are made of India-rubber in Australia,' I said. 'Since we were obliged to bounce, we learn how to do it. Please now see about that child!'

He looked at me most anxiously; but I got him at last to help me to a tree, where I could support myself. For some reason, I was determined to stay on my feet. There were things to be done, and I did not want to do them sitting down.

'The child!' I cried to Malcolm.

He nodded. He mounted his big horse, and trotted along the strip of wood to where the scream had come from. He dismounted, and peered among the trees.

'Narthing,' he said, returning. 'No' a bairn, dog, fox, hare,

151

tinker. Will your Leddyship speir the noo at wha' brocht the mare doon?'

It was a rope, thin, stiff, strong, dark-coloured so that it was almost invisible in the shade of the trees, stretched between two trees so that it spanned the gap a little more than two feet from the ground. At each end were solid and intricate knots, tied round the trunks of fir-trees. I did not think a rope could have been stretched there for any other purpose than to bring down a galloping horse. I did not think any other horse could have been intended, than mine.

Sir Archibald Hannay was right.

But he was wrong that I was safe while Charles was away. The plotters had hired their assassin, and he had very nearly done their work for them.

The scream was a trap. It was meant to do exactly what it had done – to make me gallop as fast as I possibly could through the gap in the trees.

There had been no message to Malcolm Menzies from the Urquharts. Indeed a message came, but not from them. That too was part of the trap – it was meant to do exactly what it had done, to make us come this way and not some other.

The plan was made by somebody who knew the estate, and its servants, and its tenants, and me. It was evident that the plan had been made by the son of the owner of the estate. And that, no doubt, was why he had suddenly gone away 'on business'. He had gone away so that he would be in Edinburgh, in the sight of dozens of people, when my horse came down in the trees. The news would be carried to him. He would hurry back, for the look of the thing. And then he would try again. But I thought he would not try again at long range. It would be slow, and difficult, and dangerous, to give instructions to an assassin by word of mouth, or by the penny post. He would come home, and try again, and I still needed a plan to save my life.

While I was thinking these unwelcome thoughts, Malcolm Menzies was examining Marmalade's forelegs. They were cut, bruised and tender. Like me, she was lucky but not unscathed. She could walk, slowly, but we agreed that she should not be ridden.

Malcolm lifted me up onto his horse, where I sat awkwardly on his cross-saddle as though it had been a side-saddle. He would walk, leading both horses. Though he was wearing riding boots, which are not commonly comfortable to walk in, he was undaunted at the prospect of walking three miles to Glengard.

Of course we talked as we went, and I tried to be as cheerful as before. As I prattled rather wildly on about such matters as the races behind the taverns in New South Wales, he glanced often back at me, sometimes with an expression of amazement, sometimes with a broad grin, and once with a worried frown.

His own conversation was all about the rope. Why should it have been put there? By whom? To keep something in? To keep something out? That it should have been put there in order to bring down a galloping horse was, to him, too wild an idea to consider for a moment.

I did not share my theories with him. Though I knew for a very certainty that they were true, I knew equally that in a court of law they would be no more than theories, and as wild as Malcolm would have found them.

I sat the big horse, my injured ankle paining me. I fell silent, as Malcolm rambled on about the mystery of the rope between the trees. I wondered if there was anybody in the world I could talk to.

The Reverend Pericles Davidson seemed my friend; but he would hardly credit my story about a man on whom his livelihood depended, and with whom he seemed on very good terms. The Duke seemed prepared to listen to me talking on all manner of topics; but not this one. The Glengard servants, high and low, indoors and out, would think every word the most preposterous and most evil slander. My own family, the Gordons of Callo, would come running to the Marquess if he whistled, and fawn and wag their tails and lick his boots. I would cease to be the Marchioness of their toad-eating, and become not merely a moral leper again, but a dangerous lunatic, fit only for the Lochgrannomhead Asylum for Pauper Lunatics.

The Nicholls of Invermore, the Frasers of Lossie, the McCallums of Miltoun, were not, as far as I knew, toad-eaters in my family's class. But their reaction would be very much the same. Their sons? They knew more than the parents did. They had been more in the world, and had heard more tales. They were not like to be blinded by greatness, or dazzled by an impressive appearance. They might be prepared to believe this evil of Charles, because they already knew other evils of Charles. I knew that I could rely completely on the friendship of all three.

Very well, I had friends that I could talk to. I was sure they would want to help me, but I was not sure how. Help me to hide, somewhere in safety? But if I hid for more than a few days I would be a deserter, a runaway wife. I knew the law of that, because it had arisen once or twice in Australia, where the laws were the same. My husband had the right to seek me out and drag me back, a sheep to the shambles. In hiding, how would I live? How would I pay for my bed or my bread? Batten on the charity of young men who were only beginning their lives?

I wanted, urgently, passionately, to go back at once to Australia. In wanting that, I was wanting the waters of the moon.

They helped me upstairs and to bed, because they rightly said my ankle must be rested. I thought a day or two would be enough, but the women threw up their hands, and said it must be a week. I pretended to be submissive; but, as soon as I could walk, I would be a Marchioness.

Messages now began to fly about Glengard. I sent to the stables, to ask for news of Marmalade's injuries. The head groom sent to me, to ask for news of my injuries. The Reverend Pericles Davidson sent to ask my leave for him to visit me, and when he came brought messages of condolence and concern from the Duke.

Marmalade's injuries were just about as serious as mine. She would be impatient to be active again just as soon as I would be.

Next day Mariota came. She brought unnecessary flowers to a sickroom which was already, thanks to Mr Blair the head gardener, like a florist's shop.

It was just as might have been supposed – since the whole

Glengard estate knew of my accident within minutes, the whole Crask estate knew of it within hours.

Mariota brought yet more messages, from her father and more particularly from her mother, who recommended all kinds of nostrums and patent medicines and pills for a twisted ankle.

'Is Charles a comfort?' asked Mariota, 'or is he as impatient of an invalid as I am told most husbands are?'

'Charles is away,' I said.

She looked at me surprised, frowning.

I was surprised at her surprise. I said, 'He said he would be away for about a week. He will be in Edinburgh, and perhaps some other places.'

Mariota looked at me in evident distress. She looked embarrassed, which I did not think I had ever seen before.

'I think I must tell you,' she said. 'It will hurt your feelings, but that is better than being hurt as you were yesterday.'

'How will you hurt my feelings?' I asked stupidly.

'Charles is not in Edinburgh. He is here. I saw him yesterday afternoon.'

'Where?'

Mariota looked more unhappy than ever. 'At Achmore,' she said. 'I went to see Jean Hannay, with a message from my Mama. She was out, or at least she was not at home to me. I slipped round to the back, all on my own, because I wanted to arrange to get some bantam chicks of a breed the gamekeeper has. I was in the gamekeeper's cottage, which is just behind the steading. I saw Charles, with a groom, riding, some way off. I happened to look out of the window. I saw Charles dismount. The groom rode off, leading Charles's horse. Charles walked up to the house, to the back. I suppose he went in. I did not see him again. He is not in Edinburgh, Bella.'

'Was Jean there?' I asked.

'How do you guess?'

'What about Sir Archibald?'

'The butler told me Sir Archibald was out all day, not expected back until seven.'

'Unfortunately,' I said, 'this all comes as no surprise.'

'I had a notion it might not be a surprise.'

'Charles cannot be *staying* at Callo,' I said. 'I wonder where he is staying?'

'His father owns hundreds of houses, farms, crofts. I expect thousands. The tenants of every one are completely at Charles's mercy. Think, Bella. A man in Charles's position can drop out of sight with the greatest ease.'

'Yes,' I said. 'And still remain in close touch with everything that goes on here. And still make plans, and control the working of the plan. . . .'

'And still do all kinds of things,' said Mariota. There was no fairy music in her head now. She was frowning, concentrating. She looked acutely unhappy. She said, 'I went to Achmore again this morning. Jean has – confided in me a little. I don't think I can break her confidence, even to you, even at a time like this. Because of what she told me, I thought I ought to talk to her today. To remind her that you and she were childhood friends, and – so forth.'

'I think,' I said, 'Jean would not be much impressed with that.'

'I thought that, too, but I thought I ought to try.'

'Did you try?'

'I had no chance to try. Jean went away last night, before her husband came home. She went away in a carriage, with some baggage. She told nobody where she was going, and the man who drove her has not come back. They are all very mystified. At least, they say they are.'

'I am afraid Sir Archibald is not mystified,' I said. 'Miserable –'

'I think he must certainly be that.'

'But not so very surprised. Do you suppose Jean went to where Charles is?'

Mariota said nothing. She looked at me, herself miserable. She seemed to come to a sudden decision. She said, 'I cannot tell you the things Jean said to me, Bella, about her feelings and so forth. But I can tell you things she did not say to me, but that I know just the same. I think I must tell you. I am not sure if it is breaking a confidence. I must tell you, even if it is. Jean let me see – made me see, without meaning to – that she . . . that she would do anything, go to any lengths. Jean is cleverer than she makes you think. And she is much more ruthless. She hides it behind all that

156

fluttering, and by being so small. But to get what she wants she will do *anything*. She made me understand all that, without meaning to. She made me understand that she decided to catch Sir Archibald, because he is rich. She decided to come back to Achmore, although he thought he was deciding that. Now she has decided to get Charles. I am sorry, Bella, but that is what I was made to understand, and what you must understand. She will get rid of Sir Archibald, and she will get rid of you. He's no problem – she can get him to let her go. If at first he doesn't, she'll make his life so miserable that in the end he will. You wouldn't think, would you, that somebody so small and fluttery could make a rich man's life unendurable? Jean could. But you, Bella, you're a different kind of problem.'

'They tried to solve it yesterday,' I said.

'Yes, I know. That is why I am here. The whole glen knows there was a rope between two trees. The whole glen wonders why ever it was put there. I know. You know. Come away, Bella – come to Crask where you'll be safe. Once you're there we'll think of something. At least, once you're there you'll be alive to think.'

'None of this is going to go away,' I said. 'It is very kind of you to ask me to Crask, but everything will go on exactly as it is going. Nothing will be solved. I can't live at Crask for ever.'

'Yes, you can. As things are, you must.'

'Suppose I could find a lawyer,' I said slowly. 'Suppose he could get evidence on oath from – I don't know – Jean's coachman, perhaps, or her maid.'

'Evidence on oath? To be brought out in a courtroom? Bella, do you know what you're saying?'

'I don't like saying any of it,' I said.

'But divorce is unthinkable!'

'I know it's rare, and very scandalous, and people hate it. . . . Old Lady Strathgallant's daughter was divorced, and she lived happily ever after.'

'She had to live in Paris. And her mother never forgave her. Bella, it's impossible. *Think*, dear. Do you suppose Charles would allow his name to be dragged through the courts, to be on the front page of every penny newspaper, to be made to resign from his clubs, to give up every public position he has in the county and the country? He'd die first.'

'No,' I said.

'No. He'd kill you first. For pity's sake, Bella, come to Crask.'

My ankle was hurting. I was feeling sore and sorry for myself. I was frightened. I knew that at Crask I would be safe, and that I would be surrounded by love and goodwill.

'Thank you, Mariota,' I said, astonishing myself. 'But no.'

'*Why?*' she wailed.

Well, why?

Because I was a general's daughter. Because I was Marchioness of Gard, and Arabella Gordon of Callo. Because I was damned – I put it like that, to myself – I was damned if a piece of string between fir-trees was going to frighten me out of the house of which I was mistress.

To Mariota I said, 'I shall be more careful where I gallop.'

She looked at me, stricken. She said, 'Then all I can do is pray for you.'

Chapter 8

Of course the scream was Jean's. Of course the knots were Gard's. Now they had both disappeared. They would not be far. I must walk, as soon as I could walk, with my chin on my shoulder.

I tried to think myself into their minds. Lying idle in bed, I thought this was a useful way of filling the time. I thought about how I would go about it, if I were they.

I became certain that they would try to arrange another 'accident'. I would be drowned in the Falls of Gard, or buried under an avalanche; I would trip and fall down stairs, or be hit by a falling stone from the roof. I would not be obviously murdered, by knife or bullet, for then the question would be asked who stood to gain by my death, and presently everybody would know, including the County Police.

When the 'accident' happened, Charles would be able to prove he was somewhere else, and Jean would be able to prove she was somewhere else. Probably they would vouch for one another, and then, if they stood firm, no lawyer would be able to prove them lying.

What 'accident' would I contrive, in their place?

Lying against my pillows, somewhat distracted by the throbbing of my ankle, I pondered methods of murdering my neighbours. I had some highly ingenious ideas which would not, I think, have worked. They were apt to depend on the victim running with great innocence into a trap, as I had done the day before. But I would not do that; and they would know by now that I would not do that. Or they depended on the victim trusting me implicitly, or doing something extremely silly which I had planned for him to do, or taking some insane risk. But I would not be trusting them, or doing anything silly, or taking any risks at all.

It had to be an 'accident', believed at once and always, by

159

everybody, to be so. It had to be out of anybody's sight. They had to be out of anybody's sight, but able to prove that they were elsewhere. It had to be soon, because Charles could not stay hidden for ever; before many days he would have to come out into the glare of the sunlight, to look after his estate and to look after his father.

I thought they were giving themselves a difficult problem. I thought they might not solve it. I thought that with care, and with luck, I would be safe.

My thoughts went uselessly round and round, and after two days I could stand no more of it. I found that my ankle could bear my weight; I could not have run, but with a stick I could walk. They helped me dress, although they did not want to. They did not help me downstairs, although they did want to. Servants seemed to come at me round every corner; I greeted them all with extravagant cheerfulness, nearly all by name, to show that I had come to no harm, that I had bounced as an Australian should, that I had no suspicions. They clucked in dismay, like a parcel of hens in a yard.

I sensed goodwill, great and growing.

Limping as little as I could, I went straight out to the stables. There was more clucking, and there were more grins. Marmalade greeted me with forgiveness. The grooms thought she needed another few days of idleness; she quite disagreed, but I thought it my duty to support the grooms. She looked reproachfully after me, over the half-door of her loose-box, when I hobbled back to the castle.

I suffered from enforced idleness, almost for the first time in my life. My ankle would not carry me far or fast; and, while things remained as they were, I would not walk alone out of sight of grooms or gardeners.

I decided to put my idleness to some use. I decided to begin, in a small way, with some of the changes I meant to make.

I hobbled to the laundry. I saw again the little laundry-maids stagger from the coppers to the mangles under their burdens of dripping linen.

160

To Mrs McKay the Head Laundrymaid I said, 'I expect there is a very good reason which you will be able to explain to me, but I do not quite understand why you have an arrangement which wastes so much time, and gives so much more work.'

She looked at me, puzzled, not at all understanding what I was talking about. She was not yet angry or resentful; perhaps that would come later.

I explained my notions about the position of the mangles. She waved her arms, which were wet with suds, as she personally washed the Duke's linen. The mangles had always been just where they were now. It was just as I had supposed. Tradition ruled. Besides, the mangles were bolted into the flagstone floor of the laundry.

Patiently, I explained the merit of having the mangles beside the coppers. I spoke loudly enough so that all the laundrymaids could hear. I said that, as to the bolts, there was a blacksmith in the stables.

'You will be able to do more washing in the same time,' I said, 'or the same amount of washing in less time.'

Mrs McKay frowned, pondered, waved her arms, shouted commands at her underlings, and at last said she could not for the life of her think why the mangles had ever been put where they were.

Two hours later they had all been moved, and new bolts were being made in the forge to pin them to the flagstones.

In visiting Marmalade, I had not seen Malcolm Menzies. I sent for him, and asked the question I should have thought to ask the moment I got my breath back after my fall: who had brought the message from the Urquharts? Was there in truth trouble at the croft?

Yes, it was, as I had understood, a shepherd. Not a man of the Glengard estate. Not a man whose name Malcolm Menzies knew. A man from Achmore: one of the Hannays' men.

It would be possible to find him – Malcolm knew his face. It would be quite useless. He might be – probably was – perfectly innocent. He would have been told, 'There is trouble in the Urquharts' croft; tell Malcolm Menzies at the Glengard stables, who is their friend, that they need his help.' In all good faith, quite likely, he carried this message. In all good faith, perhaps, he had even been given the message; it would be impossible to prove that it had originated with Jean Hannay.

Malcolm had been to the Urquharts'. He had been given leave to visit them, which was why I had not seen him when I visited Marmalade. There was no trouble there, more than the trouble which was always there. He did not understand about the message. It did not occur to him that it was a trap, or that the rope had been stretched to bring down my horse. Malcolm had habits of thought which included veneration for his master, and respect for the wives of neighbouring lairds. He was as much a prisoner of those habits of thought, as Mrs McKay in the laundry.

The shot changed my mind about a lot of things, and did so with miraculous speed.

In a park like that of Glengard – on an estate with so many gamekeepers, stalkers and gillies – shots could be heard all the year round. There is no closed season for vermin, and no respite in the war against it. The keepers shot buzzards and hoodie-crows, magpies and jays, foxes and rabbits. The animals were skinned; the birds were hung in grisly rows in the 'gamekeepers' larders' in the preserves, with the ridiculous object of teaching other vermin a lesson. Even in spring and summer, when nothing else was killed, the war against vermin went on, and it was no surprise to hear shots far away and near, and even in the gardens. The keepers were all experienced and careful, and there had never been an accident.

There was very nearly an accident – I should say, more exactly, an 'accident' – the day after I moved the mangles. I was hobbling, a little more briskly, towards the stables, where I felt more at ease than I did in the castle. It was no surprise to hear a shot from a clump of trees some sixty yards to my right, to the east. It was a very great surprise to hear, at the same moment, the thwack of something hitting the stone of the castle wall a yard from my head.

It was a bullet. The shot I had heard was not the deep boom of a shotgun, but the lighter crack of a sporting rifle. I

162

knew the difference well enough, from hundreds of sporting expeditions with Papa in Australia. A rifle bullet carried ten times further than the pellets of a shotgun, and it could be lethal even at extreme range.

Yes, it would have been an 'accident', blamed on a poacher or a schoolboy too frightened to own up.

I thought these thoughts very rapidly, after I had dropped to my knees behind the low wall bordering the drive. I took off my hat and peeped over the wall. I did not expect to see anything, and did not. With two sound ankles, I could have run at my best speed, which was a very good speed, into the safety of the courtyard; even the best rifle shot in the world would hardly hit a slim person, running very fast, at sixty yards. But I could not run. Even an indifferent shot might easily hit a hobbling person, at that range, in that brilliant sunshine. I had to keep below the level of the little wall. I had to crawl to safety. It made me extremely angry, to be obliged to crawl along the carriage-drive of my own home.

There was no point in sending a platoon of grooms or gardeners to the clump of trees. The marksman would be over the horizon by the time they got there. Even if he was still there, he was perfectly safe. He was their master. He had fired, yes, but in another direction entirely. I had imagined the bullet hitting the stone. The hole it had made was one of thousands in that ancient masonry. I was suffering from a little concussion, perhaps, the effect of my fall from my horse. What I had heard, if I had heard anything, was an echo of the shot.

I had been fatuously confident. Mariota had been right, and I wrong.

Crask was undoubtedly the place to go, but I could not imagine how to get there. I could not walk so far – it would have been a weary way even on two good ankles. If I rode, the groom who came with me would know where I had gone, so that immediately everyone would know where I had gone. I could not ride alone – it would never be permitted. I could not saddle and bridle a horse, and ride it away unseen. I could not drive myself, without groom or footman; I could not have myself driven. If I sent a message by hand to Mariota, everybody would know where the messenger had gone; soon everybody would know why, so they would know where I was. If she came to get me, they would know where she was taking me. If she sent a servant to get me, the servant would be recognized.

Even as I crawled I puzzled; and I found no answer, then or later.

Though Mariota had been right and I wrong, I was sure I was safe on the topmost of the terraces, only yards from the windows of the castle. Prudence now made me almost a prisoner, but at least I could breath fresh air.

Young Geordie Gault had been expecting me to have my tea on the terrace; he was waiting for me. Instead of his usual broad grin, he had a look of solemn excitement.

He said that a gentleman had come to see me, urgently and in private. The gentleman was with Mr Blair the head gardener. He would not give his name. Georgie did not know him, nor Mr Blair. He said that I knew him, and that when I saw him I would know that it was both safe and proper to talk to him privately. Geordie was a long time getting all this out, because he had never had to try to say anything of the sort before.

I followed him down the sequence of terraces, my ankle awkward on the steps.

In one of the leafy avenues which radiated from the bottom terrace, I saw a slim young man with untidy dark hair and a beaky nose, talking to Mr Blair. It was Rupert Fraser. I do not know why this was so completely unexpected. I had assumed that my visitor might be Sir Archibald Hannay, come to repeat his warning – come, perhaps, to tell me to be doubly careful, because Jean had disappeared. A possibility was that it was Peter McCallum, come to increase his misery and so make me miserable. Rupert had not come with his parents to call on me, for wretched reasons which I thought I understood; but now he had come on his own.

Rupert exclaimed when he saw me limping. He looked at me in horror. He knew.

Mr Blair withdrew tactfully out of earshot, but kept us in sight.

Rupert confirmed what I had already guessed – he had been talking to Mariota.

'Crask is the place for you,' he said. 'The Earl and Countess will simply accept that you are there, without bothering about the reason. But we have been wondering how you can get there, with nobody here knowing where you have gone.'

'I have been wondering just the same thing,' I said.

'Oh. Good. Mariota told me you refused to run away.'

'That was before somebody shot at me,' I said.

'What? Good God, Bella, you must get away from here immediately! At any rate, no later than this evening!'

'But how?'

'Peter McCallum has hired a carriage and a horse in Lochgrannomhead. Of course he had to give his name to the livery-stable, but that does not matter, as he will have no part in this evening's ploy. This evening, Geoffrey Nicholls and I will bring the carriage here. We aim to arrive just after dark. We shall try not to be seen, but it does not matter so very much if we are, because nobody in the castle knows us except Charles Gard, and he is away. I know he is not far away, but he is not at home. If, by any extraordinary chance, anybody recognizes the hired carriage, that does not matter either – it can be traced to Peter but not to us, and certainly not to Crask. Can you slip out, with a bag, without being seen?'

'I don't know,' I said. 'There are servants round every corner. I shall look very odd, going for a stroll with a portmanteau after dark.'

'Can you wear Mariota's clothes?'

'Yes, I expect so, but I cannot use her toothbrush.'

'There must be spare toothbrushes at Crask . . . On second thoughts, it is one house where I daresay there are none, or they will have forgotten where they put them.'

He laughed, without any joy. He was looking at me as he had at the ball. For him it would have been better if he had not come to see me; but for me it was very, very much better that he had. I thanked God for such friends.

We agreed that I would pack what necessaries I could into a small bag which I could hide under a cloak. I would stroll out onto the terrace after dinner, and down through the gardens, and so onto the drive by the door I knew. I would leave plenty of time, because I could not hurry. I undertook to get past the lodges without been seen; I would find the carriage on the road, a safe distance from the lodges.

It was further than I wanted to walk; but we agreed that it would be lunacy to bring the carriage any nearer to the castle.

Rupert left as discreetly as he had arrived, having tethered his horse somewhere out of sight.

Some explanation would have to be given to Mr Blair, to account for an unknown gentleman who had business with me in private, and who would not give his name. Unless I explained, the whole castle would soon be making guesses.

I said, 'It is about his sister. That is why he did not give his name, and why I mustn't mention his name. It affects a lady's honour, you understand. My friend is hoping I can help his sister out of — certain difficulties. I hope I can. Perhaps I should consult the chaplain.'

This did not quite satisfy Mr Blair, but it was the best I could do on the spur of the moment. I mentally begged forgiveness of little Emily Fraser, who would not be in the sort of trouble I hinted at for many years yet.

I felt like Mary Queen of Scots, slipping out of a castle after dark. I do not know if that sad queen had a toothbrush with her; I had scarcely anything else. A bundle that could be hidden under a cloak was a thin one indeed. I played hide-and-seek with an army of servants, who seemed to be hiding round every corner, and to be determined to waylay their mistress; and at last I was out on the terrace under the stars.

It was heavy work for my sprained ankle, getting all the way down through the gardens, and all the way down the drive. I was going very slow, by the time I reached the lodges. Then I embarked along the dark road, hobbling, not quite certain if there would be a carriage waiting. After I had limped a hundred yards, I began to face the prospect of limping back again, all the way up through the gardens, all the way to my room. The thought filled me with despair. It was lowering, too, to think that if I showed my face in the park I might be shot at again.

The carriage was there. Rupert was there, and Geoffrey Nicholls, both dressed up in black cloaks like conspirators.

I shook hands with them both. I could not see the look on their faces, in the dark. I did not want to see the look on Geoffrey's face. I had seen the look on Rupert's face, and I did not want to see it again.

Well, if I was cursed with the capacity of making people unhappy, I was well and truly punished.

They bundled me into the back of the carriage. Rupert sat on the box and took the reins; Geoffrey led the horse. They were not risking lights, or driving without lights. When we were well out of sight of the lodges, they put a match to the lamps, Geoffrey climbed aboard, and we went along a little more briskly.

I felt relieved, deeply grateful, a little frightened, and very angry. The need for this midnight melodrama was none of my making. If I had thrown a spanner into the works of a passionate affair, I had not meant to do so; and it was a cruel, miserable and immoral affair. Through no fault of my own, I thought, I was tipped off my horse, shot at, and compelled to carriage rides in the dark. If I had shown a fault, it was only curiosity, which I had been brought up to think was rather a virtue (my Papa's curiosity about birds and animals was the reason I had learned so much about them) and which did not deserve a sprained ankle, or a bullet a yard from my head.

The journey seemed endless, because I could see nothing in the dark, and I had no one to talk to. But we came at last to Crask, and to Mariota's loving welcome. Her parents were abed, and most of the servants also, so it was a discreet and informal arrival, which was good. Rupert and Geoffrey left almost at once, which was both good and bad; they would take the hired carriage to Miltoun very early in the morning, they said, whence Peter McCallum would take it back to Lochgrannomhead. Nobody would know where it had gone, and nobody would know where I had gone.

'I am so thankful you changed your mind, Bella,' said Mariota, when we were alone. 'I was terrified for you.'

I told her what had changed my mind; she shrieked.

'Papa and Mamma may seem rather ... dreamy and impractical, to somebody like you,' she said, 'but I promise they will not let anything dreadful happen to you here. Nor will I. You can feel completely safe.'

167

'I do,' I said. 'It makes a nice change.'

She said, 'They love you almost as much as I do. Everybody seems to. I would be jealous, if I didn't know you deserved it. Do you think it is time for bed?'

I agreed that it was. 'I have had an extraordinary day,' I said. 'And I think I face an extraordinary future.'

The Crasks made me as lovingly welcome in the morning as they always had, and as I knew they always would. It did not seem to me that they had taken in why I was there. I was Mariota's friend – that was enough. They must have been puzzled, if they had thought about it – puzzled that I had left Glengard, to stay in another house on my own, so very soon after my marriage; puzzled that, if I was leaving Glengard, I did not go to my own family at Callo. But they were not given to puzzling about things outside their own immediate concerns. Lord Crask, I was sure, was happy to entertain me, but his mind was full of whatever new hare-brained scheme had got hold of him; Lady Crask was happy to entertain me, but she lived in an ivory tower, and spent her time looking inwards, with a sort of gentle self-pity, so that she only ever had a faint idea of what was going on about her.

They did understand that nobody was to be told that I was there. Mariota had somehow made that clear to them. That would have puzzled them more than anything, if they had stopped to think about it.

Mariota swore that the servants could be trusted. I had to believe her, although they did not look very trustworthy.

We knew that my disappearance would cause a clamour. Mariota, going about the glen as I could not, reported that it did. Glengard was in as much of an uproar as so silent and disciplined a place could ever be in. Callo was in a desperate uproar; Uncle Ranald and Aunt Honoria did not know, Mariota said, whether to condemn a wild Australian whim, or take the line that the Marchioness of Gard could do as she pleased. Nobody could get in touch with the Marquess; nobody knew where he was; almost nobody knew that he was

168

not far away in the Lowlands. There were all kinds of wild theories, all put to Mariota, at Lossie, and Invermore, and Miltoun. There were no doubt equally wild theories among the servants at Achmore, but Sir Archibald Hannay would know very well why I had gone, if not where I had gone.

Charles and Jean, I thought, would have heard the news very soon after it was discovered, in the morning, that I had not slept in my bed. They were nearby, that was certain. They were together, that was practically certain. They would surely assume I had gone to Callo, to my family; there was no way they could guess that it was the last place I would go. It was Callo they would watch, at dawn and in the evening. It was the Callo servants they would try to bribe. It was at the windows of Callo that that sporting rifle would be aimed. I hoped none of the servants would be accidentally shot. I ought to have hoped, harder than I did, that my Cousin Grizelda would not be accidentally shot.

Mariota agreed that the enemy's eyes must be on Callo. As my ankle mended, in spite of – perhaps even owing to – the amazing treatments prescribed by Lady Crask, I had to have fresh air and exercise. Mariota, quite as concerned for my safety as I was myself, thought that I could go out as the sky paled, and cover a few miles, as long as I was back and hidden before the day properly began. And so I began to do, and so I preserved my sanity.

I had three of those walks, in the magic of the dawn, each longer than the last. My mind churned with the strangeness and horror of my situation, and sometimes with the grotesque farce of it. I wondered what would become of me, while the strengthening light in the sky found all the dewdrops on all the cobwebs in the glen.

I said to myself: I am a general's daughter. I am not a passive victim. The question is not what will become of me, but what I shall do. I was deceived by the dawn and the wind of the dawn and the dewdrops. I was a passive victim. There was nothing I could do.

My fourth dawn walk ended that brief and strange period of my life, and started one that was even stranger. I tried to be, all the time, as alert as a wildcat – Charles Gard and Jean Hannay might by now have learned that I was not at Callo. There were many ways they could have done that.

They might simply have guessed I was not at Callo. They might have guessed that I was at Crask, that I would absolutely demand some exercise and fresh air, that I would take the air at dawn. It was not terribly likely, but it was possible. My chin had still to be on my shoulder. It was very, very lucky that it was. I saw, in the first peep of the sun over the rim of the hill, a gleam, a sudden flash of light that came and went. It looked like the momentary glare of sunshine on metal. It came from amongst a tumble of rocks, a hundred yards away from me and a little above. No piece of metal had any business among those rocks. No piece of metal had any business to be moving, unless somebody was moving it.

I knew what it was, and who was holding it, and why. I was right. Even as I whipped round the bole of an oak tree against which I had been standing, the bullet smacked into the tree. It was a rifle. No doubt it was the same rifle. It was a better shot. It would have killed me, if I had not seen that gleam of sunshine on metal.

General's daughter I might be, but that was a moment to run. I ran. The thought of that rifle among the rocks lent wings to my heels, even though one of my ankles was unreliable. If there were a record for crossing a few furlongs of grass, heather and scree, with a half-cured sprained ankle, I must have held it, except that I went like a snipe, in unpredictable zigzags. At least, I hoped my zigzags were unpredictable. Anybody watching me must have thought I was raving: except a man behind the backsight of a rifle, trying to draw a bead on a zigzagging snipe.

I regained Crask, unable to speak; I regained my room, unable to stand up. I collapsed into a chair. I considered things.

It was possible that nobody had betrayed me. I reviewed my thoughts of a few moments before (which seemed like a lifetime) and found them, to my own surprise, quite sane. It was *possible* that nobody had betrayed me – that Charles and Jean had arrived at a theory that I might be at Crask, and had acted on that notion.

That was possible. What else was possible? Who knew that I was at Crask? The Earl and Countess. If I were sure of anything at all, in a staggering world, it was that they loved me and wished me well. Mariota. I was very sure that she was not passionately in love with Charles Gard, that she was not consumed by murderous envy. She was my friend, my lifelong intimate. If I started mistrusting her, there was nothing left to believe. Geoffrey Nicholls, Rupert Fraser, Peter McCallum. The first two of these knew of course where I was, the third almost certainly did. They were, all three, chivalrous gentleman. They all loved me. I was sad that they should. I was proud that they did. It was inconceivable that any one of the three should have betrayed me to Gard or to Jean Hannay: as inconceivable as that one of them had pulled that trigger. That left the Crask servants. Mariota had said that they were totally to be trusted. Perhaps in the ordinary way she was right. But I did not suppose that she had ever seen any of them drunk, nor being offered bribes larger than a year's wages. I had never seen any of them drunk, either, but I had seen drunks in the streets of Sydney, and heard their shameless ravings; it was obviously possible that my hiding place had been discovered at the cost of a bottle of whisky.

I found that a new mood had taken hold of me, which I hated. I found that I did not dare to trust anybody. Not gentle Mariota, nor her vague and enthusiastic father. Not the three young men who were suffering with a love for me which might, perhaps, have unhinged one of them. Not the Crask servants – not any of them, at all.

I could have stayed safely in Crask, perhaps, in a room looking inwards, taking my exercise between bed and dressing-table, breathing fresh air through a window; that would be no better than death. And, if a Crask servant had in truth been bought, I might be no safer there than in the park at Glengard.

I needed another hiding place. What I would do when I was hidden in it, was another problem for another day. Charles Gard would have to come out of hiding at last; it could not be so very many days before he did. When he did, the whole situation would be changed. I might still be under threat, but it would be a different sort of threat, and if I ran away, it would be in a new direction.

Perhaps my wits were blunted by that bullet slamming into the oak-tree; perhaps they were sharpened. At any rate, it

171

was the middle of the morning before I saw what I must do; but, when I saw it, it was inescapably right.

A little before noon, I went up to the sunny boudoir of the Countess of Crask. I made sure that we were quite alone – that there were no servants anywhere near, that nobody would hear a word of what we said.

I told her my story. I thought that, in doing so, I had killed her. She moaned, and clutched her brow and then her breast; she went chalk-white, and seemed to struggle for breath. I cursed myself for my thoughtlessness, in visiting my troubles on so frail a lady. But she had smelling-salts by, and something of a dreadful colour out of a bottle; and then, in a voice that was weak but perfectly clear, she said that she had known I was in deep trouble, though she had not known exactly what the trouble was, and was hoping that I would tell her.

As firmly as Mariota, she swore that her servants were trustworthy. As firmly as myself, she refused to believe in treachery from Geoffrey Nicholls, or Rupert Fraser, or Peter McCallum.

She said, 'Lord Gard and that dreadful Jean Hannay must have realised, or guessed, that you were not with your uncle and aunt, dear. Where else would they think to look for you? Where but here? They must know – the whole glen knows – how much we love you. Though it had been a joy to have you here, Bella, it was probably not a good place for you to come. We must think of somewhere else. I must think. When I have thought of a safe place for you, I will tell you about it, and no one else. Not my husband, not my daughter. They would both die rather than deliberately bring any harm to you, dear, but they are both – you may perhaps have noticed – they are both inclined to be absent-minded. At once vague and impulsive. My husband's brain is forever *churning* and *seething* with ideas, so that he is sometimes not closely in touch with the things that are happening round him. He rises quite above his surroundings! And then you see, in conversation with somebody, he might *blurt out* . . . In all innocence, you understand! They say that walls have ears. I think that, in a place like this, the trees and rocks have them. I have never, you know, had any secrets from my husband – I have never had anything to make a secret of! But now we shall be conspirators, dear. I shall rack my brains! I only wish I had more of them . . . You shall take a pony from the stables, and ride away with two saddlebags. And, even if anybody sees you go, they will not know where you have gone! Perhaps you should start off in the wrong direction, even if it means you give yourself further to ride . . .'

I blessed my good fortune, that there was somebody in the world on whose goodwill I could completely rely. I did so doubly, because it was the only good fortune I had.

For a lady who seemed to live in a placid ivory tower, Lady Crask thought long, hard, and to the best possible effect.

She remembered a croft that had stood empty for several years. It was on the edge of the Crask estates, near the march with Glengard land. It was out of sight of any other habitation – the chimney could smoke, and no one would see. Probably few people even knew of its existence. The last tenant had been idle and feckless – he had let the land grow sour, and the windows fall in, and he had not paid his rent. I guessed – though no word of this was said – that the landlord had been absent-minded and unhelpful. Lord Crask had not been diligent in trying to find another tenant; and no farmers had rushed forward to occupy a tumbledown little house, and a farm that could never be made to pay.

There was a roof and a fireplace. What more did I need, in the glorious weather of late summer? It was fortunate that I was what I was, a colonial tomboy, and my father's daughter.

There was a well. Its water was accounted good.

I could take food for a day or two. Thereafter, the Countess would arrange for food to be taken in baskets to another farm, not far away; the folk there were very honest, very old, very deaf, and very short-sighted. They would accept the duty of giving to a lady on a pony a basket of foodstuffs every two or three days. They would not know my name. They would not see which way I went. They would not tell anything to anybody, because they would not have anything to tell. Their farm would be my post office, also – I could receive messages from the Countess, and send messages to her. I would not receive messages from anybody else, because nobody else would know that I was there.

I was to drop off the face of the earth, until it seemed wise to do something else.

The Countess gave me very exact directions. I needed them, as we agreed that I should leave Crask before dawn, and arrive at the croft as soon as possible after it. I was startled at the accurate detail of the Countess's memory – she could not have been to that croft for fifteen years, yet she remembered every corner in the road to it.

'I have nothing to do but remember, dear,' she said. 'Since I cannot go about our country in the body, I do so in the spirit. The walls I jump, on the horse of my day-dreams! Really it is much more satisfactory than jumping real walls on real horses, which I *never* had the courage to do . . .'

After the grooms had stumped away from the stables (earlier than they would have done from any other stables that I knew) I made sure that there was a saddle and bridle where I could find them, and that the pony I had chosen could be got at without the other horses being too much disturbed. I smuggled a pair of saddlebags up to my bedroom, and hid them in the back of the wardrobe behind the dresses which Mariota had lent me. I felt wretched at not taking Mariota into my confidence, when she had done so much for me. But what her mother had said was true – distracted by fairy music, she might give something away.

At Crask, there were not the teeming servants of Glengard; and the few that there were did not materialise, late at night, round every corner. The moment they could, they took to the bottle or the bed. I had not the least difficulty getting out unseen and unheard, dressed in an old riding-habit of Mariota's, and dragging the saddle-bags behind me. Though lately I had been spoiled, I was well able to put a saddle and bridle on a pony, as I was of brushing mud off his legs, or picking stones out of his feet.

And, thanks to the Countess's directions, I was well able to find my road in the dark.

I had not minded getting out of bed in the pitch dark. I had not had any difficulty waking when I had told myself to wake. Often and often, when Papa took me fishing or wildfowling, we were in position before first light. There were advantages to my strange education.

I went very slow and careful, keeping to the road as long as it served me, and then to well-marked tracks. The sky began to pale, and I saw where I was. The croft I was bound for was not so very far from the Urquharts'; it was not so very far from the place where the rope had brought Marmalade down.

The Urquharts. Those skinny, friendly children. It came to me that I had other friends that I could trust. It came to me that those children could be very useful.

I went to the Urquharts' croft, and found that heroic household already astir. Peggy, the eldest child, was feeding hens with corn from a basket; Jaikie was struggling towards the croft with a bucket of water from the well, most of which he was spilling on the ground or on his bare feet; wee Morag was picking blackberries from a clump of brambles. They all came running when they saw me, Peggy spilling her corn, Jaikie his water, and Morag her berries.

I remembered that they did not know who I was. They had been told, but they had thought it was a joke.

I scrambled off the pony, and shook hands with them all. Morag tried to curtsey, and in doing so fell over, which Jaikie thought the funniest thing he had ever seen in his life.

I said that I was Mary McNeish. (Mary McNeish was the nurserymaid, in Government House in Sydney.) I said that I was fifty years old. Peggy looked a little doubtful, but the others accepted this – anybody over the age of fifteen was as good as fifty to them. I said that I was setting up house in the tumbledown croft nearby, which the Earl of Crask was letting me use because nobody else wanted it. I said that I was hiding from a wicked Indian prince, who wanted me as a slave. I remembered some of my childhood reading, and gave him a curly black beard, and an evil glint in his eye, and a private army of gigantic blackamoors. Becoming a little carried away, I said that he always rode a huge white elephant, with which he often trampled people to death if they annoyed him; I said that he wore a turban three feet high, with a diamond in the front as big as a whaup's egg.

They wanted to know the prince's name. I was gravelled for a moment. For some reason I was perfectly unable to

175

think of a name. I said at last that he was called Prince Marmalade. I thought that they had never eaten marmalade, or even heard of it; they accepted it as a name for an Indian prince.

I said that the prince was at home in his palace in India, but that he had sent spies to find me. They would be disguised, I said, to look like quite ordinary, respectable people. Did the Urquhart bairns want me to be captured, and carried away screaming, to be the slave of a cruel prince in India? They did not. Then they must be my guards. They must keep hidden themselves, but watch the ways to my new dwelling, and warn me if anybody came close – anybody at all, whoever they were, whatever they looked like.

They were delighted to be involved in this adventure. They promised faithfully that the Duke of Lomond himself would come nowhere near my house without their warning me.

I felt a little guilty, at spinning them so ludicrous a yarn, and seeing them accept it all so trustingly. But the truth would have been harder for them to believe.

When the moment came to say goodbye, wee Morag visibly positioned herself to attempt another curtsey. Jaikie began to giggle, predicting another tumble. I predicted it too, so, to forestall it, I seized Morag and gave her a kiss. Peggy then rushed up to me, crying that, as she was the elder, she deserved a bigger kiss. I tried to give her a kiss of exactly the same size, if kisses came in sizes like gloves, so as not to wound Morag's feelings. I then wondered about Jaikie. He had quite stopped giggling; he was blushing scarlet. I thought that he wanted a kiss, but that he also saw a need to be manly and aloof.

I said, 'Since I have kissed your sisters, Jaikie, it is only polite if I kiss you too. And, since your sisters have kissed me, it is only polite if you kiss me too.'

He looked only half convinced.

I said, 'It is very manly to kiss ladies. Gentlemen are allowed to do it, if they are gallant, and brave, and have good manners.'

So Jaikie kissed me, and I kissed Jaikie, and I felt a wave of love for these skinny and splendid children.

I rode away to the tumbledown farm, feeling happier than I had felt since the eve of my birthday ball.

*

It was better and worse than I had expected.

It was indeed a lost little place. I had not known it existed, though as a child I had thought to know every yard of the Crask estate. It was not a mile from the Urquharts' croft, yet it might have been on a different planet. It was not half a mile from the farm which was to be my post office and victualling point, but from neither dwelling would you have known that the other was there.

That was good. Good also was a little high-walled paddock where I could put the pony. There was grazing for him there for a few days: not more, but so much. If I were to be there for more than a few days, feeding the pony would become a problem; but since Charles must reappear, and I change my plans, that problem would solve itself.

The situation was perfect; the pony was hidden and comfortable. The house was not perfect; and though I was hidden I was not likely to be comfortable. The accommodation was very much like that in the castle on the island in the Falls of Gard – one room, and the rest a ruin. Trodden earth for a bed, and a hole in the wall for a window. Well, I had slept hard in Australia often enough, and the weather was still glorious. I spread a rug, and that was my bed. I drew water from the well, for the pony and myself, and that was my bath and my drink. I unpacked what I had brought – food, a few clothes, a toothbrush – and that was my worldly goods.

My housekeeping completed, I contemplated the result. The utter absurdity of it all set me between laughter and tears. I had no business to be who I was: but, since I was who I was, I had no business to be here. If I was not here, somebody would be shooting at me with a rifle, which was all because I was who I was. . . .

I lay hard that night, which was nothing to me. I lay safe, which was everything to me.

I dreamed of Australia. I woke in the dawn, cold and cramped, with a perfect and sweet and bitter recollection of my dream. My life there had been supremely safe, with a few moments of exciting peril. My life here was supremely perilous, with a few moments of uncomfortable safety.

I blessed the thought of the Urquhart bairns, patrolling the frontiers of my ragged little kingdom.

I had learned in Australia how to lay and light a campfire, and to boil a can of water on a pile of sticks. I had learned how to choose the wood so as to make no smoke: for, in the outback, a column of smoke may repel insects, but attract visitors even less welcome. Though I knew my fortress was invisible, I wanted to take no avoidable risk. I remembered Papa saying that, in battles, scores and hundreds and thousands of lives were saved, by generals who refused to take avoidable risks; I had only one life to save, but it still seemed sweet to me.

I made my fire in one of the ruined rooms, where my chimney was the open sky. I was content with that. When I smelled my bacon frying, I was content with everything. The sound and smell of bacon frying over a campfire under a clear dawn sky – that was a part of some of my most glorious memories. It was impossible not to be happy. It was impossible not to forget that I had nothing, nothing, to be happy about.

I cooked my breakfast, and ate it with an appetite that astonished me, and cleared the things away. I drew a bucket of water from the well, to wash my breakfast things; I drew another for the pony. He was content; I thought the grazing was better in that little scrubby paddock, than what he was used to at Crask.

I twitched straight the rug upon which I had slept. I collected an armful of sticks for my next fire. I contemplated my kingdom, and decided that I had finished my housework. There was absolutely no more to be done. There was no broom, to sweep the floor with. There was no furniture to dust. God knew there was no silver to polish. The contrast with life at Glengard struck me comically, and not so comically. I thought about that for a little, and then wondered what to do. This was an aspect of my life in hiding which I had not properly considered – how was I to fill the day?

The problem solved itself in the middle of the morning. I was on my way to talk to the pony, for lack of anybody else to talk to, and at a great distance I saw Jaikie Urquhart's carroty head. He was going on all fours, very fast; I supposed he imagined he was invisible; he was getting the utmost out of the task which I had set him, which was exactly what I would have done at his age. He arrived at the farmhouse so out of breath, that it was a long time before he could speak. When he did so, it was to say that a man was coming towards the farmhouse, alone, on foot, going very gentle, as though he did not wish to be seen or heard.

I thought quickly: there might be many reasons for a man approaching the farmhouse stealthily, and they might have nothing to do with me. But it seemed likely that his reasons had everything to do with me. A messenger from Lady Crask? No, we had made a different and much better arrangement. Who, then? Who could know where I was?

I was puzzled, and frightened, but at least I knew what to do. I told Jaikie to hide himself, and especially to hide that head of his that could be seen a mile away. He grinned, in pure excitement, and scampered away out of sight. Then I hid myself, inside a clump of hazel bushes that must have grown up since the farm was let go; I remembered that my own head could be seen a mile away.

Crouching and waiting, with a sensation of insects exploring down the back of my neck, I suddenly cursed myself for not having taken the most obvious precautions. Though whoever came would not see me, he would know I was living in the house. My rug was spread on the floor, with the saddlebags beside it. In the saddlebags were female clothes, and, though I had not brought anything grand, they were not the clothes of a tinker woman. My breakfast campfire was still warm. The pony was in the paddock.

Who could be coming? How could he know where to come? I crouched lower in the hazels, and peeped through the leaves at the path which led to the house.

And then I almost jumped out of my skin, and out of my hiding-place. A man had prowled up, not on the path but beside it, in the cover of the scrubby whin and furze and hazel which covered the ground. His way had taken him almost by the clump in which I was hiding. If he had chosen a different route, even by a couple of yards, he would have come behind me, and seen the lion-colour of my hair.

I knew the man, though he was half hidden from where I

179

crouched. I would not have believed that he could have moved so skilful and so stealthy. I was completely astonished, when I saw who it was.

It was Sir Archibald Hannay, who I had thought was my friend.

Chapter 9

Perhaps Sir Archibald Hannay was my friend. Perhaps it was as my friend that he came so stealthily. Perhaps it was not so that he would be unseen by me, but so that he would be unseen by my enemies. Perhaps he was now in the confidence of the Countess of Crask; he had gone to her, knowing as well as I did how much she loved me, knowing that I was in the greater danger because his wife had disappeared. She had understood that he was to be trusted, that he wished me well. He was come now with a new warning, with the offer of another and better hiding place, with something for my help and comfort. He had suspected himself watched, followed – perhaps by stalkers or shepherds from Glengard, perhaps by his own people who had been bought by Glengard gold. So he had come creeping to my croft, going like a spider and like a snake, going so much more skilfully than one would have thought possible for a fat middle-aged man.

It could all be so. It could be profoundly otherwise. I had no idea what to think. I crouched, and watched him. I thought he must hear the thudding of my heart. I thought an army of insects had now invaded the back of my neck.

He was watching the croft, as motionless as I. He was watching for me, as intently as I was watching him. He was hatless; the morning sun gleamed on the bald patch on the back of his head, which he had incompletely covered with the hair that remained to him.

Now that he was here, unobserved as he thought, why did he not march up to the door and knock on it? Why did he stay crouched behind a clump of furze, the sun bright on his bald patch?

He could have no conceivable reason to come to this place, except to see me. He could have no conceivable way of knowing that I was here, except from the Countess of Crask.

181

I could think collectedly enough, to be sure of those two points. There was much that he might wish to say to me. There was much that I might wish to hear from him. The warning he had given me was proof of his friendship. That he was in Lady Crask's confidence, was proof of his friendship. It was almost certainly safe for me, wise for me, to emerge from my cllump of hazels and greet him as the friend he was.

Why was he hiding behind the furze? Was he hiding from me? Why would he hide from me, if he was my friend?

As I did not know what to do, I thought it best to do nothing. He seemed to have unlimited time. God knew, so did I. To rush out now was an avoidable risk. To sit mouse-quiet, and wait upon events, was only a waste of the time of which I had far too much.

By and by he took a long and slow look round. He turned to face me. I could not well see his face, because of the broad leaves of the hazel. I could not read the expression of his face. I was sure he could not see me; he did not see me. He crept to the door of the croft, keeping low – keeping, I saw, out of the line of the single narrow window. He was like a thief. He could not be a thief. He was like a spy. Could he be a spy? On me? Why?

At the door he straightened. He looked round again, all round, slowly. He stood as though listening. He pressed his ear to the door. He stood so for a long time, listening. He put his hand to the latch of the door, and opened it suddenly. After a long moment, he went in.

He would see the rug and the saddlebags. He would see the clothes in the saddlebags. He would see, in the next and roofless room, a recent fire, and feel warm ashes.

He must have known already that I was living in the croft. That knowledge would be confirmed. He would assume that I was taking exercise, or off upon an errand. Getting food from the farm, perhaps, or sending a message to Lady Crask. He would leave a note. Or he would await my return. How long would he wait? An hour? All day? All day and night? Was I to be a prisoner in my clump of hazel for thirty-six hours?

He was inside the tumbledown house for four or five minutes. In that time, he could have seen everything that was to be seen, ten times over. When he came out he was still stealthy, alert, suspicious. It was still perfectly impossible to guess whether he was hiding from me, or hiding, on my behalf, from somebody else.

It seemed highly important to me to find out, if I could, what Sir Archibald was about. It seemed highly important to do so, if I could, without his knowing that I was doing so. I decided that, when he left, I would follow. On foot? My ankle was still unreliable. He had not walked all the way from Achmore. Somewhere within walking distance he had a horse, or a groom with two horses, or a carriage of some kind.

I saw what I must do, and I wondered if I could do it.

He left, going as stealthily as he had come. He went along the side of the farm track that led to the unmade little road by which I had arrived.

As soon as he was out of sight, I rose stiffly from my crouch in the hazels, and ran as best I could to the little walled paddock. I threw the saddle on the pony. With fingers that were slow because of my haste, I pushed the bit in the pony's mouth, and pulled the bridle over his head, and fastened the buckles of nose-band and throat-lash. He expected to be mounted, but I led him. I went slow, because Sir Archibald was going slow. As far as I could, I kept the pony's feet off dead sticks on the path.

It was an absurd idea. It was impossible that I should follow him, unseen and unheard, leading and then riding a pony. Perhaps he had already, from hiding, seen me go by, and was now following me. My plan had seemed so good. Now it seemed downright silly.

Then, from a clump of bracken, rose Peggy Urquhart, her thin little face (not perfectly clean) split by an excited grin. She gestured to me to stop. She put a finger to her lips. She pointed down the track. Fifty yards away, Jaikie emerged from a ditch. He beckoned. Peggy nodded vigorously, gesturing me to go on. As soon as I started to do so, she disappeared again into her clump of bracken, and a moment later I saw her speeding along beside the track, through and behind the scrubby undergrowth.

Jaikie's grin was as broad and excited as his sister's. He did exactly as she had done – gestured to me to stop, put his finger to his lips, and pointed forward. Thirty yards on, perhaps, wee Morag's head appeared from behind a tree. She waved furiously. Jaikie's gesture told me not to move. Morag disappeared. After a moment she reappeared, and beckoned to me. Jaikie waved me on. He disappeared, in his turn, and I saw glimpses of his red-fox hair in the undergrowth.

I knew that I should see Peggy beyond Morag, Jaikie beyond Peggy, Morag again beyond Jaikie. They were leapfrogging. They were handing me on, one to another, keeping sight of Sir Archibald, keeping out of his sight, keeping me out of his sight. It seemed to me that their tactics were brilliant: and it was not anything that anybody had taught them, but something they had devised entirely on their own.

It was all for my sake. I nearly wept, to think how clever they were being, and how far and fast they were running, for my sake. It was nice to think that, at the same time, they were getting enormous fun out of it.

They led me to the little road, and on along the road, starting me and stopping me, and keeping me quiet, and hurrying me up and slowing me down; and I thought that my father could never have commanded more skilful scouts, or more faithful soldiers.

There came a corner, and all three small heads rising from behind a rock. Three arms waved to stop me, and then beckoned me to come gently on.

I came up to them, and, peeping round the shoulder of scree where the road turned, saw what they saw. Some way off there was a groom, standing at the heads of two horses. Nearer, but not very near, there was a pony trap drawn up at the side of the road. I knew the trap, and its driver. Sir Archibald, on foot, was deep in talk with the driver. The pony and the trap came from Crask, and the driver was Mariota.

Once again a flood of possibilities poured into my head. Mariota was on the road between Crask and Glengard. There were a thousand innocent reasons why she might be on that road, bound for Glengard on any of a thousand errands, or for some other place reached by the road. She had met Sir Archibald by chance, and had naturally stopped to talk. She would be asking if there were news of Jean; she would be offering him any help that it was in the power of Crask to give. Yes, it might be so, and it might be far otherwise. I was completely puzzled. Where stood those two? Were they my friends? Were they friends of one another? If they were allies, in what cause, whose cause?

I was nearly certain that they had met not by chance but by arrangement. What arrangement? Why such an arrangement? Why meet in a secret and lonely place? Charles and Jean had done so, but they had had good reason. Mariota and Sir Archibald could have no such reason. What reason, then? They were neighbours. They knew one another. If they had things to discuss, they could discuss them in the great comfort of Achmore, or the less great comfort of Crask. But they were meeting near the place where I was hiding. Was that coincidence? Could it be? How could it not be?

Sir Archibald waved to his groom. The groom led the two horses towards the pony trap. Sir Archibald mounted, then the groom. They rode away along a track which led towards Achmore.

Sir Archibald was going home. There was no purpose in following him further. I would see the horse disappear into the stable, and the man into the house; and I would be no nearer knowing whether it was wise or unwise, safe or unsafe, to knock on the door of that house.

Was Mariota going home?

Two hundred yards on, the road forked. The right fork led in the direction of Crask, the left towards Glengard. I watched Mariota shake the reins; I thought I heard her call something to the pony. The trap jolted into motion, over the ruts of the unmade road.

Mariota forked left. She was not going home.

The children could help me no more – even they could not keep up with a trotting pony. I thanked them quickly, and kissed them all three, which took a little longer, as Jaikie was now a convert to kissing. Then, with Mariota out of sight, I mounted the pony and trotted after her. I did not know what I should see. I did not know if I should see anything. It was still entirely possible that her errand was innocent, and her meeting with Sir Archibald accidental. I deeply hoped that it was, and that I would soon learn that it was.

I could keep well behind, because she could not leave the road. She would not hear my pony's hoofbeats over the rattle of her own, and the rumble of the wheels of the trap. I could follow without her seeing or hearing me. I was frightened of what I myself might see and hear.

We were already on Glengard land, and approaching the castle from the west. This was low ground, fat farming land; there were several crofts, and a few more substantial tenant farms. Fifty souls, perhaps, lived between the castle and the point which Mariota had reached. She might have business with any of them. A nostrum for a gouty foot, recommended by her mother – that was the kind of errand she might have. That was the kind of errand I prayed she had.

I reached a corner. I reined into a walk, and peeped round the corner as carefully as I had peeped round every corner. The pony-trap should have been in full view, two or three hundred yards ahead. But the road was empty. I blinked, in disbelief, until I saw that another, smaller road ran off among trees to the left. It was a way I had never been. I had no idea where the road led. We were far from Callo; this was a region I had never explored. I went slow and careful to the junction of the roads, and slow and careful up the side-road between the trees.

Mariota was ahead of me. She was walking her pony now, because of the roughness of the road. I could not imagine where we were heading. I could go silent now, on the grassy verge of the road. The only sound we made came from the chink of the rings of my pony's bit. I could hear Mariota clearly from round the corner – the banging and jolting of the trap.

The noise stopped. She had stopped. I jumped off my pony, led him into the trees, and tied him up by his reins. I ran to the corner, as fast as my ankle would let me, silent on the grass verge.

Mariota had pulled up in front of a strange little building, which I suddenly remembered having heard about. The Reverend Doctor Pericles Davidson had mentioned it, as one of the curiosities of the estate. It was a chapel, built during the Commonwealth, in Cromwell's time, for some strange and extreme religious sect. It was long disused, because the sect had lost its followers. Probably it had long been deconsecrated, if it was ever consecrated. I thought it was not used for anything, because it was far from anywhere.

It seemed Mariota was using it for something.

As she got down from the trap, the door of the chapel opened. A man came out. He was limping, and walking with a stick, just as I had done a few days earlier. He shook Mariota's hand with great warmth. It was my husband.

I wondered fleetingly how he had hurt himself. I was not deeply interested in the answer, and I had far more important questions to ask myself.

What was happening here?

The answer was obvious, but it might be wrong.

If the obvious was right, this was worse than my worst imagining. If the obvious was right, then Mariota had betrayed me to my husband, and would do so again. I had been tricked into going to Crask, a lamb to the shambles. I was brought there to be killed.

Why?

Was Mariota so fond of Jean Hannay, that she was helping the lovers to dispose of an inconvenient wife?

If so, why in God's name did she confer with Sir Archibald Hannay, so near the place where I was hiding? Hannay's role in the whole affair had seemed at first completely innocent, and most easy to understand. After his stealthy visit to the croft, it had become puzzling. Now it was utterly baffling.

I could not understand how the three could be allies. I could not understand what game Mariota was playing. It seemed that there was now no fairy music filling her inner ear. She knew exactly what she was doing. But I could not for the life of me begin to guess what that was.

Charles and Mariota talked long and earnestly. They were full in the cleared open space in front of the chapel; I could not get near close enough to them, to hear what they were saying. I could see their faces. After a warm and smiling greeting, they were deeply serious.

I had a blinding flash of insight. As an old friend – as, at one time, something like a sweetheart – she could talk to Charles as no one else could. She was pleading with Charles for me. She was pleading for my safety.

How had she known where to find him, when nobody knew – when she herself had said she did not know, only the day before? He sent her a message. He wanted her help. But she would not help him, because she was helping me.

And her business with Hannay? Was she pleading with

187

him, too, on my behalf – begging him to look after his wife better?

Why then did he prowl to my croft, like a thief, like a spy? How did he know where to find me?

It did not do. I tried to cling to my new theory, but it did not do.

Charles now presumably knew, from Mariota, where my hiding place was. So it was no longer a hiding place, and it was urgent that I should find another.

Callo was still no use to me. My aunt and uncle would curry favour with the Marquess by telling him I was there, or by sending me back to him.

None of the neighbouring lairds was any good to me.

There were other tumbledown crofts, but none of them was any good to me without an arrangement like that the Countess of Crask had devised, for me to get food.

An idea blinked at me, from the very edge of my mind. It was an idea so ludicrous, so outrageous, that I pushed it away. It would not go away. It blinked at me, and blinked at me, a little brighter with each blink, until it was as bright as the lighthouse in Sydney Harbour.

I must go to the one place in the world where no one would think of looking for me. The one place that no one would guess that I would choose. A place so huge that, though it was full of servants, I could hide in safety for ever.

I must go to my new home. I must go to Glengard Castle.

I thought about this preposterous idea, even as I watched my husband and my closest friend deep in conversation about God knew what.

The servants? I thought some of them were coming to like me. I had felt warmth, goodwill, a welcome when I reappeared downstairs after my fall on Marmalade. I had treated them politely, as I had been brought up to do – Papa would have been seriously angry if any of us had been needlessly rude to the humblest Aborigine stock-boy. I learned their names. Mrs McKay in the laundry thought I was a kind of sorcerer, because I had suggested moving some mangles. Mr Blair the head gardener treated me with the cautious friendliness which is the most that any head gardener commonly allows himself. The grooms were more openly friendly, in the way of grooms, and they seemed to approve of the way I rode a horse. Well, all of that was all ways gratifying, and it did not add up to a single person that I could truly say that I trusted. How could it? They were all utterly dependent on Charles.

And then I remembered one who was even more dependent than any of the rest: because he was only a young boy, because he was an orphan. The one person at Glengard that I could rely on completely, with muddy gaiters, and a rebellious thatch of hair, and a tweed cap too big for him.

Geordie Gault lived with his mother and sisters, in a cottage among trees which could be seen from the top terrace. It was a place which could be reached unseen, in the dawn or in the gloaming. That was good. Geordie was a high-spirited, adventurous laddie, no respecter of persons (except Mr Blair); I would have bet everything I had – if I had had anything – that he knew ways in and out of the castle, which were not the ways used by respectable visitors, or servants going about their lawful business. That was good. He and I had made one another laugh, so that we became fast friends on the instant. That was best of all.

It was curious to find that I had four friends whom I truly loved and trusted; and three of them were skinny little tattiebogles of crofter children, and one was a gardener's boy in muddy gaiters. But so it was; and I thanked God for the friends I had.

I considered the practical problems. There were Mariota's clothes in the tumbledown house, and the saddle-bags, and the cooking things. I thought they were best where they were; I thought they would come to no harm. If anybody else prowled up to the place, they would see those things, and conclude that I was living there. It was an excellent idea that people should think I was living there. I was all in favour of them watching that place, instead of watching other places.

There was the pony, and his saddle and bridle. I would need the pony to get to Glengard. I could hide the tack under a bush, and let the pony go in the park. When people caught him in the morning, they could think what they liked. They would not think that I had ridden him to the castle. They might think some boy had borrowed him from Crask – some scamp from a farm, or an adventurous lad like Geordie Gault. They might most reasonably think that the pony himself had grown tired of the sour grazing and slovenly management of Crask, and had taken himself to greener pastures. It did not matter what anybody thought, because nobody would think me so demented as to ride him up to the castle.

Once in, I could find places to hide. Geordie Gault might have some good ideas. I could creep down to the kitchens, and find plenty to eat. I could wash and even bathe. I would manage very well. It would only be for a few days at the most, until Charles came out of hiding. And then we should see what we should see.

I would not eat or drink until very late at night. That would not kill me. I had gone hungry on expeditions with Papa in Australia, and simply made up for it later. I blessed my hearty campfire breakfast; it would keep me going at least until midnight.

At last Charles and Mariota were smiling and shaking hands. No more than that, but I thought the smiles were warm. Mariota turned her pony-trap, and started back towards the track through the wood. Charles limped back into the chapel. I retreated further back into the cover of the trees and undergrowth, sure that, in the deep shade, neither my pony nor myself would be seen by somebody in the full sunlight, who was steering a difficult course over rough ground. Mariota went by, rattling and jolting. My pony might have neighed, and I thought she would not have heard.

It was only after she had gone by, that I wondered whether Charles was alone in that strange little chapel. Had he Jean Hannay with him? If so, did Mariota know that? If Jean was not there, where was she?

Thinking of Jean made me think of Sir Archibald – made me wonder all over again, and as uselessly as before, what in Heaven's name he was about, and where in Heaven's name he stood; and what Mariota was about, and where she stood.

And thinking about them made me think about myself, and I was filled with a great rage that I was driven to hiding, and creeping to and fro, and crawling like a thief into a house that was supposed to be my home.

It was rage or self-pity. No other mood was possible. I did not care for self-pity. I did not care for rage, either, but it was the lesser evil.

I gave Mariota time to get well clear; then I led the pony

out of the wood. The wood was a perfectly safe place to be, and no hungrier than anywhere else; but it gave me an uneasy and unpleasant feeling to be so close to Charles. I rode away, and towards my supposed home. The country rose and fell, and rose again towards the eminence on which the castle stood. The way was new to me, but the Australian bush had taught me to steer safely cross any country, and to know always what direction I was taking. It was empty, and very beautiful; I had left the fat farmland behind and below me. I saw no one. If I was seen, it could only have been from a distance. I was not like to be recognised, in a borrowed habit and on a borrowed pony, and with my hair tucked up under my hat. I wondered, as I rode, how I should repay the Urquhart children, who had helped me so magnificently, and who had shown such quickness and intelligence. I had nothing to repay them with, except more kisses. They would have to serve, until I could come by something more substantial. They would have to serve for Geordie Gault, too; but perhaps he would like it better if I made him laugh again.

I remembered my own laughter as something from another life.

I came over the brow of a hill, and saw the castle for the first time. It was a great way off. It was reared up like something monstrous and forbidding, dominating the country round. In the brilliant late-summer sun, all the air between was shimmering, and the castle itself seemed to rest on a shimmering, insubstantial base.

I saw that I was not going to be able to ride nearly as close as I had hoped. Though there was the cover of the gardens, and of clumps of trees in the park, there were large areas of empty hillside in full view of hundreds of windows. Well, I would let the pony go and I would walk. If my ankle pained me, I would walk slowly.

The timing was important, and I must give it thought. I must not attempt to approach the castle until it was almost full dark, though my habit was dark-coloured, and my betraying hair was imprisoned in my hat. But I must get to the Gaults' cottage before Geordie was sent to bed by his mother. I guessed that would be early, because Geordie's working day started early – there were hosts of seedlings and young plants in the greenhouses which had to be watered before the full heat of the day. Last thing, just before he went to bed, I guessed Geordie would have chores round and about the cottage – a fresh armful of firewood to be brought in for the morn's breakfast, hens to be shut up against foxes and hunting cats, a bucket of water from the well, so that he could wash his face before he said his prayers – very much the kind of chores, I thought, that I had seen the Urquhart children performing, when Morag tried to curtsey and tumbled over. That moment seemed a lifetime ago.

My breakfast of fried bacon seemed a lifetime ago, too.

I rode into a fair-sized wood half hidden from the castle by a shoulder of hill. It was still a long way from the fence of the park, but it was the nearest I could go on horseback. There were many spyglasses kept on windowsills and window-seats in the higher rooms, intended for looking at birds, and inspecting the herds of deer in the park, and spotting for poachers; and they could very well be used for spotting runaway Marchionesses who were creeping back to burgle the castle.

I dismounted stiffly; I seemed to have been in that saddle for a very long time. I would have liked to let the pony go, to enjoy the freedom of all the grass of Glengard; but being a friendly animal he would have stayed near me, and probably followed me when I moved, which might have given me away to a watcher even without a spyglass. I tied him up by his reins in the shade, where he was pretty well hidden and could reach some grass which he approved of. I took off the saddle, and hid it in the middle of a clump of hazel. I remembered that it was a Crask saddle; looking at it closely, I saw that it was a Crask saddle; I thought it was on the point of falling to pieces, through not having been looked after properly – the leather was so dry through lack of dressing that it was almost crumbling.

From time to time I moved the pony, when he seemed to grow bored with one patch of grass and to covet another; it was the least I could do for a beast who had served me so nobly. But most of that long, long afternoon and early evening I sat with my back to a tree, with my thoughts swirling round in my head like the seagulls over Sydney Harbour.

I tried to count my blessings; I found that – if you stretched

192

the meaning of the word 'blessing' – there were more than I might have supposed. I ticked them off on my fingers:

Nobody in the whole world knew where I was. I might not be safe later, but for the moment I was safe.

I had friends. They were small, and not very clean, and there were only four of them, but they were sure enough my friends.

Though something I did not understand had happened in the Castle of Crask, so that it was no longer a safe place for me to be, but a very dangerous place, still there was one person there to whom I knew I could turn. The Countess might not be a very vigorous ally, but I knew that, if I turned to her, she would help me if she could.

Geoffrey Nicholls? Rupert Fraser? Peter McCallum? They would help me, if they could. They had helped me magnificently, or thought that they were doing so – *surely* they thought that they were doing so? – but I did not see how any of them, or all of them together, could help me now.

Charles would be emerging from the obscurity of that quaint little chapel, into the full glare of the sunlight, into the magnificence of his usual role. He would find it difficult to murder me, with the eyes of hundreds of servants constantly upon him, at least in such crude ways as he had so far tried. This was rather an uncertain and dubious blessing, but I counted it as a blessing, because there were not so very many others, and I wanted to make the list as long as possible, in order to cheer myself up.

I began to count my misfortunes, as a way of passing the time; but the list was immediately so long, and so depressing, that I gave up the attempt. I was still very clear that I preferred anger to self-pity.

As once or twice before, the farcical absurdity of my situation struck me. I suddenly laughed out loud, astonishing the pony, who raised his head from the grass, and turned to look at me in wonder. I suddenly stopped laughing. There was nothing whatever to laugh at. To become hysterical would be exhausting and dangerous.

The sun went down slower than I ever remembered, and I could do nothing except sit and wish that it would hurry up. Then, when it disappeared at last behind the high tops to the west, I wished it had stayed in the sky: because I had committed myself to a strategy which had seemed so wise, so inescapably right, five hours before – and now seemed the most lunatic folly. Well, there I was. Glengard was where I had to go, because I could go nowhere else. And if I spent the night in the open, with or without the pony, the same few blessings might still be there in the morning, but the same misfortunes would all be there too.

I took the bridle off the pony, and hid it with the saddle. He looked at me enquiringly, as though to say, 'Where are we going now?' I slapped him across the rump with the flat of my hand (nothing would have induced me to use a whip on such a creature); I tried to push him physically out into the darkening countryside, with the promise of unlimited sweet grass and fresh water, and several thousand acres in which he could roll; I used some Australian phrases to him, which the grooms in Sydney did not know I was listening to. All to no purpose; wherever I went, he would follow. I supposed he would be found in the morning grazing the rose-beds.

We set off, the pony following me. Sometimes I felt his nose gently nuzzling my shoulder. I knew no more than he did what was going to happen next. His plan was to stay with me, which he had decided was necessary to his happiness. My plan was more complicated. His plan would fail. Probably mine would, too.

That walk was far, far longer than I would have chosen; it was far rougher, too. I was in imminent danger of spraining my ankle again. We had to go slow. We were going to be later than I had meant. Geordie Gault might be in bed and asleep by the time I reached the cottage. I could not know where he slept, or with whom. I was going to lose his help, and I did not think I could manage without his help. Difficulties gibbered at me, like beasts, from the gathering darkness.

The pony followed me into the park. He could do no more harm there than on the open hill, and he would be found and cared for sooner. He did not follow me through a door in the garden wall, although he wanted to. He neighed, in dismay at being left alone in the dark. The evening was absolutely quiet; I thought that neigh must have been heard in Loch-grannomhead. I listened intently, and stared about me. There were no shouts or lanterns. I hugged the pony round the neck, and kissed his nose. I had no more reward for him than I had for the Urquhart children.

That single, reproachful neigh was providential.

I went up a woodland path, within the enormous garden, towards the clearing where the Gaults' cottage was. A small figure came flying down the path towards me, flapping, white, like a ghost. I gulped, but I think only once. I suppose I was harder to see, in my dark riding-habit. He ran almost into my arms. I seized him. I thought I knew him. He gave a high, thin '*Peep*', like a meadow-pipit.

Yes, it was Geordie. He had heard from his bed the neigh of a horse. It had sounded very close, in that breathless evening. It had sounded as though it was inside the garden. Geordie was appalled at the thought of a horse loose at night in that garden – appalled at the damage it would do, the plants it would eat, the footprints it would leave, the glass it would break. Appalled because he had a sort of idea that he might himself have left unlatched one of the doors in the garden wall. He climbed out of the window of the chamber the children shared (as he had often done before) and ran down through the wood to do something about the horse.

He told me all this in a great rush, like the waters of the Falls of Gard in spate. This was partly because he was so relieved that he had nothing to worry about with the pony; partly because he had had a fright, bumping into a dark figure in the dark. He pretended he had not, until I told him I had had a fright, too, seeing a small white ghost rushing at me through the wood. The thought of himself in his nightshirt as a ghost set him giggling, so that at once he was himself again; and that made me myself again.

He could easily smuggle me into the castle.

It was much as I had expected, knowing Geordie, knowing my own adventurous little brothers. There was a little pantry door, used for bringing vegetables in from the kitchen gardens. It had not a lock and key, but a bolt on the inside. By now the bolt would certainly be closed and, if by any chance the kitchen-maid whose task it was had forgotten the bolt, the nightwatchmen would have inspected it, as they did every outside door in the castle. Over the door was a fanlight, with a catch that could be released with a clasp-knife blade.

Geordie could get through that fanlight, climb to the floor, unbolt the door, admit me and a regiment, if I had a regiment.

He had no clasp-knife in his nightshirt. I had none (though time was, in Australia, I would never have stepped out of doors without one). He had one in the cottage. We went softly up the woodland path to the cottage. We went hand in hand; Geordie took my hand in case I was afraid of the dark.

The cottage was all in darkness. A pear-tree was trained up the side. Geordie went up the tree like a spider, and through a window which he had left ajar. Moments later he was beside me in the cottage garden. He took my hand again, in case I got lost in the gardens; and led me through walled gardens, and fruit gardens, and herb gardens, where the brush of my habit-skirt on the plants awoke Australian aromas; and down area steps to a row of underground doors, the last of which was the larder door with the fanlight.

He had so little trouble getting in, that I realised he came this route as a regular thing. I was certain that he did no harm, and stole nothing. It was simply an adventure. In a moment I was inside the cavernous stone-flagged cellar where the vegetables were scrubbed and prepared for the kitchen.

I wondered, for a crazy moment, what changes I would see the need of there.

Geordie was anxious to be back to his bed, before his escapade was discovered. I tried to whisper my thanks. Like most of the Highlanders, even young boys, he hated being thanked. I kissed him, instead. He may have hated that, too, but I could not tell in the dark.

In my previous existence – in one of the previous existences of which I seemed to have had so many – I had most thoroughly explored the castle. This was partly because, if I were to live there, it helped if I knew my way about. It was partly so that I could be a good mistress to it, if the time ever came when I was truly mistress of it. It was partly because I had nothing else to do. Well, the effort was repaid that night, even if it was never to be repaid in any other way, at any other time. In the thick darkness I groped my way confidently to the larders, and so to the store-rooms, and so to the cupboard where candles and matches were kept.

Before I made a light, I looked and listened intently. It was well I did so. I heard the night-watchmen clumping into the kitchen, and saw round the corner the glow of their bull's-eye lanterns.

There were two night-watchmen, called Maitland and Moir, and I knew them both. They had retired from more active jobs, Maitland as a groom and Moir as a gamekeeper. Maitland had never married and Moir was a widower, so to work all night and sleep all day suited them better than other men. They did not prowl. I thought they did not want to catch intruders, but to frighten intruders away. They were thorough but unhurried. They were being unhurried now. I heard the clatter of cutlery on plates. They were helping themselves to supper – or to them, perhaps, breakfast.

From talking to them, I knew their routine. After they had eaten, they would go all round the castle twice, checking all outside doors and windows and bars and bolts. They would stay always together, in case they met trouble. Together they would visit all the public rooms, where the castle treasures were – the antiquities, the massive silver, the French and Italian paintings. They would return to the attic room they shared at sunrise, taking their orders from the sun rather than from any clock.

I had not actually visited their room, but I knew where it was. I knew it would be empty until sunrise. It might be full of the smoke of their pipes, but it would be clean and orderly, because they were clean and orderly. That was one problem solved.

The clatter of their knives and forks made me realise, with sudden agony, that I had not eaten a mouthful since my fried bacon in the early morning. I had forgotten hunger, in excitement and action, and in trying to make plans. Remembering it, I thought I should go mad.

I could smell food, too – a savoury, meaty smell. The cooks had left something for them on a low fire. Knowing the gigantic wastefulness of the castle kitchens, I was sure that what was put out for them would feed a dozen people. That was another problem solved.

These were little problems. I had always supposed they would be easy to solve. The large problems were another matter.

They were taking their time about their meal. They were talking comfortably. I crept nearer, to listen, not because I had a great desire to eavesdrop, but because it would pass the time until I could satisfy my own unendurable hunger. Also I was curious to know what night-watchmen talked about – what two men found to talk about, who spent every waking and sleeping moment together.

They were talking about me. I might have expected that. I supposed that, ever since the night of my disappearance, there had hardly been a conversation in the castle on any other topic.

Maitland, who had the deeper voice, would have it that I had been kidnapped. I was startled to hear that, by his way of it, I was a beauty known far and wide; probably I had been seized on the orders of a London millionaire, or one of those Indian princes.

I almost laughed out loud, to hear my own outlandish story to the Urquhart children coming in all solemnity from old Maitland.

Moir, who came from Glasgow way and had the distinctive speech of those parts, disliked Maitland's theory, because it represented so great a failure on the part of themselves. He held that I had suffered an attack of brain-fever, probably the result of some disease I had contracted in Australia. He lamented that such an awful thing should happen to someone as bonny as myself. He agreed with Maitland's notions about what they called my beauty, but he pooh-poohed the theory of a kidnap.

I thought they had been having the same conversation over their meal, night after night, and that everybody else in the castle had been having it too. I wondered what the majority theory was. I wondered what Mrs Murray the housekeeper thought, and Simpson the whiskered butler, and Mrs McKay in the laundry, and Malcolm Menzies and all my other friends in the stables.

The night-watchmen stumped away with their plates into a scullery, and embarked on their inspection of all the doors in that underground kingdom. I kept without difficulty out of the beams of the bull's-eye lanterns, and, though I was wearing boots, I was careful to make no sound. I thought it would be a good joke to appear to them suddenly – to the one who thought I had been kidnapped, to the one who thought I had wandered off, crazed with brain-fever. They

198

would think I was a ghost. It would be put about everywhere that I was dead. Then, perhaps, if everybody thought I was dead, nobody would go on trying to kill me. It was not a difficult temptation to resist.

I heard the watchmen climbing the stone stairs to the ground floor of the castle. I knew I had the kitchen to myself for three or four hours. I lit a candle, and inspected what had been left on the fire.

I knew that, if I made another plate dirty, questions would be asked – the watchmen would know how many plates they had used, and the scullery-maids would know they had left no dirty plates. The thing was to eat straight out of the cooking-pot, which was an iron cauldron over a darkening fire of sea-coal. It was not elegant; I was past elegance; I had eaten from many a cooking-pot, over a camp-fire in Australia. Food did not taste worse, eaten so; I thought it tasted better.

After a long search, I found a drawer of kitchen spoons (the silver was kept in the butler's pantry, a room as big as a church, of which only he had the key). There were hundreds and hundreds of spoons. I chose one of the biggest, and began shovelling into myself pieces of beef, and potato, and carrot, and turnip, all in the savoury gravy I had smelled.

I burst into silent laughter, as I had in the wood (but this time my mouth was full) at the craziness of this situation. I laughed with pure delight at the size and excellence of my dinner. Large as the cauldron was, I was sure I had visibly lowered the level of its contents. That would not excite any curiosity.

An extra dirty spoon would. To get water for washing it meant turning all manner of wheels and cocks, which I did not properly understand, and thought I never would. I was stopped dead, for the moment, by the problem of one dirty soup-spoon. Probably what I finally did would earn the approval of nobody – I licked the spoon clean, and put it back in the drawer. Even in Australia I had never seen anybody doing that: but the Marchioness of Gard was doing it in her own castle. I began to giggle again, my mood much improved by the excellence of the dinner I had eaten.

My mood was improved, and my brain sharpened. Though my day had been long, I was very wide awake and alert. Though my mind had been churning, my body had been well rested during those crawling hours in the wood. I had the castle to myself, except for two old night-watchmen whom I could see and hear coming from a long way away. I had the freedom of Glengard, until dawn: what use could I put it to?

What had bedevilled my thoughts was my puzzlement, my confusion, my utter ignorance of the motives of so many people. Was it possible that I could use the hours of darkness to come by a little knowledge? Might there be papers, letters, notes in a diary, that would shed some light on all the baffling obscurity?

I thought it likely. Charles and Jean Hannay must sometimes have communicated by note, if only to arrange their meetings. Charles might have destroyed Jean's notes, but I thought that, lover like, he had probably kept them. I thought sourly that they were likely under his pillow, or carried next to his heart. If they were in his bed-chamber, I was not going anywhere near them – I was not going near that part of the house. They would not be in any drawer of any desk in the library or any of the public rooms.

They might be in his business room. I had not been inside that room, but I knew just where it was – I had seen his luncheon carried into it on a tray.

It might be locked. I could only find out by going there and trying the door.

I blew out my candle, and crept up the stone stairs. As a precaution, I searched for and found the watchmen: they were scrutinising with their lanterns the catches of the shutters in the great hall. I went by the picture gallery and the broad arched passages to that inconspicuous door which I knew.

It was not locked.

Of course many drawers might be; and, if there were letters from Jean, they might be in a safe or a strong-box. But perhaps there would be letters from Mariota, or Sir Archibald Hannay, or anybody else under the sun, that might tell me something.

I went in, and shut the door softly behind me. I lit my candle, and held it high. I was surprised. I had expected some masculine 'den', with deep leather chairs and a brass club-fender and a lot of oil-paintings of race-horses. It was very barely furnished, in scrubbed pine. The walls were white. Though it was tidy, there was an air that much business went on here – there were files tied up in ribbon, and massive portfolios and ledgers, and stacks of papers under paper-weights, and on one wall what I took to be a large-scale map of the estate. It was like the battalion office in a barracks.

Opposite the door I had come through, there was another door. It seemed wise to know where it led. I opened it a crack, leaving my candle at the other end of the room, just in case the watchmen had made a sudden flanking movement, and were taking me in the rear. There was nothing to be seen or heard. I went out into a stone-flagged passage which I had not known existed, which led to a flight of narrow stairs which I had not known existed, either (and I thought I had thoroughly explored the castle). I wondered where the stairs led. There might be a time for finding out, but it was not now.

I shut the door, and began to look through the papers on the big, scrubbed-pine desk.

It was all business. None of it meant anything to me whatever. There were figures, and statistics, and accounts, and lists, and measurements, and contracts, and invoices (I knew they were invoices because 'Invoice' was written at the top: I should not otherwise have known). There were letters. They were about farms, rents, repairs, cows and sheep, fishing and shooting rights, horses and harness. There was a file all concerned with the Duke's health – letters from doctors, and reports from specialists, and copies of Charles's replies. I understood the medical terms no more than the legal or financial ones.

'Are you looking to see,' said a voice behind me, 'what you will be worth when you have killed me?'

My back was to the main door. I spun round. In the doorway stood my husband. He must have opened the door very softly, having seen a gleam of light under the door or through the keyhole.

I could not see his face; the light of my candle did not reach so far.

I could see that he carried a heavy stick, with a great knob at the end. I knew the use he intended to put that stick to.

Chapter 10

Charles bent to pick up a dark-lantern, which he had left on the floor just outside the room. He raised it, uncovered the light, and shone the beam on my face. I sat, paralysed by astonishment, full in the glare of the lantern, in front of a letter from an Edinburgh physician saying that the Duke's heart was excellent for his age.

Charles took a half step towards me, holding the lantern, holding the heavy stick with the great knob at the end. His movement broke the spell that was holding me transfixed in the chair. I jumped to my feet, and sped round the table. If my own ankle pained me at all, I did not notice it. I ran to the other door, the smaller door, opposite to the one Charles had used. I left my candle behind. I opened the door, slipped through it, and slammed it behind me. I groped in the dark for key or bolt; there was neither. I ran along the stone passage. In riding boots I could not do so quietly. I kept one hand to the wall so that, in the pitch darkness, I kept straight. I slowed when I judged I was near the foot of the narrow stone stairs I had seen. Groping, I found the newel-post and the bottom of the rail. As I started up the stairs, the door behind me opened, and light from the dark-lantern flooded into the little passage.

Charles had been limping heavily, there at the chapel. I was still limping, but only a little. I was sure I could easily outrun him. Immediately, that was what I must do. It was all I could do. What happened after was another problem for another minute.

I sped up the stairs, my boots clattering on the stone steps, my habit-skirt hampering me. I turned at the top, to see Charles limping to the foot of the stairs and starting up them. I should have liked to throw something, to shatter the glass of his lantern. But I had nothing to throw, and my brothers always truly said that I could not throw straight. Instead I plunged on, along another stone passage, leading I knew not where. It was almost pitch dark in the passage, but as Charles climbed the light strengthened. There were doors in the passage. I did not know to what. I supposed to rooms. Any room would be a trap. I wondered how, if he caught and killed me, he would dispose of the body.

The passage turned right-handed at the end. I went through what I could just see was a massive stone arch. My groping fingers now touched rough, unfaced masonry. I realised I had come into the very oldest part of the castle, which was not used because it was so cold and comfortless, but preserved as a monument. As I ran along, my boot-soles clattering on the granite, the memory jumped into my head – as the most useless thoughts do, at moments of the greatest crisis and danger – that the chaplain had told me the original castle had been built by King Alexander II in the thirteenth century. I wondered what the king would have thought of the wild game of hide-and-seek now being played in the galleries of his fortress. I had *not* thoroughly explored these cavernous guardrooms. Parts were said to be dangerous, and were being restored by the estate masons.

It came to me that the only way out of the ancient keep was the way by which I had come in.

It came to me that Charles had found the night-watchmen, and had sent them to the cellars or to bed.

I ran and ran. I thought I was going round in circles, as I had heard that travellers did who were lost in the Australian bush. Always the glow followed me, coming on and coming on.

Just visible in the deadly glow of that oncoming lantern, I saw a ladder. It was propped against the rough stones of the wall. I could not see what was at the top. If there was nothing – simply the wall – I thought I would be safe at the top from the beam of the lantern.

I wanted to stop running. I had not noticed the pain in my ankle at first. I noticed it now.

I went up the ladder, and found that at the top there was a kind of niche or embrasure, in which I could perch like a bird. Here surely I was safe. But as I was easing myself off the top of the ladder into the embrasure, the dark-lantern came round a corner. I could not see the man behind the lantern. I could hear the uneven thud of limping footsteps, and the sharper tap of the stick. Lantern and man came to the foot of the ladder. And then he did what I might have known he would do – what anybody would have done – what I must have expected, if I had thought for a moment. He shone the light upwards, full in my face.

'Will you come down, or shall I come up?' he said. He was panting.

He had come fast, for a man with so bad a limp.

I was panting too, deeply, with a harsh sound in my throat. I could not at once speak. I did not want to speak. I had nothing to say.

Sitting now securely in the embrasure, some fifteen feet above the floor, I stretched out my foot, and began to push the ladder away from the wall. He made to seize it. Before he could do so; he had to put down his stick and lantern. That gave me time to. push the ladder beyond the vertical, and it crashed onto the flagstones.

'Stalemate,' he said. 'How long do you want to stay there?'

My breathing had steadied, so that I could speak. 'I would sooner die here in peace,' I said with difficulty, 'than by whatever means you have chosen.'

'By whatever means *I* have chosen?' he said, with a sneering ring in his voice. 'I have been preoccupied with keeping myself alive, since your friends brought my horse down and damaged my knee. Or did you stretch that rope yourself? Was that a trick you learned in Australia?'

This contemptuous attempt at bluff threw me into a rage. 'It passes belief that you should say such a thing,' I shouted. 'You who brought my horse down with a rope to trip him. I suppose Jean Hannay was doing the screaming, to bring me through the trees at a gallop.'

'Jean Hannay?' he said, in a voice which he contrived to make surprised.

'You have surely not forgotten her,' I said. 'Last week she was your mistress.'

'She was never my mistress.'

'Of course you would say that. Unfortunately I know the truth.'

'From whom?'

'From people I believe more than I shall ever believe you.'

'From whom?' he repeated, in the high angry voice I remembered from the island in the Falls of Gard.

'From Sir Archibald Hannay,' I said, in what was meant to be a note of triumph.

I had to fight to achieve such a note, and I probably failed. I could not fail to realise, even as I spoke, that though he could not reach me, I could not do anything at all. Even if he went away and left me, I could not get down to escape, without a friend to put up the ladder. I had no friend in that castle. My friend in the cottage in the garden would never know I was there; and he would not be strong enough to raise the ladder. Charles had a hundred loyal servants. In a few hours they would run to do his bidding. He would say I had brain-fever (as some of them already believed) and I must be brought down, by force, for my own safety.

I would show no sign of fright. I would not.

'Hannay?' he said, in a voice into which he tried to put utter amazement.

'I suppose neither of you realised that he knew,' I said scornfully. 'It was very stupid of you. Of course he knew.'

'He told you that he knew that I . . . That Jean and I . . .?'

'He came to warn me that you would do exactly what you tried to do. You are so arrogant that you think everybody else is stupid or blind. Do you think I did not see Jean Hannay waiting for a glimpse of you, minutes after that obscene mockery they called our marriage?'

'Do you think I did not see that insolent puppy McCallum, slavering after you, minutes after our marriage?'

'He is in love with me.'

'I have good reason to know he is.'

'At least he has not tried to kill anybody.'

'No. I would respect him more if he had. He takes the coward's way, of hiring poachers and tinkers to do the work for him. To do your work for you.'

'That is outrageous rubbish,' I said. 'You are hiding behind lies. I do not understand why you bother, since you are going to kill me anyway.'

'*I?*' he said. 'Kill *you*? Are you both mad and bad, or only bad?'

The note of shocked amazement in his voice was very well done. But it was true – I did not understand why he bothered.

I tried a laugh. It was meant to be defiant and contemptuous. It was a terrible failure. He was better at pretending than I was.

I said, 'What were you and Mariota talking about this morning?'

'What?' This time I thought the surprise in his voice was genuine. 'How did you know I saw Mariota this morning?'

'I was there. I watched you.'

'I wonder who betrayed me to you.'

'Mariota did.'

'Impossible!'

'She did not know she was doing so. I followed her, after her meeting with Sir Archibald Hannay.'

'She did not meet Hannay!'

'Oh,' I said, losing patience. 'It is stupid to keep denying things which you must know I know are true. What were you and Mariota talking about?'

'She came to warn me again. To say that Peter McCallum had disappeared from home, and that you had disappeared from Crask. That you were obviously together. That you were recruiting your mercenary army. That I could expect a shot in the back or a knife between the ribs.'

'I wonder,' I said, 'what you were really talking about. Were you alone in the old chapel?'

'No.'

'I thought not. Jean must have found it uncomfortable.'

'I have not seen Jean for a week.'

'Oh God,' I said, 'how I would like to hear one word of truth from you. You can have me pulled down from this ledge in the morning, and then you can do what you like with me. Why bother acting and lying to me now?'

'Acting and lying? Those words come strangely from you.'

'They come angrily from me.'

'You have no right to anger. You have a right only to shame, guilt and misery.'

'The misery you have contrived.'

'The misery you have earned. You had a furtive, hole-and corner intrigue with McCallum before our marriage, and you

206

continued it after. Do you suppose he was not seen, creeping about in the policies?'

I was so stunned by this preposterous charge that I was silent for a moment.

'The silence of guilt,' said my husband. 'The silence of the unmasked.'

'Did you invent that evil-minded slander?' I managed to say at last.

'I tried to doubt it when I was told it. I was made to see that it was true.'

'It was a convenient thing to pretend to believe. I suppose it still is. You will use it to explain my disappearance.'

'Yes, it will explain your disappearance, and my death, and your reappearance with your paramour as mistress of this place. How rich you will make McCallum, and how unhappy you will make him. I suppose Australia schooled you in the methods of violence and murder. I suppose you will succeed in the end. I am so sickened that I would be almost past caring, if it were not for my father and my duty to this place and its tenants and servants.'

'Well, I am not past caring,' I said. 'I am only eighteen years old, and I would like to go on living. But I will not plead or cringe. I am a soldier's daughter.'

'People speak well of your father. That is one of the horrible things about the person you have become.'

There was a bitterness in his voice which sounded real. I thought he believed that I was horrible, and that it was a pity.

I suddenly said, 'This must be the oddest conversation ever held between a husband and a wife.'

'The thought had occurred to me,' he said.

'That would have been a better thing to mention than the things you have been mentioning. But I have been struck by the oddest notion. I think you may believe what you have been saying.'

'I think you had better tell me your story. I am not sure yet if I will believe it, but I may be getting a little closer to believing you.'

'I will tell you the exact truth,' I said. 'I thought you knew it all, but perhaps you don't.'

'I thought I knew it, too. Possibly I don't.'

I told him about Sir Archibald Hannay's visit, and all our conversation on the terrace. About himself and Jean, and their plot to kill me. About my caution and about my defiance. About the scream, which was like a child or an animal being flogged, and about the rope which brought Marmalade down.

'When exactly did that happen?' he said. 'Give me the day and the hour.'

I did so. It was not a day or an hour I was like to forget.

'I was in Edinburgh,' he said.

'Can you prove that?'

'Of course I can. I was in the office of my bankers.'

I told him about Mariota's visit to my sickroom, and the warning that she added to Sir Archibald's. I told him about the bullet fired from the copse in the park; Rupert's visit; my decision to go to the safety of Crask.

'I think that was what that bullet was for,' he said. 'Not to kill you, but to frighten you away to Crask.'

'I was very angry at being frightened away to anywhere,' I said. 'I was very angry at having to crawl so as not to be shot at again.'

'Yes. When exactly was the shot?'

I told him the day and hour. Those also I would not forget.

'Ah,' he said. 'I had come back from Edinburgh, but not back to the castle. At that moment, as it happens, I was in Lochgrannomhead. And yes, in answer to the question you were no doubt about to ask, of course I can prove it.'

'But why did they want me at Crask? And who wanted me at Crask?'

'As to the first, I think subsequent events may answer your question. As to the second, when we have pooled our stories we may have a clearer idea. What did happen at Crask?'

I told him about the second bullet, my appeal to the Countess, the pony and the saddlebags and the ruined croft, and about the Urquhart children.

'I know them,' he said. 'You could not have recruited better allies.'

I remembered my indignation, and interrupted my story to say, 'It is monstrous that that family should have to struggle so hard to eat so little.'

'I have been trying for years,' he said, 'to reduce the

struggle and increase the meals. But Tam Urquhart will not accept charity. I have tried to wrap it up so that his pride will allow me to help him. But he is as prickly as a sea-urchin.'

'Oh,' I said, digesting this, and finding that I was believing him. 'My Uncle Ranald had a tenant like that at Callo. In the end, when the tenancy was to be renewed, he would not renew it. I don't know what has become of that family.'

'Tam Urquhart is quite safe from eviction, and well he knows it.'

'Yes,' I said, still believing him.

'And were those children useful to you?'

'Yes,' I said. I told him about Sir Archibald creeping up to the croft, and creeping away again, and meeting Mariota nearby; and about my following Mariota to her meeting with himself; and about my burgling the castle. But I would not tell him how I had done that – I did not want to get Geordie Gault into trouble, nor the night-watchmen.

There was a silence. I wondered what was going through his head. I was not sure what was going through mine.

He said at last, 'You were told, by Mariota and by Hannay, that Jean Hannay threw herself at my head.'

'Yes. I saw her. I think it is true.'

'Unfortunately it is true.'

'I was told that you, um – this is difficult to say.'

'Try.'

'I was told that you, um, made a collection of ladies, and that you grew tired of them quickly, and dropped them, and some of them were driven almost to death by misery and shame.'

'Is that my reputation?' he said, sounding very much surprised.

'It is what I was told. So the business of Jean Hannay came as no surprise.'

'It came as a great surprise to me,' he said.

'You met her secretly, in the little castle in the falls.'

'I have given you an exact account of that. I did not believe her suicide threat, but I did not think I had the right to take such an appalling risk.'

'You met her again. By the east gate of the park.'

'How can you know that?'

'I saw you.'

'I can imagine the conclusions you jumped to. I had by that time arranged a system for sending and receiving messages, but without showing my face. The message from Jean was such that, again, I could not take the risk of refusing to meet her. I think I have never before seen naked, shameless, utter misery. That she should destroy herself did seem possible. Not likely, but possible. How could I have lived with myself, if I knew that she had killed herself, and that I was the cause?'

'You had not seen her since?'

'No, nor had word from her.'

'Then when she left Achmore, where did she go?'

'I did not know she had left Achmore. I don't know where she has gone, or why. I devoutly hope that I never see her again. I do not think I could stand another scene like those I had with her. Well, let us put what I have been told beside what you say you have been told. First, you must know that there was a tentative understanding between Mariota and myself. She is beautiful, intelligent and of ancient family. If I was not precisely in a storming passion of love for her, at least I was not in love with anybody else. My father was anxious to see me married and settled, for my own sake and for the sake of the succession. But it seemed to me that we both needed to be a great deal more certain of our feelings before we embarked on so gigantic a step.'

My husband's attitude to marriage, before his marriage, seemed to me so ironical that I gave a sort of yelp of laughter.

'I am sorry,' I said. 'None of this is anything to laugh at.'

'No, but I see why you laughed. There were, anyway, things that made me a little doubtful about that match. Mariota's father is a man of great sweetness of character, but his mismanagement approaches a kind of massive, involuntary selfishness. Mariota herself. . .'

'Hears fairy music.'

'Not all the time. In the intervals of the fairy concerts, she was sometimes – proprietory. I do not like being owned. You are the same, I think, so you will understand. Mariota assumed that, since she did not wish me to go to your ball, I would meekly observe her wishes, and refuse your aunt's invitation.'

'Good gracious,' I said. 'Is that why you accepted it? It

did seem odd at the time, as you scarcely knew the family and you didn't know me at all. . . For once I agreed with Grizelda. Well, it came to the same in the end, as you never got to the ball. . .'

'Giving a reason for her command, Mariota said that I might find myself attracted to you, since it seemed that other people were. Only unhappiness, she said, could result from that. Because you were already profoundly and totally committed. Your liaison with Peter McCallum began the moment he returned here for the summer. It continued up to the eve of our marriage. That was the reason for your extreme distaste, at the thought of our marriage. Knowing that, it was the reason for mine. The liaison has continued since, continues still, and will continue. You and he contemplated with dismay a life of stealthy intrigue. A life in which, also, he would have at first only the very small salary of a very junior government official. You were going to put both right. I did not quite believe that last part of the story, until my horse was brought down.'

'Was a child screaming?'

'A child or an animal.'

'And you hurt your ankle?'

'My knee.'

'Then we were not exactly the same. . . That is why you are carrying that stick?'

'Yes, of course, why else?'

'I had a different notion about it. . . I think that Mariota – '

'Mariota. What of Mariota?'

'Some of what she told me was true.'

'Some of what she told me was true.'

'Yes,' I said, remembering Peter McCallum's wretched face at the side of the carriage-drive. 'She might have truly believed that all she told me was true. She was not in Jean Hannay's confidence. She might have thought she was not in yours. If you told her that you had rejected Jean – '

'I did tell her so.'

'You would have told her so whether it was true or not. You would hardly admit to having a secret affair with a married woman. She may really have thought that you and Jean. . . Sir Archibald certainly thought so, and he is married to Jean. He said somebody would try to kill me, exactly as

211

Mariota did. And then Marmalade was brought down, and somebody shot at me. . . That part of what Mariota told me was true, too. There's no reason she shouldn't have believed every word she told me.'

'Then what of what she told me? She cannot have believed that too.'

'Why not?' I said. 'I might have told her, if she had asked me, that I was not having an affair with Peter McCallum or anybody else. But what else would I say? She might easily have believed that I loved him as much as I'm afraid he loves me. Then to be forced into this marriage – then to see what would come to me with you out of the way – and I have come from the colonies, where everybody is all the time shooting at one another. . . Why should she not have believed all that?'

'So she saved your life by warning you against me, and she saved my life by warning me against you?'

'Yes. Why not? She likes us both. She would not want either of us killed.'

'But to believe that we were actually planning to murder one another. . . No, the idea is grotesque.'

'But somebody did try to murder you, Charles!'

'Perhaps not. Perhaps simply to lend verisimilitude to the story. Perhaps that is the reason your horse was brought down.'

'That would be a terrible thing to do – to risk giving a horse a serious injury, just to lend veri – what you said, to a story.'

'Was your horse injured?'

'Only a little. Was yours?'

'A small cut only. I am sorry about your ankle.'

'And I about your knee. I suppose,' I said, 'Jean Hannay does hate me enough to want to kill me. And she has disappeared. The only part of those stories that was wrong was the part about you.'

'Do you believe that now, Arabella?'

'I find I do. I never expected to. It is quite a relief. I hope I am right to believe it.'

'For my part,' he said, 'I suppose Peter McCallum hates me enough to want to kill me. And he has disappeared. It seems that the only part of the stories told to me that was wrong was the part about you.'

'Do you believe that now, Charles?'

'I believe some things and not others. Will you trust yourself to the ladder now?'

'Yes. This stone is becoming very hard. How are we to explain my disappearance?'

'With part of the truth. You were threatened. I was away, and unable to protect you. You did not know the people here well enough to trust them. You went to Crask. Now that I am back, you feel it safe to come back.'

'Yes. I suppose people might believe that. But who threatened me?'

'Someone from Australia. Someone with a grudge against your father – a deserter from the army, perhaps, or a criminal he caught and punished.'

'This is getting a little like the story I told the Urquhart children. . .'

By this time Charles had replaced the ladder against the wall. I descended stiffly. He helped me, with a hand to my arm, as I reached the ground. I gave a start when I felt his hand. Not many minutes before I had been certain he was going to kill me; you do not get rid of such a feeling, altogether, in an instant. I could not well see his face, because the lantern was on the floor, but I thought he frowned. He frowned at the start I had given, because it suggested I did not trust him.

'I am sure you are tired,' he said, in a voice to which some of the coldness had come back.

So we went to our rooms – he to his and I to mine. It was like the nights of the first days of our marriage. Nothing had changed. Nothing would change. Despair joined relief in my mind.

I was thankful for a clean nightgown and a comfortable bed. But, as I lay wakeful in the dark, I looked at the life that lay ahead of me. I thought that perhaps I had been wrong to skip round the tree at Crask.

I did not know how the servants knew that we were both back. But they must have known very early in the morning – I was called with a tray at eight o'clock, and my clothes had been ironed and aired.

When I came downstairs, I felt again a mood of welcome. They were glad I had not been abducted; they were glad I had not got brain-fever. They were glad, I thought, that I had not forgotten their names.

There was no welcome over the breakfast table. Charles had already eaten, and gone out. Things were as they had been.

I found myself hoping that, as he rode about the estate, nobody shot at him. I found myself wondering why I hoped so.

Geordie Gault was on the second terrace, helping an under-gardener with the autumn pruning. We could not talk freely. I winked at him (something which Aunt Honoria had tried to cure me of). In his effort not to burst out laughing, he went purple, and pretended to have a choking-fit. The under-gardener beat him on the back. The under-gardener laughed; this allowed Geordie to laugh; this allowed me to laugh.

It still seemed to be as close as I was ever going to come to being intimate with anybody at Glengard.

I did not see the chaplain. I was not summoned to the Duke. Charles was out all day; I had a solitary luncheon, in great state.

I thought about my own position, my own safety. Jean Hannay had tried to kill me. She must have an accomplice. One could only barely imagine her tying a rope between trees; one could not imagine her firing a sporting rifle. Who had fired? If not Charles, who? Someone else who wanted me dead, or simply someone she was paying?

What about Charles's safety? What about Peter McCallum?

In the middle of the night, when I sat perched on the cold rough stone of the embrasure, the threats had seemed to go away. But of course they had not gone away. Were we both mad, behaving as though they had?

Nothing was changed between Charles and myself. Nothing was changed between ourselves and our enemies. We were to live out our lives in a false and loveless marriage; we were to live our lives with our chins on our shoulders.

We trusted one another, it seemed, though we did not like one another. Who else did either of us trust? Could we trust anybody?

Could I trust Charles?

I was extremely surprised, that afternoon, to receive a call from the Earl of Crask.

He came alone. He was visibly distressed, unhappy, embarrassed. He looked more untidy than usual, more wind-blown, more moth-eaten. He looked like an old kitchen chair, from which a leg might fall off. He stammered at me, unable to get his words out; I felt a surge of affection for him, but a certain impatience.

'I am in great perturbation of spirit, Arabella,' he said. 'I had rather not be here. . . Oh dear! That was unfortunately put! I had rather anybody else was giving you this message. My own instinct was to mind my own business. But my dear wife, to whom as always I confided the whole, persuaded me that it was my duty to give you the truth. I so much wish Mariota was here. She would have come with me, of course. She would have perhaps come instead of me. She would have been able to give you comfort, which I despair of doing. The messenger who bears evil tidings is hated – I beg you will not hate me, my dear, even though what I have to say to you is so. . .'

'Is Mariota ill?' I said. 'Has she had an accident?'

'No no. That is to say, not as far as I know. She is away.'

'Since yesterday?'

'Since yesterday. She has been promised to stay with. . . Oh dear, the name escapes me. Distant relatives. Not far. She left after luncheon. She is to be away for a week. . . I think she said it would be about a week. I was pleased for her. She does not see as many people as she should. Our neighbours are charming, to be sure, but new faces. . .'

'What is it you have to say to me, Lord Crask?' I asked. I did not want to be rude to so kind a person, but I could see

215

that the conversation, if not pushed along, would last until dinner-time.

'My instinct was to mind my own business,' he repeated. 'I allowed myself to be persuaded by my dear wife that that course would, in truth, have been moral cowardice rather than kindness or discretion. She convinced me that we could not, as friends, keep from you facts to which you are entitled.'

'What facts?' I said. I could not imagine what he was going to tell me. I hoped I was pushing him along.

I was not pushing him very fast. He was going round and round the subject, because he dreaded saying what he had come to say.

'If I could in conscience have minded my own business,' he said miserably, rubbing his head with his hand, so that his hair became even more wildly untidy than usual. 'The episode only occurred this morning. My dear wife and I discussed it, as you may imagine. She took the clear view that, painful as it will be for you. . . In sum, I allowed her to persuade me, to override my own instinct, which was to . . . Just so.'

'Is this some news about my family?' I said. 'Has my cousin fallen off his horse?'

'No no! I believe them to be in perfect health. Though, to be sure, I understand that your cousin Grizelda's health gives rise to. . . Your dear aunt has more than once mentioned. . . Migraine headaches, I believe? Quite crippling. Most disagreeable. The doctors helpless in the face of. . . Just so.'

'Then what is it, Lord Crask?' I said, as gently as I possibly could.

'Oh dear! I wish some other messenger than I. . . If my dear wife's health. . . If Mariota had not gone away. . . But it falls to me. The episode occurred at noon today. A little before or after, perhaps, but approximately at noon. . .'

He looked at me as though he were drowning, and I had charge of a rope.

. 'A carriage was seen,' he said. 'At noon today. A little before or after, I daresay, but about noon. It was apparently deserted. The horse was tied up by the head to a tree. Whether with the reins or with a halter-rope. . . But the carriage was not deserted. There were two persons in it. They were engaged in, ah, I do not know how to define their

216

activity in seemly terms. . . I do not know how to say this in a manner that will save you pain. . .'

'Who were they?' I said, knowing the answer.

'Your husband. And Lady Hannay.'

I came into the small drawing room immediately before dinner. Charles was already there, talking to the Reverend Doctor Davidson. He was in profile to me. He did not immediately see me, nor hear me come in. They were very deep in talk, about some family whom Charles wished to help but who would not let him help, who were too proud to be helped. I realised they were talking about the Urquharts.

I felt a greater rage than ever I remembered feeling. I was seething with anger, that my husband should make love to another woman.

Why was I? What was it to me?

The answer hit me with such force that I physically staggered, and had to sit down suddenly in the nearest chair.

Evening dress suited him, as it does all tall and well-made men. He was smiling, with a kind of affectionate impatience, as he talked of Tam Urquhart's pride. He was handsome. Yes, smiling so, he was very handsome.

Jean Hannay had fallen headlong and helplessly in love with him.

And now I had done the same thing.

At dinner the chaplain and I talked; and the chaplain and Charles talked. After dinner Charles excused himself. He had fallen behind with his work, because of his absence from the castle; there were letters that would not wait.

Love letters, to Jean Hannay.

The chaplain and I sat. I pretended to be busy with embroidery. Really I was busy with rage, and jealousy, and a sick feeling. I thought the trick that fate had played on me was the cruellest I ever heard of.

The chaplain was talking. I was too preoccupied to listen, until I realised he was talking about myself.

'I am, in a manner of speaking,' he said, 'his Grace's eyes and ears. I go up and down the glen, and everybody tells me everything. I talk too much, you know, and that has the curious effect of inviting confidences. They all think I am very discreet. I am, too, except to his Grace. But now I think it proper to be indiscreet to you, my Lady. About the opinion people have of you. About the effect you have had hereabouts, ever since you appeared from Australia like a fairy coming through a trapdoor in a Christmas pantomime. But also like the demon king. Did you know that? The demon king, acquiring slaves, and earning the most bitter and poisonous hatred. I have been, and remain, saddened and shocked by what I have seen and sensed. It must be a curious feeling, to be hated. It has never happened to me. I am not important enough to have earned anybody's hatred, I think. You should know about it, for your own safety. I realise that, to an extent, you do know about it, and endeavoured to secure your own safety. We were thankful for your return. You are safer here. You are not hated here.'

'I am only hated by Lady Hannay,' I said, 'and I can understand that.'

'Does she feel so? I did not know that. Yes, one can understand it. She met his Lordship, after an interval of several years, only after she was herself married. What she felt was wrong, what she wanted was wrong, but comparing his Lordship to Sir Archibald Hannay. . . The heart is not its own master.'

'No,' I agreed, considering the state of my own.

'Alas, the other hatred you have inspired is equally easy to understand. Wicked, monstrous, but, given everything, all too easy to understand.'

'You have left me behind, Doctor,' I said. 'What other?'

'Three young men have lived in the glen all their lives.'

'Yes.'

'And a fourth, a little older, his Lordship. All four, all their lives, have known Lady Mariota Seaton. For the last half dozen years she has been queen of the glen and of those four. At any moment, she could have picked any one of the three. She knew it, and so did they. The one she picked would have been honoured and enchanted. In the event, as we know, she picked his Lordship. She had to.'

'Why?'

'Because the Earl of Crask is headed for bankruptcy.'

'Oh. I did not know it was as bad as that.'

'He himself does not know it is as bad as that. The Countess does. She would have been in despair. She was not, because of the developing understanding between Lady Mariota and his Lordship. Nobody doubted how that would end. We were ready to welcome her here. We were – his Grace was – ready to rescue Crask from its creditors. And then, my Lady, out you came from your trapdoor. I imagine your reunion with Lady Mariota took place very soon after your arrival?'

'Yes.'

'And I imagine you were asked to Crask very soon after that?'

'Yes.'

'And you saw the Countess?'

'Yes, of course. That was why I went there. We talked for a very long time. She made me talk and talk and talk, until I was quite exhausted.'

'As I supposed. And I picture her staring at you.'

'I think she did.'

'Curious, is not it? She scrutinised you closely and at length, and prompted you to talk about yourself at length. His Grace did just the same, as I expect you remember, with exactly the same intention and exactly the opposite effect.'

'Oh,' I said. 'What was his Grace's intention?'

'To determine if you were a suitable wife for his son, my Lady.'

'What did he decide?'

'Whereas the Countess of Crask,' he said, ignoring my question, 'wanted to know how much of a threat you represented. After that prolonged scrutiny, that long conversation, she concluded that, if I may so put it, you presented a very great threat indeed.'

'But. . .'

'The Countess wanted her daughter settled and her husband's bills paid. That is why, to Crask, you were the demon king. Think of your effect, my Lady, on those three young men.'

'Oh. I am sorry for them.'

'I know that. Just as I know you were sorry for the laundry-maids, carrying piles of wet linen to the mangles.'

'I thought Mrs McKay was going to have a fit.'

219

'No one in the laundry has stopped blessing you. We all wonder where you will turn next. This castle, my Lady, has been without a mistress for far too long.'

'I will turn to the larder next,' I said, 'and then that basement dormitory where there is damp in the wall. . . Doctor, I cannot believe a word you are telling me about Lady Crask. She is too indolent to hate people.'

'She has nothing else to do but lie hating you, which she has been doing all summer. Did she by any chance see the gown which you wore to your own ball? I understand it was extremely becoming.'

'Yes. She wanted to see it. She liked it, I think. . . Oh. Then Mariota tried to stop Charles coming to the ball.'

'In case he saw you, in that becoming dress. Lady Mariota and her mother knew very well what effect you had had on those three young men. Why not on his Lordship, too? And if that happened, you see, all their cake was dough.'

'She did send me to the tumbledown croft, and swore not to tell anybody, and the next thing was visitors. . . How oddly things have worked out.'

'Things have not yet worked out, my Lady.'

'No, not quite. . . How can you be so sure about Lady Crask?'

'I was not, until today. That is why I have not spoken thus to your Ladyship, until today. I visited her, as I do once a fortnight, to celebrate Holy Communion in her room.'

'Communion. Good gracious. Surely she did not add a few sentences to the Confession?'

'We chatted afterwards. She made one or two incautious remarks, which, in the ordinary way, I would probably not have correctly construed. In asking after his Grace's health, she let fall something which revealed that she expected her daughter, at some future time, to be resident in this castle.'

'It all still goes on, then. I thought it must. What a very great nuisance.'

'Talking of that led her to make a chance remark about yourself, my Lady. In which, reading as it were between the lines, I saw with disgust the bitterness of her feeling. I was shocked, you understand, because I had just given her Absolution, as the Prayer Book directs, and the bread and wine of the sacrament.'

A thought suddenly struck me. Hope flared like a lamp.

'What about Lord Crask?' I said. 'Am I to believe what he tells me?'

'Yes,' said Doctor Davidson. 'I am absolutely certain that that childlike and innocent quality is genuine. He is incapable of deceiving anybody or of hurting anybody. He is an ineffective manager, but in personality he approaches the saintly. You can believe with total confidence anything that he tells you.'

'I was afraid you'd say that,' I said drably; and my flame of hope sank in a pool of grease.

Chapter 11

Charles was still working when I went to bed. I was pleased and sorry.

Solitary between the sheets, I realised that my love for Charles had been in hiding. Because of Jean. Because of his reputation. Because I thought he was trying to kill me. Because of his dislike for me, his contempt for me. When things are like that, you do not admit to yourself that you are in love. You do not invite misery. You lie to yourself, and you go on doing so.

Why had I stopped doing so? Suddenly, in the early evening, when he was smiling and talking about the Urquharts?

His concern about that family was genuine, and it did him credit. But that would not have been enough.

It was anger that had opened my eyes to the state of my own heart. Anger that he loved not me but Jean.

I tried to revive the anger. But all I felt, lying alone in the dark, was misery.

I breakfasted alone. Of course I did. I supposed that I always would. To the servants, I put on the mask of Marchioness. But I nearly added needless salt to my breakfast bacon, by weeping into my plate.

In the middle of the morning I was in the larders with Mrs Murray the housekeeper. She seemed glad to see me, glad to talk, which was a change from her previous reception of me. She made some remark about the laundry. Word had got about, of course, and she had inspected the changes I had made.

I wanted to contrive that the changes in the larder were at least as much Mrs Murray's work as mine – or, at least, that she should think they were. So we began a cautious negotiation about where the butter and eggs should be kept, which were wanted several times a day, and where the jars of red-pepper should go, which were hardly wanted once a fortnight.

She produced the opinion, as her own opinion, that things which were wanted constantly should be in easy reach. I vehemently agreed with her, praising her judgement. She looked at me in triumph, as though she had won a long and exhausting battle.

I knew this was how my Papa sometimes got things done, although it was foreign to his impetuous temperament. I was pleased to find that his methods worked, as well in the Glengard larders as in the offices of Government House in Sydney. Especially, perhaps, because going a roundabout way at things was foreign to my temperament. But Papa had also tried to teach me self-discipline, and to a small extent succeeded.

I needed it, even more of it, again, at once.

A footman came to find me, to say that I had callers. I was surprised. Half-past eleven was an unusual time for a call. I was amused to find myself, of all people, reacting so conventionally. It came, perhaps, of being a Marchioness all morning.

My callers were Geoffrey Nicholls and Rupert Fraser. I had not seen either of them since they carried me to Crask in the middle of the night. I had not expected to see them. They looked acutely miserable. I thought I knew part of the cause of that; it turned out I did not know all of it.

They looked quite as embarrassed as Lord Crask had, the previous afternoon.

Geoffrey, the man of moods, seemed to constitute himself spokesman. Perhaps they had agreed that, as between a lawyer and a soldier, a lawyer would be a better spokesman. But he was a very bad one. He was as long and as reluctant in getting to the point as Lord Crask had been.

'We have come because we agreed that we must,' he said, looking away from me. 'We have come to confess . . . Not a crime, exactly . . . A sin. A sort of sin. Which we both committed. Peter McCallum did, too. At least, I think so. He

223

said he was going to. He would be here. At least, I think so. But he has gone away.'

'Yes,' I said. 'Where, and why?'

'To England,' said Geoffrey. 'His family persuaded him to go. His parents. He was too miserable. He was too much in love with you, Bella. Everything reminded him of you. Every hill, every turn of the road. He came creeping into the gardens here, for a glimpse of you. He was torturing himself. He was making himself ill. They were right to send him away. They hope he will forget you. He won't forget you, but perhaps new places may distract him for a minute or two at a time.'

'I came creeping into your gardens, too,' said Rupert unexpectedly.

'So did I,' said Geoffrey. 'But I never saw you.'

'Oh,' I said. I should have said something comforting, but I had no comfort for either of them.

Geoffrey was as slow coming to the point as Lord Crask had been, and for the same reason. He did not want to say what they had come to say. Their visible misery increased. They were not becoming easier in their minds, but each minute less easy.

'If you had stayed at Crask, or gone back to Callo,' said Geoffrey at last, 'we might never have had this conversation. I wish to God it had been so. Not for your sake, but for ours. But we both heard yesterday that you were back here, back with Charles Gard.'

'How did you hear?'

'I think from the servants. Both of us, I think, from the servants . . .'

I nodded. The mysterious electric telegraph, without wires, still operated between all the servants' halls in the glen.

'Since you are here,' said Geoffrey, 'since we suppose you will stay here –'

'I suppose I shall,' I said.

'You must know the truth about your husband.'

'I think I have had too much of that,' I said.

'No. You have had lies about him. The moment I saw you, when you came back here from Australia and I from Edinburgh, I was desperate with love for you.'

'So was I,' said Rupert. 'So was Peter.'

'We all knew it about one another,' said Geoffrey. 'We

224

could not have kept it a secret from one another. We did not
try. It was a fair race. None of us tried to cheat, I think. Even
though we were rivals, we were loyal to our friendship. But
we were frightened of another runner in our race. We were
frightened of Gard.'

'You . . . From the beginning, you were frightened of
Charles?'

'Of course. How could we not be? We expected you to have
the effect on him that you had on us. How could you not?
And then we considered the effect he would have on you. We
compared ourselves to him. We despaired. He is ten years
older than any of us. He is experienced and travelled. Though
still a young man, he is widely respected, and not just because
he is heir to a Dukedom. His judgement is sought. His opinion
is listened to. Compared to him we are all young boys, hardly
embarked on our adult lives.'

'Taller,' said Rupert thickly.

'He tops us all by inches,' said Geoffrey. 'I am no judge of
masculine beauty, but I take it he is very handsome. Women
certainly think so. All women think so.'

'Yes,' I said.

'And then there is Glengard. You would not marry for
wealth or position, Bella. We all know that, perfectly well.
But it would be foolish to ignore Glengard, as a factor in the
situation. Glengard, compared to our inheritances, is exactly
like Charles Gard, compared to us. The worst of it was, that
we saw a kind of rightness in your coming here. You, the
most glorious creature any of us had ever seen, should by
rights be queen of a place like this. There was even a sort of
inevitability about it. We agreed to fight the inevitable. We
agreed to weight the favourite out of the race. We agreed on
a method. It was my idea, I think. That is why I am forcing
myself to make the confession.'

'You need not make it,' I said. 'I know what you are going
to say.'

'It may have been you who had the idea,' said Rupert
miserably. 'But it was I who first. . . . Who first. . . .'

'The young wife,' I said, 'who was driven to the point of
suicide –'

'Never existed,' said Rupert in a voice I could hardly hear.

'We wanted you so badly, all of us, that we went to those lengths. . . .'

'We thought,' said Geoffrey, 'that if we made Charles Gard seem odious, cruel, conscienceless, if we made you believe those things –'

'It was all lies?' I said, wanting very badly to be absolutely clear on the point. 'All that both of you said about Charles, all that Peter said?'

'All lies,' muttered Rupert.

'And, now that you are back here, you should know that,' said Geoffrey.

We sat in silence, on wrought-iron chairs on the terrace. Neither of them would meet my eye.

'We do not expect you ever to forgive us,' said Geoffrey. 'We do not expect you ever to talk to any of us again.'

'I expect I shall,' I said: because it was as though, very far away, I could hear the singing of a magic bird.

My return to Glengard was the immediate reason for the visit of Geoffrey Nicholls and Rupert Fraser, and for their astonishing confession.

My return to Glengard was the reason for another visit, which surprised me even more. My Cousin Grizelda called, in time for tea. She would not take tea on the terrace, because the sun would have given her a headache. She was dressed as elaborately as always. She looked sourly round the lovely Tambour Room. I could not imagine what had brought her, or what we should talk about for an hour.

'Duty brings me here, Arabella,' she said, as all my callers seemed to say.

'I did not think it was pleasure,' I said.

'No. It is no pleasure, and it is thoroughly inconvenient. When you had disappeared, I could not have spoken to you even if I had wanted to, and I did not want to. I can think now of many thousand things I would rather be doing. But now you are back, mistress of this house, Marchioness of Gard, and the situation is changed.'

'You heard I was back from your servants?' I said.

'Yes, of course. You may have heard that Lady Hannay disappeared, as you did. You may not know why.'

'I know very well why.'

'I think not, Arabella. I think you do not know, either, that when she left Achmore she sought refuge at Callo, with us. I do not know that she particularly likes us. I do not know that anybody does. I do not see how they could. My father is a pompous and self-important snob of one kind, my mother is the same thing but of another kind, my brother partakes of the worst qualities of both, and I am an embittered old maid. All this must have been as obvious to Jean Hannay is it is to everybody else. But we have the advantage that we can be trusted. Jean Hannay thought so, and she was right. So, when she was in fear for her physical safety, she ran to us and we took her in. We made sure that there was no gossip from the servants' hall. We promised she would be safe. She was safe. She is safe still.'

'Safe from what?' I said.

'Her husband. He is violently possessive of a much younger wife, whom he suspects of having married him for his money. The marriage worked well enough, as I have understood from Jean, though for her it was a marriage of convenience and for him a piece of the most infantile self-delusion. At first he supposed her in love with him. She was able to sustain this delusion, and was willing to do so in return for what it earned her.'

'That is all very cynical,' I said.

'You may have observed that I am very cynical. My life has obliged me to be so. Jean Hannay was cynical, too, until she met the Marquess of Gard. I have not met him, so I cannot judge the effect he would be likely to have. On her it was cataclysmic. All honour, decency, shame, loyalty went out of the window. Her husband, of course, found out at once – the power of her emotions had unbalanced her – it was impossible for her to hide her feelings.'

'I know. He told me.'

'Did he tell you that he beat her?'

'He actually beat her?'

'With a dog-whip. I have seen the marks. She was terrified of worse beatings, and of worse than beatings.'

'I never would have supposed he would be violent,' I said. 'A fat little middle-aged man. . . .'

'Surely even you can understand,' said Grizelda

impatiently, 'that it is because he is what you call a fat little middle-aged man that he was so angry, so hurt, so touched in his pride.'

'Yes, I think I understand.... Why are you telling me this, Grizelda?'

'Because it is now your duty to help Jean Hannay. We have done all we can. It is not convenient to have her permanently at Callo. We cannot indefinitely keep the secret of her being there. Sir Archibald can compel her to come home. That seems to me a monstrous law, but it is the law. The moment he finds out where she is, he will arm himself with his legal rights, and he will drag her home. She will not be safe. I am not fond of her, but I am sorry for her, and we have accepted responsibility for her safety. We can no longer exercise that responsibility. We hand it to you.'

I looked at her, unable to believe that I had heard what I had heard.

'I think,' I said slowly, 'it is odd to ask me to take responsibility for someone who is in love with my husband.'

'That has nothing to do with it,' she said. 'It must be you because your husband and his father are practically all-powerful in this part of Scotland. They must frighten Hannay, or send him away, or something of the sort.'

I said suddenly, 'Where was Jean Hannay at noon yesterday?'

'She was writing letters at my writing-table, from eleven until nearly one. It was extremely inconvenient. I wanted to use the table myself.'

'You must keep her for another day,' I said, 'even though it means you lose the use of your writing-table. I will talk to Charles. I do not see how he can make Sir Archibald go away. Perhaps his lawyers will help....'

I was not listening to my own voice. I did not think about what I was saying.

Lord Crask's story was false. He thought it was true but it was false.

After Grizelda had gone, I was asked by the Reverend Doctor Davidson if I would favour my father-in-law with half an hour of my time.

'His Grace's throat has been largely cured,' said the chaplain. 'He can speak without pain, which, as you know, was for some time not the case. Since he has never spoken to you, he is most anxious to do so.'

I wondered what the Duke's voice was like. Charles's was deep, and I had found, the previous evening, that it did curious things to my knees and the small of my back.

He was in the same chair, and in the same brocade dressing-gown. He looked better, livelier; his colour was higher; his eye was just as bright.

He said, 'Come in, dear child.'

His voice was low, but perfectly clear.

It made a change, to be listening in that room, instead of talking.

He said, 'Now that I am capable of giving one, I owe you an explanation for your residence in this castle, to which I am extremely relieved that you have returned. Perhaps I owe you an apology, but I am not going to give you one. You came one day with a neighbour, who had business with my head-gardener.'

'Yes, sir,' I said. 'I came with Lady Nicholls.'

'You explored these terraces. I watched you from this window.'

'Oh. Yes, I had a feeling somebody was watching me.'

'I have always enjoyed the view from this window. That afternoon it was better than ever before.'

'Oh. Thank you. That is nice.'

'It continued to improve. You sat on the swing.'

'Oh. I would have preferred you not to see that.'

'On the contrary, my dear Arabella. I saw you come up the steps to that top terrace. I saw the way you moved. You have the colour of a lion, but I think your movements more closely resemble the tiger. You prowl.'

'I thought I was strolling,' I said dubiously.

'You prowled towards the swing. And I made a wager with myself. I wagered that, having seen the swing, you would not be able to resist swinging on it. My wager was that if you did swing, I would have an extra glass or claret with my dinner. If you did not, I would have no claret at all.'

'Then unless claret is bad for you, sir,' I said, 'I am very glad I gave way to temptation.'

'I am permitted it in moderation. There are differences of opinion as to what constitutes moderation. You broke the swing.'

'I am very sorry I did that.'

'Why? We needed a new one. Some child might have used it, and suffered an injury. I was relieved that you evidently suffered none. I saw you laughing with a young lad, a gardener's boy. I laughed myself, at the sight of the two of you laughing. I laughed long and loud. My laughter did me more good than the extra glass of claret – though I should add that, thanks to you, I much enjoyed the claret. I was immediately and exceedingly curious about you. My chaplain found out at once who you were, as he always does. He found out that, with certain notable exceptions, you made slaves of everyone who met you. I wondered if you would make a slave of my son. This was a little disquieting, since I believed him to be committed, or nearly so, to Mariota Seaton.

'Then there was the episode of poor Crask's dam. Your uncle, of course, took a very high line. We both know why, dear child. I thought at first that it was an astonishing coincidence, that the girl I had so much admired on my own terrace should have been the one imprisoned by the flood with my son. I saw that it was no coincidence at all – the young lady who would sit on the swing and collapse with laughter with a gardener's-boy was the young lady who would cross the footbridge at midnight to investigate a light. It was a young lady I was very curious to meet – whom I now had an excuse to meet – whom I could even pretend I was obliged to meet.

'I asked my chaplain to form an opinion of you first, to persuade you to talk and to listen carefully. Then I did the same. I think we both owe you an apology for that afternoon's work, but I do not advise you to count on getting one. Did you find Davidson taciturn? Did you find yourself obliged to talk incessantly, in order to fill a silence which could otherwise have been oppressive?'

'Yes,' I said. 'I talked dreadful rubbish, just so that somebody would be saying something. . . .'

'He did not think it was rubbish. He was enchanted by your accounts of the episodes in those little French pictures in the Tambour Room, and by the conversations you imagined between the persons depicted. He says that he cannot now look at any of those pictures, without hearing the words that you put into the mouths of the people. His deliberate silence, you see, had exactly the effect we intended. It obliged you to talk, and in talking to reveal much of yourself. That is because you combine a warm and out-reaching personality with imagination, wit, and naturally excellent manners.'

'Oh,' I said, startled by a description of myself to which Callo had unaccustomed me. 'But in spite of those nice things you have just said, sir, I think I should be angry.'

'I daresay you should, dearest child, but I beg you will not be angry with our good chaplain. If you are, fairness will oblige you to be angry with me also.'

'Oh. You did the same. *Could* you talk that afternoon, sir? And those other times when I had to go on and on?'

'I could in truth talk very little, and that little pained me and was bad for my throat. I could have said something to you. It seemed more adroit to say nothing. Having revealed something of yourself to the chaplain, you revealed a great deal to me. After you had gone, we compared notes. He is a very good judge of character. I think I may say the same of myself. We both formed the clear view that you were the ideal wife for my son. You are not only the most beautiful girl I have ever seen, you are also the most spirited, the most entertaining, and the most honest. I could not suppose that Charles could fail to fall in love with you, whatever he may have fancied he felt for Mariota. I flattered myself that there was every chance that you would fall in love with Charles. I am inclined to be partial, but I trust I can also be objective. So I directed that, on grounds of morality, the marriage must take place.'

'It need not have taken place, sir?'

'Of course it need not. There are many advantages to being a very rich Duke. One of them is that, if I do not wish my son to marry a person, he does not marry that person. I did wish him to marry you. I was certain that if he travelled the world all his life he would not find a more perfect match for himself, a more admirable mistress for this castle. Everything that I have seen of you since – everything that I have heard from you, and heard about you – confirms the rightness of the conclusion that my chaplain and I came to. I was especially delighted with your mirth, that afternoon when your aunt and uncle called.'

'Oh. . . . Yes, I remember. I felt guilty at laughing at my own relations, who took me in and looked after me.'

'Laugh at everything you find funny, Arabella, and especially at folly and presumption. Laugh in my presence, if you can arrange to do so – I greatly enjoy the sight and sound of your laughter.'

A servant came in with a glass of medicine. He said, with a firmness I would not have expected in a Duke's servant, that his Grace had been talking for far too long, that he would tire his throat and renew the infection, and that he must immediately fall silent and remain silent.

The Duke shrugged to me, and himself gave a small, low laugh. He kissed my hand when I left him.

'Charles,' I said just before dinner, 'can you tell me where you were at noon yesterday? Just before, and just after, and just at noon?'

'Yes. I went to see Tam Urquhart. I may have found him another farm. He was not there. I saw the children.'

'Peggy, Jaikie and Morag.'

'They had a high time trailing Archibald Hannay.'

'They did it very well.'

'They are very intelligent children. They deserve a good education. I am going to make certain that they get one. There at least Tam agrees with me. Why do you want to know where I was at noon yesterday?'

'Because Lord Crask told me you were somewhere quite different, and doing something quite different, with quite a different person.'

'If Crask said it, he believed it.'

'Someone made him believe it. His wife, or Mariota. Oh, speaking of Jean Hannay –'

'Were we?'

'Yes, of course. Grizelda says we must take responsibility for her.'

'In God's name why? And how?'

'You are powerful enough to stop her husband beating her with a dog-whip.'

'Has he done that?'

'Grizelda saw the marks.'

'Then I will stop him.'

Written down, the words seem friendly enough – informal chatter between husband and wife. But we did not smile at one another. There was no intimacy between us.

I wanted to tell him that I knew that all I had been told about his treatment of women was false, and that all I had been told about his affair with Jean Hannay was false.

But he was coldly polite, reserved, unbending. He spoke at dinner only the minimum, and only for the sake of the servants. He excused himself immediately after dinner, having yet more letters to write.

His father's plan had worked with me, but it had not worked with him.

As usual, I did not see him again until just before dinner the following day.

'I have been to Crask,' he said. 'It seemed wise to have more questions answered. I am responsible for your safety, and my own, and it appears I am to be handed responsibility for Jean Hannay's safety, too. Mariota, as you know, is away. I spoke therefore only to Lord Crask. It is as we supposed. Mariota came to her father soon after noon, on the day she went away. She said she was upset and unhappy. She needed guidance. She described what she said she had seen. Her father believed her – why not? He was persuaded by his wife to come to you. He accepts that the story was a complete fabrication. He is driven to accept also that his wife and daughter were deliberately making vicious mischief. I have never seen a man so distressed, so ashamed. Lady Crask is obsessed, her mind poisoned. She is to be seen by doctors. She is probably to go into the private asylum in Lochgrannomhead. Crask says that, with that influence removed, Mariota will return to sanity and decency. At any rate, he makes himself responsible for her conduct.'

Charles was addressing me as though I were a public meeting, as my Uncle Ranald had so often done. He was doing his duty by imparting to me information which it was my right to know. That was all he was doing. He was finding it distasteful to do so much.

'What are you telling me about Lady Crask,' I said, 'I believe, because I have heard it already. It is horrible, but I know it is true. What you are telling me about Mariota is simply impossible. She listens to fairy music. There cannot be two such different people inside one person.'

'All her life Mariota has been listening to fairy music,' said Charles, 'because the sounds of the real world which immediately surrounded her were intolerable. The whines of crofters who could not get new roofs to keep the rain off their children. The muttering of servants whose wages were six weeks late. All her life she has gazed at visions, because the sights of the real world were intolerable. Patches on the walls where pictures had been, thread-bare carpets, piles of bills unpaid and unpayable. Think what she faced – what she faces still. Ruin, despair, humiliation for her parents and for herself. She does deeply love her parents, I believe. We can perhaps a little excuse her treachery, because she was doing it for the sake of her parents.'

'We can try,' I said dubiously.

'In answer to my questions,' Charles went on, 'Crask gave me one further piece of relevant intelligence.'

A piece of 'relevant intelligence', my mind crossly echoed. Was that how husbands spoke to wives? It sounded like a newspaper report of an international incident.

'During perhaps the last two weeks – Crask is uncertain of the dates – there has been one frequent visitor there. He had not been so before. He spent considerable time with Mariota, and considerable time with her mother. They accounted for his visits by his personal unhappiness, the change towards him of his wife. He came to them for comfort. That is what they told Crask. One cannot at all blame him for believing them.'

'Oh, I see,' I said. 'It was Sir Archibald Hannay.'

'Mariota must have had a colleague. Let us hypothesise that it was Hannay.'

'Let us do what?'

'Proceed on the assumption that it was Hannay.'

'Hum. Somebody sent a message from Achmore to Malcolm Menzies in the stables here, that the Urquharts

234

wanted to see him, that they were in trouble. I assumed it
was Jean. It could just as well have been Sir Archibald. It
could have been he who tied the rope between the trees. It
could have been Mariota who was screaming.'

'Mariota asked you to Crask. You would not go.'

'So Sir Archibald fired a bullet into the wall beside my
head, so that I did go to Crask. Mariota put Geoffrey Nicholls
and Rupert Fraser up to getting me there. Sir Archibald knew
I was there, because Mariota told him. He fired the bullet
that hit the tree. The Countess was the only person who knew
about my tumbledown bothy. I mean, she was supposed to
be the only person. But she told Mariota and Sir Archibald.
Yes, it all must have happened so. It answers every question
except one. What was Sir Archibald about? Why did he want
to shoot me? Whatever was the point of it for him?'

'I went from Crask to Achmore,' said Charles, 'with three
sturdy grooms. I made to Hannay a statement which would
legally be construed as a threat. I informed him that I had
statements from Lady Crask and from Lady Mariota, which
I would communicate to the Procurator Fiscal, and which
would result in his arrest for attempted murder. Such statements would, in fact, be entirely impossible to obtain. Even
with them, his crime would be very difficult to prove. He
is putting Achmore on the market, and leaving this area
immediately and permanently.'

'But why,' I asked again, 'did he want to shoot me?'

'Jean Hannay will return to her home, on the other side of
Scotland. She will not be reunited with her husband. She will
not be seen in this area again.'

'But why did Sir Archibald,' I began to ask, doggedly, for
the third time.

At this moment, dinner was announced. I could not repeat
the question, in front of the footmen in the dining-room. I
could not ask it later, because Charles went away to his
business-room.

In the early afternoon next day I was sitting on the terrace
with some sewing. To my great surprise Charles crossed the
terrace to join me. His air was curious. I could not understand
the expression on his face. He seemed excited, embarrassed,

235

even nervous. He seemed not like a great and very handsome nobleman, but like a little boy approaching the door of his schoolmaster's study.

'I heard today, for the first time,' he said in an odd gruff voice, 'that Peter McCallum has gone away into England, nursing his broken heart.'

'Oh. I heard that, too. Who told you?'

'The same source as yours, your friend young Rupert Fraser. He is a very good fellow.'

'Yes, he is, although he did one dreadful thing. . . .'

'Something he said seemed to contradict something which I knew, knew absolutely, to be the truth. So I rode to Miltoun, to see the McCallums, to face the most embarrassing interview of my life. The second most.'

'Which was the most?' I asked, wondering what could be coming.

'This one. I was – I felt myself – obliged to ask the McCallums deeply personal, deeply confidential questions. They had, as you must know, earnestly wanted you as a wife for their son. They were close to him. He confided in them. They are, at the moment, distressed about him, distressed about his acute unhappiness. He feels that his life is wasted, over, because he has never so much as kissed you, and now he knows he never will.'

'Well, I told you that,' I said.

'I did not believe you. I beg your pardon, Bella. I beg your forgiveness.'

'You have never called me 'Bella' before. Why were you so certain that I was, um, so deeply involved with Peter?'

'Because he told me so.'

'*Peter* did?'

'You understand why I believed him.'

'Yes, of course, you had to believe him. Good gracious. I can hardly speak for surprise.'

'Peter told me, as I thought and as he himself said, as an act of kindness. He had your heart, and you were betrothed. The announcement was to be made on your eighteenth birthday, until the flood took a hand. The, ah, physical liberties which you permitted yourselves were the consequence of your time in Australia, where these things are viewed in a different light. Peter told me this, of course, in

236

the strictest confidence. His whole object, he said, was to save me from unhappiness. He understood that, when I met you, I was extremely likely to fall in love with you. He had done so. Rupert Fraser had done so. Geoffrey Nicholls had done so. They were, and are, wild with love for you.'

'I wish,' I said, 'there was some way I could help any of them.'

'I know you do. There is none. Time will help. They have, all three, united and loving families – that will help. Scotland and England are full of girls. None is as beautiful and bewitching as you –'

'What?' I asked, hoping I had heard correctly, and wishing those astonishing words to be repeated.

'But,' he continued, ignoring my interruption, 'there will be soft arms to go round each of those necks, in the fullness of time. They are all very young. They are all too young, in fact, to be thinking of marriage. They are all too decent and too attractive not to find happiness. It is true that, just now, they are as unhappy as Peter warned me that I was liable to become. His story was very like Mariota's, you see. It was even more convincing. It was totally convincing. And of course he was quite right. I have been fighting the most passionate battles inside myself, to try not to fall in love with you. I did not want to run headlong into a life of endless misery. I fought and fought, and lost, and I did foresee endless misery.'

'Oh. That is why you have been so horrid. It was self defence. I have been trying it, too, but I don't think I am as good as it as you are.'

He looked at me. I saw that he was blushing. I had never seen him blush before. I had never expected to see him blush.

'Have you,' he said, in that odd throaty voice, 'been fighting battles, Bella?'

'Yes, but I lost days ago,' I said. 'I couldn't make out why I was so angry. And I realised. I had to sit down. You were talking about the Urquharts.'

He suddenly smiled at me with a warmth and a love that made the world and the castle spin.

He said, 'Now do you understand why Archibald Hannay wanted to kill you?'

This seemed a strange turn for the conversation to take. I

did not want to discuss Sir Archibald Hannay's motives. I wanted to hear about Charles being in love with me.

He said, 'When I first rejected Jean Hannay, it was because I was not in love with her and because she was married. When I continued to reject her, there was an additional and even stronger reason. I was in love with you. I told her so. I thought it would make her leave me alone. She told her husband so. He had by this time conceived a venomous hatred of me.'

'But you had behaved perfectly well!'

'Yes, I think I can honestly say I had. Don't you see, my darling – "

'Say that again.'

'Don't you see, my most precious and beloved child, that if he was insulted by Jean's feeling for myself, he was insulted a hundredfold by my rejection of her. The hurt to his pride was compounded. He wanted to hurt me, very badly, permanently.'

'I will never let anybody do that, ever,' I said.

Another huge smile made the world spin.

'He could have shot me,' said Charles. 'He did not want to do that. He wanted me to live in misery. I would do that if I lost you. If harm came to you. The way he could hurt me most was through you. This was all something I only realised yesterday. And at the time, of course, I thought that you. . .'

'And Peter McCallum. Yes. Oh, I have just understood. When you told me about Archibald Hannay, you would not tell me why he was trying to kill me. I asked three times, and then they said dinner was ready. . . You did not want to admit that you – "

'Are passionately, deliriously in love with you.'

'It is so lucky you are,' I said.

And then I burst into tears. And then he kissed me for the first time, in full view of all the windows of the castle. And I drowned and drowned in that kiss, and I nearly drowned him too, because tears continued to flood out of my eyes and down my cheeks and down his cheeks.

He said, 'I want you to come with me in the dogcart.'

'I will go anywhere you want, whenever you want,' I said.

238

The dogcart, with a horse and a groom, was waiting, all ready, in the front courtyard.

'Forethought,' said Charles 'I didn't want to waste a minute.'

'Where are we going?'

'Wait and see.'

Submissively I sat in the dogcart with my hands folded in my lap. Charles dismissed the groom and drove away down the drive.

We argued, as we went, as to which of us more greatly loved the other. We reached no conclusion. I had never heard Charles laugh loud and long before. I had not done so myself, since I broke the seat of the swing. Really there was nothing to laugh at. We were laughing in pure happiness.

I saw to my dismay that we were on the way to Callo.

'I am not questioning any of your decisions, my darling –' I began.

'Say that again.'

'I am not questioning your plans – '

'Not that part, goose!'

'My darling. My most precious and beloved love. But I don't want to see my relations.'

'You won't see them or anybody else.'

He stopped the dogcart outside the park at Callo. He tied up the horse, and gave him a bag of hay.

We went into the park and along the river, hidden from the house by the trees. I was completely mystified.

We approached the Falls of Gard, and the island with the little ruined castle.

The water boiled silver between the rocks. A kingfisher flashed upstream, like a jewel on a wire. The sun was hot. Charles held my hand as we walked. He stopped and kissed me. My arms were so tight round his neck that I thought my sleeves would tear from my bodice. I did not mind if they did.

We recovered a little, and walked on hand in hand.

'I have had a new bridge made,' said Charles in a voice that shook. 'It is retractable.'

'A drawbridge.'

'Historically correct, you know. It is a castle.'

I thought of the merit of a retractable bridge to the island. My knees began to feel weak.

'When I got back from the McCallums,' Charles went on, 'I did not come to see you immediately – '

'Whyever not?'

'Desperately as I wanted to. I had some arrangements to make first. I sent some men down here, with some things on a cart. They were very surprised. I trust they have been and gone.'

I thought I knew what Charles had sent to the island. I could hardly walk, for the trembling of my knees.

I nearly fell into the river, as we crossed the smart new bridge. Charles pulled on a rope, and the bridge hinged upwards to the vertical.

'Safe from intrusion,' said Charles.

He put an arm round my waist, and drew me to the door of the single habitable room.

'Ah,' he said. 'My trust was not misplaced. The things have arrived. It would have been a horrid anticlimax if they had not.'

'The things' were furniture. The minimum of furniture. An upright chair. A bed. A brass bedstead, with a mattress, made up with sheets and pillows.

'Oh Charles,' I somehow said. I could not say any more. I had no need to say any more.

'I thought this was the right place,' he said. He seemed to have as much difficulty speaking as I had. 'I felt I had to seduce you.'

'Why? I am your wife. You don't have to seduce your own wife.'

'It seemed to me that I had to. Not seduce, precisely. Ingratiate myself. I am frightened of you.'

'That is ridiculous.'

'No. You are a lion and a panther, and I love you to distraction.'

'Wait,' I said. 'I know you are honourable and decent and honest and kind, and so forth, and not a murderer and not in love with Jean Hannay, and whatever you say I love you more than you love me. I know all that. But there is still one thing I cannot forgive you for.'

'Oh Lord. For not believing your given word?'

'No, of course it is not that. I didn't believe yours. It was something that happened years ago. When I was a child. Here, only a few yards from here.'

'You pretended you were frightened of drowning,' he said. 'Your hair was exactly the same colour as it is now. My lioness.'

'I made you break your fishing-rod and lose your hat,' I said. 'I am truly sorry about them.'

'You laughed when I fell in.'

'I am sorry about that, too.'

'Why? You disappeared. I scrambled out of the water. I laughed too.'

'You *laughed*? You were furious!'

'Just because I got a little wet? My gillie was shocked. He had exaggerated notions of my consequence, because he thought it raised him in rank too. A very grumpy man, called Tod McLean. Darling, I admired you that day. I wished I knew you. And I don't believe you have changed a single bit. Do you know, I think I may have fallen in love with you then? No wonder I could never be very passionate about Mariota. . .'

'But you sent a man to Callo, after. You sent a message. I must be punished. I must pay for the rod and the hat. It took all my pocket-money for a year. I thought it was the most pompous and treacherous thing I ever heard of.'

'I think so too,' said Charles.

'Then why did you do such a horrid thing?'

'I didn't. This is the first I've heard of it. Tod McLean must have gone to Callo, on his own initiative. I didn't realise he was as shocked as that. What a silly man. And what a beast, to have you punished so much for high spirits.'

'Is that true? Darling, I beg your pardon! Of course it is true. Do you know, I think I am completely happy.'

Charles smiled. He touched my cheek. I pressed his hand to my cheek.

'I am almost completely happy,' I said.

'What do you still lack, my darling?'

'You said you were going to seduce me.'

'Yes.'

'Then don't you think,' I said, 'you might get on with it?'